# RETURN *to* CANNOW'S END

# IAN YEARSLEY

Published by Ian Yearsley
First published 2017
© Ian Yearsley 2017

ISBN 978-1-78222-534-8

Book design, layout and production management by Into Print
www.intoprint.net
+44 (0)1604 832149

Printed and bound in UK and USA by Lightning Source

## ACKNOWLEDGEMENTS

I would like to thank my wife, Alison, for proofreading the manuscript and suggesting ideas. Thank you Alison for your on-going support with all my various book projects.

## Letter from Miss Amelia Cartwright to Mr. Stephen Varley, Sunday 1st October

Church Cottage
High Street
Cannow's End
Near Thamesmouth
Essex
CN3 WDN
Sunday 1st October

Dear Stephen,

Hello dear, I hope you are well.

I am writing to ask you and Sophie for your help with a predicament that has arisen for me. I know you do all that e-mailing business on computers these days but, as you know, that's all a bit new-fangled for me. Give me a fountain pen and a pot of ink any day!

My dear friend, Winifred Weston, passed away last month at the grand old age of 79 – the same age as I am myself, apparently! – and the dear old girl has so very kindly left me the old Home Farm farmhouse at Cannow's End in her will, which was a lovely gesture. We'd known each other since we were at school and remained close over the intervening decades. I do miss her!

Thankfully the farmland around it has been owned and operated by the massive conglomerate of Benton-Rainham Ltd. since the 1990s, but when Winnie sold out to them she kept the farmhouse for herself. It had been in her family for centuries and I remember that she was loath to part with it. Now she has left it to me and, oh dear, it was very kind of her but what am I to do with it at my age? It's in a terrible state. She lived in a home in Thamesmouth for the last five years of her life and she had Home Farm boarded up before she moved there so that it didn't get vandalised or occupied by squatters. I walked round to have a look at it today – it's just the other side of All Saints church from my little cottage, if you remember – and it's got 'KEEP OUT!' written on the boarding on the front door. It's a big old Victorian building, two-storey, neat and symmetrical in design, with a bay at each end rising the full height of the house. It's timber-framed and clad with typical Essex weatherboarding, like my cottage, dear, but poor old Winnie has not maintained it very well in her old age and it's looking rather worse for wear. Some of the paint is peeling off the weatherboarding and bits of the latter are damp to the touch. The protective boarding has either fallen off or been pulled off some of the windows. The glass is broken in a couple of them. I'm sure the weather will have got in. The dear old farmhouse is looking a bit shabby, like one of those old haunted houses you see in films. And you should see the garden! Oh my goodness gracious me, the grass is so long that you can hardly see the cloches any more. I wanted to have a look at the great old hollow oak tree that stands at the north-west corner of the garden near the track down to the river, but I just could not get round to it through the undergrowth! It needs a fit youngster with some shears to cut a path across to it for me. It's sad to see Home Farm in this state – it's not a patch on what it was like when we were growing up – I always remember it bright and clean and shining in the summer sun.

Winnie's solicitor gave me the key to the building, but because the front door is still boarded up I couldn't get to the keyhole. I did, however, peer in through the windows and, oh dear, there was bric-a-brac everywhere: furniture, books, ornaments, everything. It will be a huge job to clear it out and I don't have the strength or the money to get anyone in. I don't know what to do, dear. It looks like there's probably a lot of heavy lifting to do and it needs a strong young man like you to clear everything out and the touch of a young woman like Sophie to set it all right again. I did notice a lot of interesting old books in one of the rooms and I know how you love to read and research things.

Would you and Sophie be able to come and help me sort it all out, dear? You haven't been back to see me in the two years since you left Cannow's End to live in Northumbria and it

RETURN TO CANNOW'S END

would be so nice to see you. You can stay with me or even in the farmhouse if you'd prefer to do that? From what I could see through the windows, the lounge looks quite snug: I think Winnie must have virtually lived in that room before she went into the Thamesmouth home. It's got some big old armchairs and a TV in it. Another room has got a bed in it; it was the dining room at one time, but Winnie had her bed moved into it when she could no longer go upstairs. It's probably all a bit musty though; I should think the bed needs airing. It shouldn't take you long to sort that out though, dear. It was very sad when Winnie had to move out.

Anyway, Stephen, I've enclosed a map with this letter to remind you where Home Farm is in relation to my little cottage and the church.

Sorry to trouble you with this, Stephen, but I don't know who else to turn to.

Thank you so very much, dear. Please do get in touch.

Yours sincerely,

Great Aunt Amelia

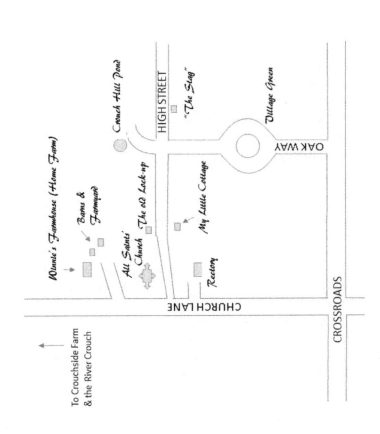

# Stephen Varley's Journal, Wednesday 4th October

*3pm*

I received a letter on Tuesday morning from Great Aunt Amelia, all those miles away in Essex, telling me that she had inherited an old, haunted-looking farmhouse and asking if Sophie and I would go and help her sort it out. It brought back a lot of memories of my previous experience in Cannow's End — my first-hand encounter with witchcraft there still gives me the shivers — and I felt sick to the pit of my stomach. I was in quite a state of mental turmoil all day. I discussed it at length with Sophie in the evening and we talked well into the night. Cannow's End is such a spooky old village that I would rather not have to go back there if I don't have to.

Great Aunt Amelia has put us on the spot though really. Leaving aside the witchcraft dimension, it's all a bit of a pain in the arse logistically — it's a good six hours from Northumberland by car and I've got plenty of other stuff I need to be getting on with. To be honest, though, if we are going to go, the timing is pretty good because Sophie has finished her University studies and has not yet got a job — I think I've written elsewhere in this journal that she recently passed her MA in archaeology; she's always digging about in ditches with university professors and stuff — and I've just finished one novel and am in the process of starting another, so, after much discussion and a lot of angst on my part, we kind of decided that now was as good a time as any and that we probably ought to go. We

10

haven't seen Great Aunt, or even been back to Essex, for two years and it will probably do us good to have a bit of a break. Sophie is keen to visit her parents in Thamesmouth so I guess we essentially have a family holiday in prospect on both sides of the family. We can always extend the rental period on our current house (we were gazumped on the house we were originally going to buy and have been renting in and around the Berwick area ever since).

So, once I had calmed down a bit, talked it over with Sophie and thought about it logically, I kind of felt obliged to go and help Great Aunt Amelia with her predicament.

I am still a bit anxious about returning to the Cannow's End area, especially with Halloween looming, but I kind of feel obliged to go and help my great aunt out and hopefully it will provide me with the opportunity to exorcise a few ghosts in the process (preferably not literally!). Sophie's quite excited about it, I think – she's looking forward to the whole adventure.

I'll reply to Great Aunt tomorrow when I've slept on it, but I'm already thinking – albeit somewhat reluctantly – 'Cannow's End here we come!'.

# Letter from Stephen Varley to Miss Amelia Cartwright, Thursday 5th October

Millburn House
The Wynding
Bamburgh
Northumberland
NE69 1LY
Thursday 5th October

Dear Great Aunt Amelia,

Thank you for your recent letter. Sorry to hear about your friend Winifred. I know from previous correspondence that you had been friends with her for a long time and were very close.

Sorry also to hear about your predicament with Home Farm. I remember the barns well, but I can't say that I can picture the house.

I have discussed the situation with Sophie and I'm pleased to be able to tell you that we would be delighted to come to Essex to help you out. I would be lying if I said I didn't have some trepidation about returning to Cannow's End after last time, but, as you have said to me since, it did all work out well in the end.

You have actually caught us at a good time as we are both 'in-between jobs' at the moment, so to speak, so our plan is to come to you next Saturday 14th October, probably arriving about mid-afternoon. If we can stay at your cottage that night it would be useful please. Sophie would like to visit her parents in Thamesmouth on the Sunday. We can stay with them on Sunday night and then come back to you in Cannow's End. We can use Monday daytime to have a look at Home Farm so we can understand the scale of the challenge and decide whether we're going to stay there or not after that.

So, thanks for writing. I hope you are keeping well. We are both looking forward to seeing you again.

All the best.

Love from Stephen (and Sophie)

X

# Stephen Varley's Journal, Saturday 14th October

9:30pm

Sophie and I arrived safely at Cannow's End this afternoon as planned and are now ensconced in Great Aunt Amelia's cottage in the High Street. It's a little bit cramped with the three of us, to be honest, but Aunt - as Sophie and I tend to call her - assures us that there is more space in 'Winnie's farmhouse' and tells us that we can stay there if preferred. She says it has got central heating and she has made the observation - more of a suggestion, I think - that it would be better for us to be on site while we are 'helping' to clear it out; though I'm already getting the impression that we are actually going to be <u>doing</u> the clearing out while Aunt supervises!

It was strange being back in Essex again: all those memories of the last time I was here grew ever more real in my recollection the closer we got to Cannow's End. Sophie was looking forward to seeing her parents, so we were both in a state of nervous excitement as we travelled down the A1 and M11 and on via the A130 past Chelmsford, though we both became noticeably quieter after we turned off at Battlesbridge and drove through the beautiful farmland landscape that stretches for miles hereabouts on the southern side of the River Crouch. I began to feel a knot forming in my stomach; it grew ever tighter as we passed through Hullbridge and Bashingham and drew ever closer to Cannow's End. I hugged Aunt when I saw her - rather more tightly than I had been planning to, but it was quite a relief to arrive at our destination without any mishaps, and it was actually genuinely nice to see her again. She made us very welcome and was clearly as pleased to see us as we were to see her.

Stepping into her cottage was a bit strange though. It's a lot closer to the churchyard than I remembered. I have been rather apprehensive over the past week about coming back here again. Lots of memories came flooding back when I stepped over the threshold and entered the cramped, white, weatherboarded, little building with its low ceilings and small, cosy rooms. I think I would rather stay in the farmhouse, to be honest, as it holds no memories for me.

Sophie wants to visit her parents tomorrow so we're going to stay one night here with Aunt, have tomorrow night over in Thamesmouth with Sophie's parents and then probably move into the farmhouse the day after that and see what the size of the problem is there. Aunt has given us a book to read about the local area, which includes a section on the history of the farmhouse; I'll have a read of that tomorrow. Home Farm is only on the other side of the church from Aunt's cottage but we didn't get time to go to look at it today as we only had a couple of hours after our arrival before it got dark. Aunt did, however, take us up to the first floor of her cottage (where I had to duck so as not to hit my head on the beams) to show us the view across All Saints churchyard towards the farm. We could make out only the roof of the farmhouse, as the rest of it was obscured by trees and barns – I remember the latter pretty well.

So, I have completed this, my daily journal entry, for the first time in Essex for two years. Sophie and I are both tired so should get to sleep pretty well, and then tomorrow it's off to the in-laws for a stroll along the seafront at Thamesmouth.

**Extract from *A Guide to Cannow's End and its Church*, written by Phyllis Beacham in 1998, and read by Stephen Varley at Sophie Varley's parents' house in Thamesmouth on the evening of Sunday 15th October**

The ancient hilltop village of Cannow's End probably gets its name from Saxon settlers in the 6th century. The name derives from the personal name of 'Cana', probably a local tribal leader. The hill on which the village stands offers good views over the surrounding countryside towards Thamesmouth to the south, and the beautiful valley of the River Crouch to the north.

The church of All Saints owes its magnificent stone tower to King Henry V, who is said to have built it in commemoration of a victory in battle. The tower is a significant landmark in this part of Essex and was used in the olden days as a beacon and a watchtower.

The current population of Cannow's End, no more than 2,000, is nonetheless the largest to date in the village's long and interesting history, and there are many families still living here who can trace their ancestry in the village for many generations back.

Cannow's End has many well established traditions, amongst them that of a village of smugglers, though this pastime has long since died out. It also possesses an even older tradition as a village of witchcraft and the supernatural. Rowdy Halloween revellers are annual, if unwelcome, visitors to the village even to this day, mistakenly believing that these ancient beliefs have a basis in fact.

An 'olde worlde' village with a picturesque High Street of ancient cottages, low-ceilinged pubs, and a proximity to the river and countryside which only adds to its charm, Cannow's End is a popular haunt for ramblers and photographers. Nevertheless, it is a surprisingly quiet village – some might say eerily so – even at weekends.

The church of All Saints, which stands at the extreme western end of the village at the top of the High Street, is the oldest building in Cannow's End, parts of it dating from the 14th century. The massive west tower, however, like much of the rest of the building, belongs to the following century and rises to a height of about 80 feet. It is built of ragstone blocks, carried by river from quarries near Maidstone in Kent. The small porch is of much historical interest, while the grotesque gargoyle carvings on the waterspouts are important, if somewhat frightening-looking, architectural features.

Just outside the eastern end of the church, where the High Street ends, is a small village lock-up, dating from c.1775. Limited parking is available at the western end of the churchyard, which is fed by the only other access road, Church Lane, which leads up the hill from the crossroads.

- - -

The manor of Cannow's End is mentioned in the Domesday Book of 1086. The manor house, Manor Farm, now called Home Farm, stands immediately to the north of All Saints church. It was historically the home of the Lord of the Manor but has in recent centuries been in the ownership of the Mason family. John Mason, who died in 1807, set up a charity for poor people in the parish and contributed funds towards the restoration of the church. Several prominent members of the Mason family are interred in the crypt beneath the chancel of All Saints.

The current manor house building is Victorian, timber-framed and clad in the white weatherboard which is traditional and therefore prevalent in these parts. It is thought to be the third manor house to stand on the site. The building is approached uphill from the south via Church Lane. The metalled road peters out and becomes simply a dirt track just to the west of All Saints and continues from there down to Crouchside Farm which abuts the River Crouch to the north of and below Cannow's End village. An eastern branch of the track to the immediate north of the church leads into Home Farm farmyard. The farmhouse itself stands north of the farmyard, with spectacular views over the river valley below it.

The main entrance to the farmhouse is on the south side. There are full-height bay windows on both the north and south sides of the building, which is rectangular in plan. The bays are topped by symmetrical pediments which rise higher than the roof of the main building. It appears to have been modelled on the 'hall house' of the medieval period, which was often H-shaped in plan, with the main rectangular hall in the centre and wings extending forward and aft of the hall at either end. It certainly occupies the footprint of the previous manor house which stood on this site and incorporates that building's brick-lined cellars. Those cellars have been dated to the 16th-century from the classic Tudor deep orange-red brickwork and uneven courses of lime-and-sand mortar.

Home Farm is referred to in some ancient records as 'Smuggler's Hall', presumably due to its involvement in the smuggling activities which were once rife in this part of the world.

# Stephen Varley's Journal, Monday 16th October

*9:20pm*

After a pleasant day spent with Sophie's parents yesterday and a nice warm cosy bed at their house overnight we today visited Home Farm first thing in the morning and found it to be just the rambling and dilapidated place that Aunt had described. Paint was peeling off the weatherboard, a couple of the windows were broken and the grounds were completely overgrown. A small, slightly ruinous stone garden wall separated the farmhouse from the farmyard in which we stood. The gate which led through this wall into the garden was hanging off its hinges. The whole place looked rather spooky, a bit like something out of 'Psycho'! The misty gloom of the October morning seemed to be hanging over the whole village like a blanket.

Sophie scared the Hell out of me a one point while we were standing in the farmyard by suddenly pointing to the top-left window and asking who it was who was standing there. Aunt and I followed her gaze to the window in question, but we couldn't see anybody.

'Please don't make any tiresome witchcraft jokes, darling,' I said, 'even in jest.'

Sophie looked genuinely concerned that she might have upset me and rested her hand reassuringly on my arm.

'It's not a joke, Stephen,' she said, earnestly. 'I wouldn't do that to you. But I swear to you that there was somebody there - in the middle window of the upstairs bay at the left-hand end there. I think it was a woman. She had long grey hair obscuring her face and a long white dress.

We all methodically scanned the windows at the front of the house, upstairs and down, to see if we could see anyone, but without success.

'There's nobody there now, dear,' said Aunt at length. 'I do hope that squatters haven't got in. Can we go in and check please, Stephen?'

I exhaled heavily and squeezed Sophie's hand.

'Of course we can, Aunt,' I said.

Sophie's dad, who is a builder, loaned us some tools yesterday and I had brought them with me with the intention of effecting some repairs to the damage to the building that Aunt had described in her letter. However, simply standing in the farmyard, looking through the gate to the farmhouse garden, I was already thinking that a lot of the necessary repair work to the fabric would be beyond me, as it was much more than cosmetic. We might have to get Sophie's dad himself round at some point!

The first task was to cut a path to the door through the vegetation. I looked around the farmyard for a suitable implement and soon saw a sickle lying by the farmhouse wall. I put my tool bag down, picked up the sickle and made my way to the garden gate. It fell off its hinges the minute I touched it.

'Oh dear!' said Aunt sadly, from over my shoulder.

I moved the gate out of the way and propped it on the farmyard side of the garden wall. I then began to hack away at the undergrowth in the garden with the sickle until I had cleared a path to the front door of the farmhouse. The exertion temporarily left me a little breathless.

'I could do with a drink now,' I said, as I returned to Aunt and Sophie where they still stood in the farmyard beyond the now gate-less garden gateway.

'Don't be a wuss!' said Sophie, smiling, and handing me a bottle of water.

'Next task,' said Aunt, almost in the manner of a building site supervisor, 'is to get that "KEEP OUT!" boarding off the front door.'

I could see that I wasn't going to be given much time to rest.

'I'll get Dave's tool bag,' I said.

- - -

After yet more exertion and some assistance from Sophie I had soon crowbarred the board off the door. The board was solid - and heavy - so the door behind it had been well protected. Sophie and I carried the board into the farmyard, where we propped it up long-ways against the wall next to the gate. We returned to the front door of the farmhouse just as Aunt was successfully turning the key in the lock.

'It's opened!' she said, triumphantly.

She pushed the door open and stepped into the wide hallway beyond it. Sophie followed her in, and then me.

'Oh dear!' said Aunt, catching her breath slightly and standing still for a moment. 'It's so sad to see Home Farm like this. This was Winnie's home. We had some smashing times here when we were younger.'

Sophie put her arm round Aunt's shoulders.

'We'll soon smarten it up again, Aunt,' she said.

While the two of them were talking, I was taking

in our surroundings. The hallway's green, flowery wallpaper was peeling off in places and there was some yellow-brown staining on what was once a white ceiling. Doorways led off from the hallway to the left and right, each into a large, grand-looking room, parts of which were visible through their respective doorways. Ahead of us, just in front of Aunt and Sophie, and occupying the right-hand side of the hallway, was a flight of stairs leading up to the first floor. The left-hand side of the hallway was home to a passage, which I presumed led to some rooms at the back. It was deathly quiet in the house and it smelt a bit damp.

'What would you like to do first, Aunt?' I said.

'Get rid of any squatters!' came the reply.

'I'll go upstairs,' I said. 'You stay here in the hallway so you can watch for anyone trying to get out.'

I bounded up the stairs and found myself on a bright, spacious landing, with a small table with a dead plant on it in a porcelain pot. There were four doors leading off the landing and a loft hatch above me with a string with a toggle hanging down from it. The hatch was closed but the doors were all open, giving me glimpses of the rooms beyond. I perused what I could see of each one in turn from where I stood. They had clearly all once been bedrooms: three of them still had beds in, but other than that and the odd sideboard they were pretty empty; the fourth one, in the north-eastern corner, which was nearest to me, was even more empty apart from a large wooden wardrobe which stood against one of the walls and a pile of clothes which lay on the floor next to it. I presumed that this had been Winifred's bedroom and that she'd had her bed and everything else she needed moved downstairs as Aunt had described in her letter when she could no longer make it up to the first floor. There were imposing windows at the north and south ends of the landing, each extending its full width and offering spectacular views over the river and churchyard respectively. There was nothing but farmland between us and the river. I could make out, down and away to my left, the farmhouse at Crouchside Farm and, ahead of me in the distance, beyond the farmland, lay Marsh Island, in the middle of the river, and the marina at Alenorth on the opposite shore. The tide was at a low ebb and I could see some of the mud on the riverbed. I mused for a moment about how the tidal creeks behind the island might have afforded some shelter to the boats of the smugglers that I'd read about in Aunt's book. There were no signs of smugglers today though, just yacht masts, a couple of ramblers in brightly-coloured red and blue jackets, and, by the seawall on the mainland to the west of the island, a flock of bird-watchers looking at something out of sight upriver through countless sets of binoculars and long-lensed cameras.

As I walked around the landing, I noticed that each room had an original fireplace on the outer wall and a radiator underneath the window. There was wallpaper on the walls of the landing and each of the rooms, but this was peeling off in places. The floors were carpeted, but the carpets were tatty and threadbare in places too. The wallpaper and carpet designs were predominantly bold floral patterns and looked rather faded and dated. There was a layer of dust on every visible surface.

I made a mental note of the layout and have drawn it up below.

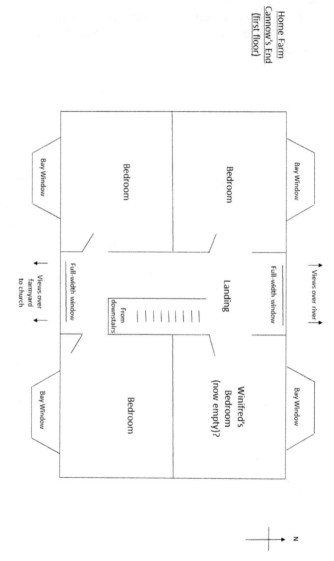

Home Farm
Cannow's End
(first floor)

Bay Window

Bedroom

Bedroom

Bay Window

Full-width window

Landing

Full-width window

From downstairs

Views over river

Views over farmyard to church

Bay Window

Bedroom

Winifred's Bedroom (now empty)?

Bay Window

N

26

I had a good look round all four rooms in case anyone was hiding in them, opening wardrobes and checking under beds. I was particularly keen to look in the bedroom in the south-western corner, where Sophie had said that she had seen the grey-haired woman at the window. Having made sure that the two north-facing rooms were clear, I crept carefully along the landing to the half-open door of that room and, keeping my back against the outside wall of it, I edged ever closer to the doorway, bit-by-bit like cautious police officers do in detective films. I got to the point where my nose was virtually touching the door frame, so that I had nowhere else to go from there but into the room. I made my move quickly, jumping across the gap, framing myself in the doorway to confront anyone who was there. There was a sudden kerfuffle as someone or something was taken by surprise and it was like the air was filled with projectiles. I ducked as some of them came in my direction. My heart missed a beat. I staggered back a couple of steps to assess my foe and realised that it was nothing more than a small flock of half-a-dozen or so pigeons that had got into the room through one of the broken windows. Most of them had flown straight out again when they had seen me, but two had flown directly at me and gone past me across the landing into the south-eastern bedroom.

'Everything OK?!' called Sophie up the stairs in evident alarm.

'Yes, darling,' I said. 'Just some pigeons that have got in through the windows.'

I followed the two escapees into the south-eastern bedroom — which was otherwise empty except for an old bed — and shooed them out through the empty frame of another broken window. I gave myself a few moments to compose myself and then returned to the south-western bedroom. Apart from some general untidiness, a lot of dust and some newly arrived pigeon mess on the old carpet, it was all OK. There was no sign of any trespassers anywhere upstairs.

I returned to the top of the stairs and called down to Aunt and Sophie.

'All clear up here,' I said.

'Apart from the pigeons!' said Sophie.

I made my way down and left Aunt and Sophie waiting at the bottom of the stairs while I made a similar exploration of the ground floor rooms. The left-hand front room (south-west), originally a dining room according to Aunt, had been converted into Winnie's bedroom. Behind that, down the passageway next to the stairs were the kitchen, on the left, and, on the right, a rather bizarre looking room comprising a bathroom and a utility room, which had clearly been converted from its original purpose, as the bay window was obscured by a washing machine, fridge and freezer. The partition wall between the utility room and bathroom was clearly a fairly modern one, perhaps from the 1970s. It was a bit sad to see the room reduced to such practical functions.

Although Winnie had clearly not used the upstairs rooms for some time, the rooms downstairs were in generally more 'lived-in' and serviceable condition. All were fairly tidy but very dusty, with many spiders' webs visible here and there, and all had a nice amount of space in them. As with upstairs, each room had a fireplace against the outer wall, though if the barren state of the one in the bathroom was anything to go by, they had clearly not been used in years. I presumed that the radiators, again placed under the windows in the downstairs rooms, had succeeded the fireplaces in the 1970s or 1980s, perhaps around the time that the north-eastern room was partitioned into a bathroom and utility room. The bathroom had an additional, standalone electric-powered radiator that was plugged in in the utility room, its lead trailing between the two spaces.

Taking everything into account, I thought that Sophie and I probably could move into the downstairs rooms temporarily, though we'd need to patch up the broken windows, and try out the heating and water.

Like the north-facing windows upstairs, the windows in the kitchen and the utility room would offer beautiful views over the River Crouch valley, if only a hedgerow and some trees along the northern boundary of the property were removed.

Between the kitchen and the utility room was a back door, which opened on to an extensive lawn. I tried the door and found it to be locked. Although the glass was cracked in one of the windows, there was no sign of any forced or illegal entry. I checked all the spaces where someone might hide and tried the door to a (locked) cupboard under the stairs. There was clearly no-one in the building but us. Again I made a mental note of the layout and have drawn it up below.

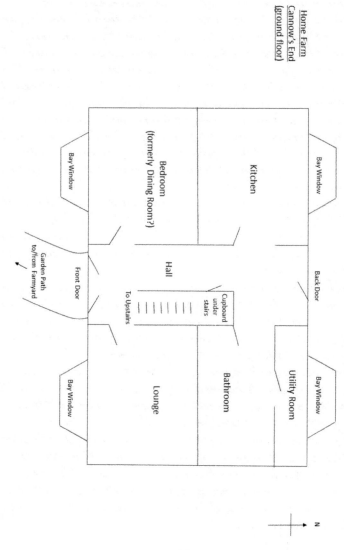

Home Farm
Cannow's End
(ground floor)

Bay Window

Bay Window

Bedroom
(formerly Dining Room?)

Kitchen

Garden Path
to/from Farmyard

Front Door

Back Door

Hall

Cupboard
under
stairs

To Upstairs

Bay Window

Lounge

Bathroom

Utility Room

Bay Window

N

30

I made my way back through the passageway to where Aunt and Sophie were still standing at the bottom of the stairs by the lounge, the one remaining room to explore.

'All clear back there,' I said. 'Let me just check in here.'

I quickly scanned the lounge, with its big old armchairs and TV. It looked quite lived in but, like the rest of the house, under the visible layer of dust, it was as quiet as the grave.

'All clear in there as well,' I said, returning to stand with Aunt and Sophie.

Sophie looked a little crestfallen.

'I could have sworn I saw someone in that window,' she said.

'Perhaps it was a trick of the light,' said Aunt, helpfully, 'or the pigeons.'

Sophie shrugged, seemingly unconvinced.

'What next, Aunt?' I asked.

Aunt sighed heavily.

'Could you take a look at the broken windows, dear,' she asked, 'while Sophie and I have a look around. I hate to sound mercenary but I don't have the money to do the place up and if there is anything here of value then it would be nice to find it and sell it quickly. There's a shop in Thamesmouth that buys second-hand furniture and there's an antique shop in Battlesbridge that might take any old copper kettles or hearth sets or anything like that. Maybe we could even do a boot sale? I hope Winnie wouldn't mind if I sold a few things.'

Sophie hugged Aunt again.

'I'm sure she'd completely understand, Aunt,' said Sophie.

'I agree,' I said. 'There may be some things of sentimental value that you'd like to keep, but if there's anything you don't want we might as well try to get some money for it for you as let it stand here and rot. I don't mind listing a few things on eBay for you.'

Aunt grimaced.

'That's a bit new-fangled for me, dear,' she said.

'I'll do it, Aunt,' I replied, smiling reassuringly. 'You just need to tell us what you want to keep. I'm sure Sophie and I can clear out everything else.'

Aunt sighed again.

'Well, there is a nice oak table and chair set tucked away behind the bedding in the corner of the dining room that caught my eye when I peered through the window shortly before I wrote to you,' she said. 'It's buried under boxes, blankets and various other loose items, so we'd need to have a proper look at it to see what state it's in. There are also some impressive-looking clocks in the lounge: two free-standing grandfather clocks and an ornate gold ormolu one on the mantelpiece.'

'Ok,' I said. 'We can have a look at all of those for you.'

There was a brief pause and we all remained motionless in the hallway temporarily.

'There is one thing I've seen that I really do not know what to do with,' said Aunt at length.

'What's that, Aunt?' asked Sophie, kindly.

'The house! It's far too big for me and I'm very

happy in my little cottage. I don't suppose you two would want it?'

Sophie and I exchanged glances.

'Er... I don't know, Aunt,' I said. 'We'd need to think about it.'

'Yes,' replied Aunt, nodding understandingly. 'You've got your life in Northumberland now, I suppose.'

'Well,' said Sophie, 'you say that, but my parents were trying to talk us into coming back to Essex only yesterday. As Stephen says, I think we'll need to think about it really.'

'Ok, dear,' said Aunt. 'Let's worry about the building later then. Shall we go and see what we can find?'

I left the two of them to it and went back out into the front garden to get Dave's tool bag, which I'd left just outside the front door when I was crowbarring the board off. As I did so, I noticed some complete panes of glass, stacked up on the inside of the garden wall, part-overgrown with undergrowth. I retrieved the sickle and hacked my way across the garden to them, dropping the sickle and cautiously parting the vegetation to look at them more closely when I got there. I visually gauged the size of the panes against the broken windows on the house and quickly realised that they were the same size. I rushed back into the house to find Sophie and Aunt, who were examining various trinkets in Winnie's bedroom (the original dining room).

'I've found some replacement glass in the garden!' I said excitedly to Sophie. 'I don't know that I can replace it on my own though. Do you think your dad would be willing to come over and help?'

'I'm sure he would,' she said. 'I'll ring him on his mobile and see if he will look in on his way home. He's working in South Hambridge today, so it'll only be a slight deviation.'

Once Sophie had confirmed that Dave could indeed stop off on his way home, I went back out into the garden and hacked my way with the sickle all the way round the perimeter walls of the house, clearing a pathway about two feet wide all the way around it. In this way, Dave and I could access the windows more easily when he arrived. I also hacked a path across the back garden on the north side to a shed that appeared to have some potentially useful tools in it and another one from the north-west corner of the building to the old hollow oak tree that Aunt had referred to in her letter, as I thought she might want to go and have a look at it later. The tree was truly ancient, with a kind of majestic but faded grandeur about it, like a Georgian hotel at a once popular coastal resort. It must have been hundreds of years old and the trunk was absolutely massive, maybe about 20 feet in circumference. The side facing the house had a gap in it that you could squeeze through to go inside the hollow trunk. I went inside it briefly and was amazed by the experience: it was quite magical. You could fit at least six people in there at once, I should think. I didn't stay in there long, though, because the ground was quite uneven with tree roots and very damp and muddy.

After I'd looked at the tree, I returned to the house, put down my sickle and turned my attention to the windows. I donned some gloves from the tool bag and began the process of picking up all the bits of glass that I could find that had fallen out of the broken windows. I also pulled out the panes and old dried putty from any windows where the glass was broken or loose, so that they were ready to start on when Dave arrived. This was more of a challenge upstairs, as I didn't have a ladder with me, so in some cases I had to push loosely hanging panes out into the garden. Fortunately, there was so much undergrowth there that they all landed fairly gently and quietly and were easy to retrieve when I went down afterwards.

The downside of taking out the broken windows was that the chill October breeze entered the house, but it wasn't that warm in the farmhouse anyway and I thought that doing this preparatory work would give us a head start when Dave arrived.

After a while spent doing this I returned to the house and found Aunt and Sophie in the kitchen, drinking some mugs of tea.

'The water's still on,' said Aunt, beaming at me as I entered.

'So I see!' I said. 'What about the heating?'

At that very second the sound of a boiler bursting into life came from a cabinet in the corner of the kitchen.

'Yes,' she said. 'That seems to be OK too. Winnie was always particularly careful about keeping the heating on when she lived here. She had a condition that affected her lungs and it was not good for her if the house got damp. She obviously switched it off when she left here, but I switched it on again earlier and it's evidently as good as it was then!

It can't have been started for a good five years, I don't suppose, but it's just kicked into life again straightaway. How wonderful is that?! It's like an old Austin A35 car I used to own: you could leave it untouched for months but it would always start straightaway again when you went back to it. It was very reliable!'

I exchanged a hidden smile with Sophie.

'That's good,' I said. 'We're going to need both heating and water if we're going to stay here.'

'Especially now that some of the windows have been taken out,' said Sophie, sarcastically.

I stuck my tongue out at her.

'I can always get my dad to check the boiler over when he's here,' she continued, 'just to make certain it's OK.'

Aunt clapped her hands with excitement.

'I'm so pleased that you're going to stay here!' she said. 'Winnie would have been so pleased!

'Remind me how many sugars you take in your tea, dear?'

- - -

Dave called in as planned on his way home from work and we soon made light work of fixing the broken windows. He also checked over the boiler for us and found it to be in full working order. While we were fixing the windows, Sophie and Aunt polished every surface in the house and brushed away all the cobwebs they could find.

'It should at least be watertight and warm in' ere tonight,' said Dave, with confidence, as we all sat in the kitchen having another mug of tea. 'You jus' need to clear out all the junk from the rooms now.'

Aunt looked a little hurt.

'It's not junk, Dad,' said Sophie. 'It's Aunt's friend's treasured possessions.'

'Sorry Luv,' replied Dave, turning to face Aunt as he did so. 'No offence Missus.'

'None taken,' said Aunt, cringing slightly at the builder's rough and ready manner.

'Thanks for fixing things up, Dave,' I said, changing the subject slightly. I could see some of Sophie in the way his mouth moved and his eyes sparkled when he laughed.

'No problem, Lad,' he said (he usually calls me 'Lad', for some reason). 'I'll send you a skip over tomorra morning so you've got somewhere to put all that junk.' He looked briefly at Aunt while he was talking. 'I mean the old window frames and broken glass, Missus.' He then turned back to me and Sophie. 'If you need anything else fixing up 'ere at any point, give me a tinkle. Looks like it could do wiv a bit of work.'

- - -

So that was our first day at Home Farm in Cannow's End. Aunt had been airing the bed on-and-off with hot water bottles since Dave arrived, and the early switching on of the heating had helped reduce the smell and feel of damp in the place, so by about 9pm Sophie and I, who'd both been umming-and-aahing all day about whether or not to spend another night in Aunt's cramped cottage or a first night in this old farmhouse, finally decided on the latter. Sophie's used to digging around in water-filled archaeological trenches, so a bit of damp in the air didn't bother her too much. To be honest, I

37

think I was the one who wanted to stay at Aunt's another night!

We decamped our things from the car, which we'd parked in the farmyard, into the lounge and jokingly established that room as 'Base Camp' for our latest adventure. Tonight we'll sleep in Winnie's old bed in what used to be the dining room, using some clean bedding that we found in the wardrobe in her old upstairs bedroom and some additional items that Aunt brought over from her cottage, most notably a lovely fluffy duvet that looked like it would be a real blessing in comfort. We're going to leave the heating on low overnight to keep taking the chill off. Hopefully the place will be warm and toasty when we get up in the morning.

# Stephen Varley's Journal, Tuesday 17<sup>th</sup> October

*8pm*

Although Winnie's bedroom was nicely kept, we both felt a bit unnerved about sleeping in it. I understand from Aunt that Winnie died in hospital, but it was still a bit spooky sleeping in her bed.

Neither of us slept particularly well and what little sleep we did get was terminated abruptly about 7am by the arrival of Dave's promised skip in a crescendo of beeping reversing noises and clanging chains. Sophie and I looked at one another with tired resignation and got up together to welcome the driver and fill out the paperwork.

The driver left the skip in the farmyard, where it was easily accessible from the house. We spent a good hour throwing all the old window frames and broken glass into it, forgetting that it was still early and we might wake up some of the neighbours. I remember from my previous time in Cannow's End that you have to have a pedigree of residency in the village dating back several centuries before you are accepted as a 'local' and I didn't want to get off on the wrong foot. I quickly realised though, as Sophie pointed out, that Home Farm was rather remote from the village and that our only 'neighbours' were sleeping underground in the graveyard next door. I prayed that we wouldn't make enough noise to wake the dead!

We left the garden gate and the 'KEEP OUT!' board propped up in the farmyard by the garden wall where we'd left them for the time being, just in case we needed either of them again. The gate, certainly, should be repairable: I'll hang it back on its hinges once we've finishing coming-and-going through the opening while we're clearing out Winifred's house. I thought we might be here a week or so, as I had hoped to be back in Northumberland before Halloween, but I'm already getting the feeling that we could be here until November: there's so much to do in repairing and clearing out the house.

– – –

All in all, we had a very productive day today at Home Farm. Aunt arrived about 8:30am (what is it with old people that they always get up early?) and set out her plan for the clearing out of the building. She suggested that we start by sorting out the upstairs rooms in the house, as a) they had evidently not been touched for some time and b) they were pretty empty anyway.

'I remember Winnie donating a lot of stuff to the church jumble sale one year,' said Aunt, almost to herself.

The downstairs rooms were liveable in and had more in them. It made sense to leave those until last and not to disturb them for the time being as Sophie and I were evidently going to be staying there for a while until we had cleared out everywhere else.

We consequently made a start on the upstairs bedrooms. We decided out of respect to leave Winifred's old north-eastern bedroom until last, while the incidents with the figure at the window and the flock of birds instinctively drew us to start in the south-western bedroom. Thankfully, nothing else unusual came to our attention there.

The three of us worked together, categorising items as 'keep', 'sell', 'recycle' or 'throw out'. Sophie mostly helped Aunt with the identifying, organising and cleaning of whatever items we came across, while I stripped the beds and vacuumed the old carpets.

It was a difficult and at times painful process, especially for Aunt who had known the house and Winifred well. Occasionally she would come across some artefact or another that held special memories for her and would choke back the odd tear as she told us with enthusiasm about its significance. Things that had sentimental value to Aunt were placed in the farmhouse hallway, ready for her to take back to her cottage. Things that she did not want to keep which looked like they might have some resale value were relocated to the lounge. Items like the pigeon poo and a broken plate with the bones of a fish in it, which we found in the same room, the bones still bizarrely laid out cartoon-fashion in the shape of the original living creature, went straight into a black sack!

# Stephen Varley's Journal, Wednesday 18th October

*7am*

Well! After another fitful night's sleep in an unfamiliar though albeit fairly comfortable bed Sophie and I were awoken suddenly at about 5am by a loud thud in the room above us. We both sat bolt upright and looked at one another in the darkness.

'What on EARTH was that?!' said Sophie, frightened.

We both listened intently for a couple of moments. The house was deathly quiet.

We got out of bed to investigate and switched on the lights in our bedroom, in the hallway and on the landing. We made our way up the stairs to the landing, me in front, Sophie behind. I had picked up a poker from the disused fireplace in our bedroom on the way and I now brandished it in front of me, ready to strike anyone we encountered without a second thought.

Although the landing light was on, the rest of the upstairs was still in darkness. I switched on the light in Winifred's old bedroom on the right at the top of the stairs as I went up, giving it a quick look round as I did so to make sure no-one was in there. I did the same with the north-west bedroom on the left-hand side of the stairs which looked out over the old hollow oak tree. I nodded to Sophie to indicate that both rooms were clear.

We then crept together towards the south-western bedroom where the thud had come from. I raised the poker higher in my right-hand, ready to bring it down onto anyone who might be hiding there and reached around the door frame with my left-hand to find the light switch. I flicked it on suddenly. Nothing happened. I flicked it off and then on again a couple of times for good measure, but the room remained in darkness.

'The bulb must have gone,' whispered Sophie from behind me.

'Go and get me a torch,' I whispered in reply. 'I'll wait here.'

Sophie did as she was instructed and returned with a torch.

'I found it in Dad's tool bag,' she said.

She handed it to me and we both refocussed our attention on the doorway into the south-western room once more. The place was so quiet that I could hear my heart pounding in my chest.

'Ready?' I whispered.

Sophie nodded.

I stepped into the doorway, much like I had done when the pigeons had been there two days earlier, and shone Dave's torch into the darkness. I gradually panned the beam of it from left to right, picking out the shapes of furniture and various boxes and bags that we had left there during our tidying-up session yesterday. When the torch beam reached the fireplace it reflected off two small piercing beams of yellow light. I strained my eyes and craned my neck forward a bit so I could try to make out what they were, when I suddenly realised that they were eyes!

I dropped the torch in shock and it fell onto the landing at Sophie's feet.

'What is it?' she said.

'Eyes!' I said. 'Give me the torch back, quick!'

By the time Sophie had picked the torch up off the floor, handed it up to me and I had panned it around to the fireplace again, the eyes had disappeared. I panned the torch beam around the room a bit until I heard some sudden scuffling emanating from the fireplace. I quickly moved the torch beam back to the place in question and was just in time to see the long, furry black tail of what I took to be a cat disappearing up the fireplace into the chimney.

'What's going on?' whispered Sophie, impatiently.

'It's a cat, I think. It's gone into the fireplace.'

'Well that explains the fish bones,' said Sophie, laconically.

I panned the torch around the room again, including up to the light-fitting on the ceiling.

'I can't see anything else,' I said. 'You're right that the bulb has gone though – there isn't even one in the fitting!'

Sophie laughed.

'I'll get one from Aunt in the morning,' she said.

I turned back to face her.

'How are we going to get the cat out though?' I asked. 'And how did it get in here in the first place?'

Sophie shrugged, the landing light behind her catching wisps of her bed-head hair in silhouette.

'It could have come in through any one of the broken windows before you and Dad fixed them,' she said, 'or through the front door yesterday while we were clearing out up here. Maybe it lives here?'

We both thought for a moment, looking at each other as if telepathically interchanging ideas.

'We could get a chimney sweep in?' said Sophie, at length.

I nodded.

'Yes, I was wondering about that. Should I block this fireplace up in the meantime? It's obviously still open even though it's no longer in use. I thought there was a draft coming from somewhere.'

Sophie shook her head.

'No!' she said, very definitely. 'We don't want to trap it in there. I couldn't live with myself if something happened to it. Maybe the chimney sweep could clear the whole flue and the cat could escape out of the bottom? Maybe it will leave of its own accord? We can block the whole thing up after we're sure it's got out.'

'Okay,' I said. 'Aunt should know if there's a chimney sweep in the area. The other thing we can do is trace the chimney network and see where it comes out.'

So that was our eventful start to the day! We never went back to bed but decided to get up and get dressed instead. I'm just writing this up over breakfast while we decide what to do next.

# Stephen Varley's Journal, Wednesday 18th October

3pm

Sophie and I decided in the end to conduct our own initial search of the layout of chimneys in the house before contacting a chimney sweep. We followed the line of chimney brickwork down from the south-western bedroom and into our bedroom (the former dining room) below it. We found, by calling up and down to each other into the two fireplaces that the whole passageway was clear between the two rooms and that consequently it was most likely that the cat had come in at ground floor level, perhaps when the front door was open yesterday, and had climbed up into the first-floor bedroom, probably taking the fish bones with it, and then, when I spotted it, it had come down and gone out through our bedroom again. God knows where it went after that – it must still be in the house somewhere – but it wasn't in any of the other chimneys: we tried calling up and down those in the same manner and found them to be blocked.

We were just musing over the success of our investigations when the front door knocker sounded I went to answer it and found Aunt standing on the doorstep.

'Hello Aunt,' I said. 'Come in.'

Aunt joined us in the kitchen and Sophie made her some tea. We then all relocated to the more comfortable setting of Winifred's lounge while Aunt asked us how we were getting on sleeping in the building. We began by telling her about how we had found the cat in the south-western bedroom upstairs and had tracked it down into our bedroom before we had lost sight of it.

'I expect it's in the house somewhere,' I said. 'I'll have a look in a minute.'

'Oh I doubt it, dear,' said Aunt, fairly definitively. 'If you haven't been able to find it here I expect it's gone down into the cellar.'

Sophie and I looked at one another in amazement.

'The cellar?!' I repeated.

Aunt looked at us in turn and then laughed.

'Yes,' she said. 'All the old buildings in the village have cellars. They're a relic from the smuggling days. Winnie used to keep wine in hers – there's probably still some down there. Didn't you read about it in that book I loaned you?'

Sophie and I exchanged looks of surprise.

'I remember it, now you mention it,' I said,' but I didn't really take it in at the time.'

'Is there a cellar in your cottage, Aunt?' asked Sophie, interrupting.

'Oh, yes,' she said. 'There was a lot of smuggling going on in the creeks hereabouts in the olden days. I think that was mentioned in the book too?'

I nodded and Aunt continued.

'There are two fireplaces in the Home Farm cellar, one at each end. The chimneys split into two at each end at ground and first floor levels – you've seen the fireplaces in the rooms – but they originate from below ground from just one fireplace at each end of the cellar. I've seen them with my own eyes. I expect your cat has gone down into the cellar if it's nowhere to be seen in the house.'

I opened my mouth as if to speak, but didn't

quite know what to say.

'Stephen, we need to find it!' said Sophie, imploringly. 'It's probably stuck somewhere in the chimney system!'

We both rose instinctively from our chairs and Aunt followed us out into the hallway. I stopped suddenly before going any further and turned to ask Aunt an obvious question.

'Where is the cellar entrance, please?' I asked her.

'The entrance is just along here under the stairs,' she said, pointing along the hall passageway. 'I've been down the stairs there a number of times in my younger days.'

We made our way along the passageway to the door under the stairs.

'I thought this was a cupboard!' I said.

Aunt laughed.

'Oh no, dear. It's the entrance to the cellar.'

I scratched my head.

'The door is locked though,' I said, remembering from my perambulation of the building on Monday, but trying it again unsuccessfully just in case.

'There's probably a key to it on that set of keys Winnie's solicitor gave me,' replied Aunt.

'They're in the kitchen,' said Sophie. 'I'll go and get them.'

I looked at Aunt in amazement while Sophie was away.

'You never mentioned a cellar before.'

There was a twinkle in Aunt's eye as she replied.

'You never asked me, dear,' she said.

Sophie returned with the keys and we identified

the one that looked the most likely. It had a red key fob in the shape of a beer barrel.

'Oh yes!' said Aunt, excitedly, chuckling to herself at some former memory. 'That's the one. I can picture Winnie standing here with it turning the lock just like you are now.'

I turned the key in the lock and it clunked back first time.

'Bingo!' said Sophie.

The door swung open to reveal a set of stairs leading down into the darkness.

'Is there a light-switch, Aunt?' I asked.

Aunt looked thoughtful for a moment.

'Yes, dear,' she said. 'If I remember rightly it's just the other side of this wall, on the right-hand side at the top of the stairs.'

I reached around to the place indicated and sure enough my hand fell upon a light switch. I flicked it on and, unlike the south-western bedroom switch earlier in the day, it had an immediate effect. A light above me at the top of the cellar stairs came on and some neon strip-lighting at the bottom of the stairs flickered into life. There were about a dozen wooden steps leading pretty steeply down to a dirty, brick-lined floor. From the flickering effects elsewhere in the depths below I could tell that two other strip-lights had come on, though these were currently out of my sight.

'Are we going to go in then?' asked Sophie, as if trying to prompt me into action.

I glanced briefly at her.

'I guess so,' I said.

I took a deep breath and began the descent.

'The steps feel pretty firm,' I said. 'No loose treads or anything.'

'Be careful,' said Sophie, reaching out to touch my arm.

I laughed.

'I intend to be!'

'Go on, dear,' said Aunt enthusiastically to Sophie from somewhere behind me. 'I've been down there a number of times in my youth. It's great fun!'

# Stephen Varley's Journal, Wednesday 18th October

*3pm, continued*

Sophie and I made our way down the steep wooden steps until we reached the cellar floor. The floor was lined with somewhat uneven red brick, but layered in places with clumps of damp earth which had seeped through the flooring from beneath in places over the centuries. The walls of the cellar were also lined with red brick, but had been painted white. This helped give off a bit of reflected light to illuminate the space better, but the paint itself was peeling in places and we could see the red brick coming through from behind it.

Sophie bent down to brush some loose earth off the brick floor with the back of her hand and then stood up again.

'Tudor bricks,' she said. 'Just like it said in the book.'

I was impressed.

'Wow!' I said, taking her archaeologist's word for it. 'So the cellar does pre-date the house.'

Sophie nodded and beamed a lovely, triumphant smile at me. I kissed her on the cheek.

We turned in unison to scan the cellar. It extended, just like the book had stated, across the whole length and breadth of the house. There were a number of pillars of brickwork dotted about the space to support the ceiling (the floor of the Victorian building above us) and there were dust and cobwebs everywhere. The pillar bricks were a kind of faded yellow in colour and contrasted noticeably with the red brickwork of the floor and walls.

'Those brick pillars are Victorian,' said Sophie, as if reading my mind.' Can you see how they are much more uniform in size than the Tudor ones, and the mortar is thinner? They are also local: yellow stock brick is predominant in this part of the world. The earth in this area is what's called London Clay. It's been used a lot over the centuries for brick-making locally. There are still the remains of some old clay brick quarries in and around Thamesmouth if you know where to look.'

We initially remained in the vicinity of the stairs and scanned the space to look for any sign of the cat. Immediately in front of us, all along the south wall, which was the most easily accessible from the stairs, were piles of what looked to me like 'junk'. Most of it was covered in what had once been white dustsheets, now rather grey and dirty-looking from decades, perhaps centuries, of dust. All kinds of shapes from long-discarded items tried their best to make themselves known to us: some legs from a chair; the base of a table lamp; and a collection of flowerpots. There were even some bottles of wine lined up in front of it.

'Winnie's wine collection,' said Sophie, remembering Aunt's words.

Once our eyes had become accustomed to the darkness, we looked beyond the immediate vicinity and the reach of the strip-lights' beams into the dark spaces and corners which lay beyond. We turned round on the spot, appraising our surroundings as we did so. Three items in particular grabbed our attention. Two of these were matching Jacobean-style chests of drawers - one away to our right by the western wall, near the north-western corner of the building, and the other right behind us smack bang in the centre of the north wall. The other was a huge, dominating, dark wooden wardrobe about seven feet tall and three wide away to our left, which was positioned near the south-eastern corner of the east wall. All three were covered in dust and I noticed that the surface of the one by the north-western corner was pretty badly tarnished.

'Depending on their condition,' I said, 'those chests of drawers and the wardrobe should sell for a bit.'

The north, west and east walls were generally less cluttered than the rest of the cellar, presumably because they were less immediately accessible from the (south-facing) stairs. Here's my drawing of the cellar layout.

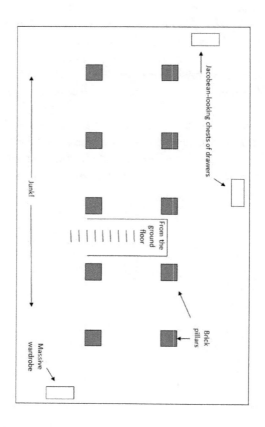

Home Farm
Cannow's End
(cellar)

Sophie interrupted my thoughts by calling suddenly up the stairs to Aunt.

'When were you last down here?'

Aunt laughed in reply.

'Oh, decades ago!' she said. 'And I don't imagine that Winnie has been down there for ages either. She had real problems with her hip in her last few years. She barely went up to the bedrooms at all towards the end, so I can't see her coming down here.'

I looked at Sophie despondently.

'More junk to clear out. We must be the first people to come down here in years.'

Sophie nodded.

'Something else for our "To Do" list,' she said, 'but first and foremost – where's the cat?'

In all the excitement about discovering a new space in the building I had completely forgotten that we had gone down into the cellar to look for the cat. I thought for a moment.

'Well,' I said, 'it went down the chimney in the south-western area of the building. If the two chimneys at each end of the house merge into one fireplace at each end down here in the cellar as Aunt has described – and looking across to them, I can see that they do – it must be over there somewhere by the west wall.'

I indicated vaguely in the appropriate direction with my arm.

Sophie laughed.

'What a shame it couldn't have just been waiting for us at the bottom of the stairs!'

We worked our way together towards the west

wall. Some parts of the brick flooring were more uneven than others and, although the strip-lighting helped us to see generally where we were going, the corners of the cellar were largely still in darkness. Nevertheless, the outline of the fireplace, which had looked rather vague from the stairs, soon made itself known to us very clearly when we stood in front of it.

'It's a bit bizarre, having a fireplace in a cellar,' I said.

'Depends how long you spend down here,' said Sophie.' It'd be a bit chilly without it if you were going to spend any time down here.'

On the floor in front of the fireplace, about six feet in from the wall, lay a couple of disjointed skeletons of what looked like small birds or mice, the main bones still revealing the shape of their once-live owners, just like the fish bones upstairs had done, but with the odd leg bones and feet scattered about a short distance away.

'Well,' said Sophie, 'the cat has certainly been down here.'

I was turning to reply when a small chink of light near the ceiling to the left of the fireplace caught my eye. I moved closer to look and I could see a small narrow passage, a few inches across, leading to the outside and with some tufts of vegetation covering some of the far end of it.

'Look!' I said. 'There's a small passage here to the garden!'

Sophie came over and peered through it alongside me.

'Well,' she said, 'that explains how the cat got

in! It's a bit of a narrow squeeze, but a cat could definitely get through there. Let's hope it got out the same way!'

'Yes,' I said. 'Let's leave it. It probably knows its way around here much better than we do and all this dust is starting to get to the back of my throat. I'm going to need the dust masks your dad put in the tool bag for us if we come down here again. Let's go back upstairs for a moment and let Aunt know what we've found.'

We climbed back up the steep cellar steps and into the hallway. I had to squint initially because the sunlight coming in through the front door and from the large upstairs windows was really bright compared to the cellar lighting – Aunt looked initially like a black silhouette against the light of the bright-blue, crisp October sky.

The three of us made our way into the kitchen again and Sophie made us some tea before we all retired into the lounge at the front of the building, with its big old comfy armchairs. Odd items that we had moved down from upstairs were dotted around the room away from the walking areas and looked a little out of place.

I took the opportunity to ask Aunt about Winifred. She got up and went to the fireplace, where the gold ormolu clock that she had mentioned occupied the centre of the mantelpiece. Aunt had wound the clock up while Sophie and I had been in the cellar; it provided a reassuring metronomic tick in the background while we talked.

Either side of the fireplace were some bookshelves which were jam-packed with books. Aunt perused the spines on a number of them for a few moments before pulling out, with some effort, because they were so tightly wedged in, two faded and dog-eared A4-sized booklets. She dusted them off and brought them over and gave them to me.

'These will tell you all you need to know about Winifred,' she said.

# Extract from 'The History of the Weston Family of Cannow's End, Essex' by Winifred Weston (an unpublished manuscript, written in 1999), read by Stephen Varley in the lounge of Home Farm on Wednesday 18<sup>th</sup> October

I, Winifred May Weston, was born in the village of Cannow's End in south-east Essex, in September 1938. My father, Abraham Noah Weston, was a farmer from Cannow's End who farmed land all over the local area, including in the neighbouring parishes of Pockingham and Bashingham. My mother, Ethel Maud Blyth, was a seamstress and was herself the daughter of a farmer from Cannow's End. They met at the annual ploughing match in September 1935 and got married in All Saints church two years later, almost to the day. The three of us lived at Home Farm, Cannow's End, where I was born and still live to this day.

My father's family have owned and farmed Malbourne Farm in the parish since 1658 and they have also farmed Hats Well Farm in Pockingham since about 1719. It was a great disappointment to him that I was his only child (my mum and dad were 30 and 32 respectively when I was born), as he never had a son to pass his farming interests on to. As I never got married or had any children myself, I will be the last of the line after all these years. I am sad about that myself as I write this down.

I am, however, very proud to record that the Weston family have been active members of the local community hereabouts for generations. My great-grandfather on my father's side paid for repairs to the church tower after it was struck by lightning in 1904. His father and grandfather were magistrates in Thamesmouth, the biggest town in the area. The younger brother of my five times great-grandfather was rector of All

Saints. There is a memorial bust to him inside the building. All my Weston ancestors are buried in the churchyard.

My mother's family had a similar lineage in Cannow's End. Her father, George, was, as I've said, a farmer there. His ancestors have owned Home Farm since at least the 16th century. Those ancestors also included magistrates. My great-great-grandfather's brother was one of the first Thamesmouth policemen. So you can see that between them, the two sides of my family owned a lot of land and held positions of responsibility in the locality right down the generations.

Unfortunately not all of my ancestors were so community-minded. Two of them have gone down in local folklore for all the wrong reasons. Sadly for me, they are the only two whom people round here seem to remember.

In 1820 my great-great-great-grandfather on my mother's side, Reginald Blyth, married a lovely girl called Adelaide Cartwright. I've got a small, roughly-drawn portrait of her in my dresser and she looks really beautiful, with long black glossy hair and equally black eyes. She was said to have bewitched Reginald from the second they met. I could tell from the picture that she certainly had the capacity to do that to a man.

By all accounts, Adelaide had quite a temper on her. My father told me that the family mantra about her was that she was at her most beautiful when she was angry. I have looked at that portrait of her many times over the years and I have always thought I could see a spark in her eyes that shows she might have been quick to fly off the handle. However, it was only when I began to research her life about 10 years ago that I began to get an inkling of where that hot temper may have come from.

I found Adelaide's baptism recorded in the parish registers for All Saints church in Cannow's End. She was baptised in 1792. Her father, William Cartwright, and mother, Mary Benson, were mentioned in the same entry. I also found William's baptism, which was recorded as taking place in 1768. The space where his father's name ought to have been written was left blank, which local historians have informed me suggests that he was probably born out of wedlock. I have been able to find no trace of his father whatsoever.

The details given for his mother were also a bit curious. Her age was given as 68 at the time of his birth, which can't possibly be correct. With the rector's permission, I took the parish register to the Keeper of Human History at Thamesmouth Museum. He examined it with a fancy electron microscope or something to see if the original age had been blotted out over time with dust and dirt, etc., but he reckoned it still said 68. Neither of us could fathom out how this could be the case, so I thanked him for his help and left. I never did get to the bottom of that. I know a lot of people were illiterate then – maybe whoever filled the parish register out just wrote down the wrong number?

William's mother's name was also oddly recorded in the register as 'Old Mother Cartwright'. The fact that the surname was the same gave further evidence that William was illegitimate, as he had taken on his mother's surname rather than his father's. I discussed his mother's unusual title with the Thamesmouth specialist and he said that he had seen similar descriptions before and that they were almost always attributed to women who lived on the fringes of their local community, either as so-called wise women or even as outright, practising witches. He quoted me a lot of information about witch trials in Essex in the 1640s and even showed me some other old documents from that period which referred to various alleged witches as 'Mother', 'Goodwife' or 'Widow'. He said it was highly likely that Old Mother Cartwright was a witch and promised to investigate.

A few days later he sent me a photocopy of a report of an old trial at Chelmsford which dated from 1759 and referred to a case against 'Goodwife Cartwright' of Cannow's End, who had been indicted for 'bewitching men and cattle with very many strange and diverse afflictions'. The case was dropped due to lack of evidence. The report did not unfortunately contain much concrete information, although it did state that the Goodwife was known to make potions from local herbs which helped alleviate sickness and cure all manner of ills.

Old Mother Cartwright is one of the two main ancestors that local people seem to want to talk to me about. I wish they'd focus more on the JPs, policemen and rectors, rather than on a silly old witch!

# Stephen Varley's Journal, Wednesday 18th October

*3pm, continued*

When I reached the part in Winifred's manuscript about 'Old Mother Cartwright' being a witch I had to break off sharply to collect my thoughts. Aunt (Great Aunt Amelia, technically) and my grandmother Eileen, her sister, were both Cannow's End Cartwrights and I knew from my previous time in the village that they also had a direct witchcraft lineage and that magical abilities could be, and often were, passed genetically down the family line.

It was too much of a coincidence for Old Mother Cartwright, against whom apparent witchcraft charges had been dropped in 1759, to be from another family with the same surname at a time when village populations were always very small. How many Cartwright witchcraft families in Cannow's End could there possibly have been??

I had to stop reading and ask Aunt some questions about this probable family connection!

'I know what you're thinking,' said Aunt, as I looked up from Winifred's manuscript and opened my mouth to speak. 'You're right - we are also descended from Goodwife Cartwright: her granddaughter Adelaide's younger brother, Adam, was my great-great-great-grandfather.'

I clearly failed to disguise my surprise.

'It's a small village,' said Aunt, almost by way of consolation.

'"Goodwife" Cartwright?' repeated Sophie, clearly needing to be brought in on the discussion.

'Winifred and Aunt are descended from the same

family, the Cartwrights,' I said. 'Old Mother or Goodwife Cartwright, who's mentioned in this book, was an 18th-century witch in the area.'

'Oh dear,' said Sophie.

'I knew there would be witches involved somewhere,' I said. 'This bloody village is full of them!'

There was a brief silence while I thought for a moment.

'Isn't the 18th century rather late for witchcraft?' I said. 'I thought most witch hunts and indictments took place in the 17th century?'

Aunt laughed.

'Don't forget that Cannow's End was once known as "The Witching Village",' she said. 'There is a long tradition of witchcraft in the area, from even before the 17th century, right up to the present day, as you may remember.'

I shuddered at the thought of it.

'Did Winifred ever talk about her witchcraft line with you?' asked Sophie, at length.

Aunt looked pensive.

'Once or twice, when we were younger. It's the kind of thing that youngsters can get very excited about, but when you get to my age you become more philosophical about life.'

Sophie shuffled in her seat and was obviously dying to ask a follow-up question.

'Did you ever try any magic tricks together?' she said.

Aunt laughed.

'Not together, we didn't, but Winifred told me that she had experimented with some spell or other

one Halloween on her own when it was full moon.
I think we would have been in our late teens, maybe
about 17 or 18. She told me that she had made a cat
appear out of thin air! I didn't believe her at the
time, but now I'm not so sure. She tried it again
the following year with me watching, but nothing
happened. She put it down to there not being a full
moon that year. Halloween full moons occur only
about once every 20 years, I think.'

'So was there a cat?' asked Sophie, curious.

'Yes, dear, there certainly was a cat,' said Aunt
in reply. 'It lived for about 15 years. I've got no
idea where she got it from. Winnie always stuck
to her story about the magic trick whenever I
discussed it with her. Her cat was as black as
your hat and had really piercing yellow eyes. It
was friendly enough though, if a bit timid whenever
strangers were around. Winifred called it "Magic",
unsurprisingly.'

'Yellow eyes!' I said, aloud.

'What happened to it?' asked Sophie, ignoring my
interruption.

'It had some kittens and they all lived in and
around the farmhouse, some in the barns and some
in other outbuildings that have mostly fallen down
over the years. The kittens were very handy for
keeping the rats and mice numbers down.

'Most of the kittens were black and white, so
we assumed that the father was white. He was
probably from one of the neighbouring farms.
They had a lot of white cats at one time down on
Crouchside Farm. Only one of the kittens was pure
black like its mother. Winifred kept that one as a

65

pet. It used to be with her all the time. She called that one "Midnight".

'Oddly enough, Midnight had only one black kitten too and sure enough Winnie kept her as a pet as well. That one was called "Panther". There were two or three others after that whose names I forget, but the pattern was the same in each generation: one litter of kittens per cat, with each litter having only one pure black cat in it, which Winnie duly kept.

'The latest one, Satan, is bound to be around somewhere. I imagine that's the one you saw. I haven't seen him myself since Winifred passed away though.'

'"Satan"!' I interrupted. 'What kind of name is that for a cat??'

Aunt shrugged.

'I can tell you're not a cat person, Stephen. Cats have all kinds of silly names: Tiggywinkle, Fluffy, Snowflake... Why not give them a name that means something? I should think "Satan" for a black cat was highly appropriate.'

'Only if it was evil!' I said.

'It's just a play on words with the blackness, Stephen,' said Sophie, reflecting. 'No different from Midnight or Panther. Maybe Miss Weston was running out of ideas for names.'

'I expect Winnie was having a little joke, dear,' said Aunt, smiling. 'Imagine calling "Midnight" at midnight to get your cat to come in, or calling "Satan" over the churchyard. There is a kind of dry humour about the whole thing.'

I shook my head.

'Well as long as it is just humour and there

aren't any real Satans about, I don't mind!' I said, unimpressed.

Now it was Sophie's turn to laugh.

'I think you're over-reacting, darling,' she said.

'That's as may be,' I replied, not entirely convinced. 'We've already had a figure at the window, family connections with witchcraft and an elusive black cat named Satan in the few days that we've been here!'

There was a slight pause before Sophie asked Aunt another question.

'Why didn't you mention Satan before?'

Aunt pulled a face.

'I didn't think to, dear,' she said, in a matter-of-fact manner. 'Cats are pretty independent and resourceful. He was always a bit timid around other people anyway. Winnie's cats were all a bit timid, expect with her – they rarely seemed to leave her side.'

I raised my eyebrows but said nothing.

'Go back to the book, dear,' said Aunt to me at length.

After the minor distraction of the Cartwrights and the cats I did indeed return to my reading to find out about Winifred's other notorious ancestor.

# Extract from 'The History of the Weston Family of Cannow's End, Essex' by Winifred Weston, continued

My other notorious ancestor who everybody seems to know about is William Blyth, brother of my five times great-grandfather on my mother's side. I haven't needed to do much research into William myself because he appears in a number of local history books, not least *William Blyth – King of Smugglers* written by John Winderforth in the 1950s. I have sellotaped a photocopy of an extract from that into this booklet below.

# Photocopied extract from 'William Blyth – King of Smugglers' by John T. Winderforth (published in 1957)

William Blyth was born in Cannow's End, Essex, in 1753. The Blyths, who owned Home Farm, were a significant local farming family, though William himself was to choose a number of different trades throughout his life. After a brief, curtailed apprenticeship on the farm with his father, William clearly decided that a life in agriculture was not for him. He nevertheless became a prominent individual in the locality as an oyster fisherman, the owner of the village's grocery shop, a churchwarden, a member of the parish vestry (forerunner of the parish council), a parish constable and perhaps also a magistrate. He managed to combine all these activities with an arguably even more successful one – smuggling illicit goods into the country in conjunction with other local fishermen, most of whom were related in some way or another. The countryside around Cannow's End is riddled with small creeks that only a local would know were there. Blyth and his cohorts spent years ferrying goods such as brandy, tobacco, silk, lace and china across the English Channel and the North Sea from France and Holland in their fleet of oyster fishing boats and sneaking them into the country through these creeks. They would usually operate under cover of the night, transferring their contraband from sea-going vessels to the flat-bottomed barges which were once common in this part of the country for onward transmission up the shallow creeks into the nearby villages of Cannow's End, Pockingham and Bashingham.

Arguably the most profitable route for Blyth was the Dunkirk run. From there, Blyth and his fellow smugglers would bring tea, gin and tobacco. Perhaps surprisingly now, tea in particular was a very lucrative commodity at that period, as it was much in demand and commanded a tidy profit. With the coastline of south-east Essex being punctuated at regular intervals by narrow, winding creeks, it was almost impossible for Customs officers, who were short in number, to be able to catch Blyth and his cohorts.

There are stories from other parts of the country of 'the revenue men', as the Customs officers were called, being murdered by smugglers at night and their bodies being dumped in the sea. There is little evidence to suggest this took place in the creeks around Cannow's End, but nevertheless the revenue men had to be bold, fearless and also full of integrity. In nearby Thamesmouth, the main Customs station hereabouts, there was a rule that Customs officers could not be local, as the authorities feared that they would collude with the smugglers if they came from within the smuggling communities.

There is evidence from the handful of cases where smugglers were caught and their activities were discussed in court that local people turned a blind eye to their activities, as they frequently profited themselves from low prices on smuggled goods. Revenue officers were few and far between at this period, so the Cannow's End smugglers essentially had carte blanche to come and go as they pleased. No-one knew the tidal creeks in this area as well as the local fishermen. It was only after the summer of 1798, when the local magistrate, John Harridge (1745-1817), from nearby Great Stonebridge, set up the Thames River Police to monitor smuggling activities in the locality, that the forces of crime prevention began to make inroads into the smugglers' activities. By the time any real effect was felt, in the early decades of the 19th century, Blyth and his like had made a tidy profit and long retired to a life of relative tranquillity as gentleman farmers, businessmen or shopkeepers. There are, however, tales of smuggling activities in the creeks around Cannow's End and Pockingham continuing into the early 20th century before the trade was finally expunged. One writer in 1909 stated that 'the whole area is honeycombed with the traditions of smuggling' and found that gin was once stored under the altar of Pockingham church.

Blyth gained a number of nicknames, including 'King of Smugglers' and, due to his rough, tough demeanour, 'Hard Nut Blyth'. There are many stories in the local annals of Blyth, who was also a churchwarden, wrapping either smuggled or illegally-acquired goods in pages from the Bible of All Saints church. His family home of Home Farm is referred to in some records as "Smugglers' Hall".

Cannow's End has been described as 'the smuggling capital of south-east Essex' during this period and most of its inhabitants, and many of those of neighbouring Pockingham and Bashingham, appear to have had some involvement or connection with the trade. Some fairly well-to-do residents owned ships which took part in the smuggling of contraband. Others provided weapons to the fishermen who nightly risked their lives in the escapade. William Blyth was the ring leader of much of this activity, especially c.1780-c.1805.

Hard Nut certainly seems to have been a bit of a character – stories about him abound. He is said to have downed two glasses of wine consecutively at the local hostelry, *The Stag* (known at that time as *The Smugglers' Rest*), and then to have calmly eaten the glasses afterwards as well. In another tale, he is said to have tried to deal with a particularly angry bull that had got loose by grabbing it by the tail and holding on for dear life as it rampaged across a number of fields and ditches before it finally came to a halt and he was able to capture it properly and bring it back to its home field. At a cricket match between Cannow's End and Pockingham in 1785, Blyth and his fellow smugglers were said to have taken guns and swords with them as they were particularly fearful at that time of being challenged by a group of excise men who were known to be in the local area. On one occasion after a smuggling run to Dunkirk, when Blyth and his fishing crew were caught by the revenue men, he invited the officers to partake in some of the smuggled brandy and got them so drunk that he left

71

them partying on their revenue cutter and continued on his way with the rest of his booty. There are even tales that the smugglers of Cannow's End became so well known that they used their smuggling runs to operate a 'ferry service' across the Channel. One of their unsuspecting passengers was said to be local lawman John Harridge himself! Whether this is true is anyone's guess, but it gives an example of how brazen and untouchable the smugglers evidently thought they were at this period.

The local landscape provided a number of hidey-holes for smuggled goods. Three large, hollow elm trees at Leas Halt Farm in Pockingham parish are said to have been used to store barrels of brandy and packages of silk. An old hollow oak tree at Home Farm in Cannow's End was similarly used. The cellar at Blyth's grocery shop in Cannow's End also came in handy for this purpose. Other accounts have Blyth and his colleagues weighing down brandy barrels and sinking them temporarily out of sight into the depths of Crouch Hill Pond. Many of these stories can be substantiated through articles in the *Thamesmouth Chronicle* from this period, copies of which can be viewed on microfilm at Thamesmouth Library.

After a life of smuggling, Blyth seems to have settled down as a (fairly respectable) churchwarden and grocer, serving on the parish vestry and possibly even on the magistrates' bench. He was clearly a real character in a comparatively unlawful era and lived until 1830, when he died at the age of 77.

# Stephen Varley's Journal, Wednesday 18th October

*3pm, continued*

I looked up from Winifred's booklet.

'Hard Nut Blyth sounds an interesting character,' I said, making eye contact with Aunt to try to prompt some reminiscences from her.

Sophie almost choked on a cake she had been otherwise surreptitiously helping herself to from a plate that lay on a low table in front of us.

'Who the Hell is Hard Nut Blyth?' she exclaimed. 'What a ridiculous name!'

I laughed.

'According to this he was a local smuggler of some repute who was also an ancestor of Winifred's. He was both churchwarden and grocer in Cannow's End. He used to wrap smuggled goods in pages torn from the church Bible and sell them in his grocer's shop!'

Sophie looked amazed.

'Really? Nice chap! Didn't anyone cotton on to this? Pages disappearing from the Bible, exotic goods turning up out-of-the-blue in the back of beyond, that kind of thing?'

I laughed again.

'You would have thought so,' I said, mulling it all over briefly, 'but perhaps everyone turned a blind eye to it all, like they did in that Kipling poem – "brandy for the parson, baccy for the clerk", etc.. The whole village would have benefited from getting exotic, quality goods at knock-down prices. You couldn't just go to Sainsbury's then, you know! He was probably a bit of a local hero – dodging the revenue men, helping the poor and all that.'

Sophie snorted at me.

'You make it sound like a nice cosy arrangement,' she said, 'but smugglers were essentially criminals – they were breaking the law!'

I nodded.

'Yes,' I said. 'I agree with what you are saying and many of them were presumably rough and ready, violent men. They were probably risking jail or maybe even the death penalty if they were caught? Whatever the case, it clearly went on.'

'The trouble is,' said Aunt, picking up a cake herself, 'it's difficult to know how many of the stories about Blyth are true. Winnie found out that a lot of them had their origins in a memoir written by John Harridge, the man mentioned in the book' – she indicated it – 'as setting up the river police. Personally, I think the basic facts are probably true but that they have been embellished over time with numerous retellings.'

I nodded sagely.

'So what exactly did Mr Blyth get up to then?' asked Sophie.

'He seems to have had a profitable smuggling business bringing goods across the Channel from France,' I said. 'Whisky, textiles, china and even tea. But he also held a number of respectable positions in the village – churchwarden, grocer, things like that. He seems to have brought various goods in through the local creeks and I suppose he sold a lot of them in his shop.'

'Winnie found an old barrel in the cellar once,' said Aunt, interjecting. 'I think she broke it up and used it for firewood. It's possible that that was an old brandy keg from the smuggling days. Half the village was involved in the smuggling trade in one way or another, if the stories are to be believed.'

Sophie looked wide-eyed.

'Winifred found a brandy keg in the cellar?' she echoed. 'The cellar of this building, Home Farm?'

'Yes,' said Aunt. 'There are stories of other smuggling relics being found in local buildings - a length of silk, some 18th-century coins, a rusty sword and so on.'

Sophie and I looked at one another.

'So there might be more smuggling relics down in the cellar,' I suggested, 'still waiting to be discovered?'

Aunt looked wide-eyed momentarily.

'Who knows, dear,' she replied. 'I should imagine there's all kinds of old junk down there. If you do find anything worthwhile let me know and we might be able to add it to our list of items to sell on D-Day.'

I suppressed a snigger.

'We'd sell them on eBay, Aunt,' I corrected.

Aunt waved her hand as if dismissing me.

'Well, whatever it's called,' she said.

Sophie put her plate down, stuffed what little was left of her cake into her mouth and jumped to her feet.

'Come on then, Stephen!' she said. 'Let's get back in that cellar and see what we can find!'

# Stephen Varley's Journal, Wednesday 18th October

*7pm*

Sophie and I returned to the cellar and spent a couple of hours clearing things out, eager now to locate some potential smuggling relics. It was stupidly dusty down there once we started moving things around: I was so pleased we had Dave's dust masks. We decided to start with the junk pile along the south wall, as it was closest to the stairs and most easily accessible. This enabled us to clear the whole area around the base of the stairs, so that we could manoeuvre anything of significant size into a position from which it would be easiest to carry it up them. There were dusty old empty milk bottles, black sacks full of threadbare vintage clothing, cardboard boxes full of God knows what that fell apart in your hands when you picked them up, rusting garden implements that looked like they came out of the Ark, several lengths of rope, a ladder and even a small fibreglass dinghy! It was hot, sometimes heavy, work.

We moved each individual item that we came across up into the hall for Aunt to evaluate for keeping, selling, recycling or disposing of. This was OK with small things like pots and pans, including one which seemed to have the world's supply of spiders inside it, but when it came to heaving a sideboard up the steep, narrow cellar stairs it was a different matter entirely. God knows when, why or by whom all that stuff was put down there!

We did, however, come across a few interesting things that captured our attention for a few moments. One of these was an old oil painting of a smartly dressed if slightly shifty-looking thirty-something man sitting on horseback in what looked to be 18th-century attire, including a black tri-corn hat, a white wig, a long blue frock coat, beige trousers and long white socks pulled up to his knees. He looked a proper dandy! What caught our eye most though was not his clothing, nor even the fact that he had the handle of a pistol protruding from the belt of his trousers, but that the horse he was sitting on seemed to have no ears! This prompted a host of unfunny jokes from Sophie along the lines of 'What do you call a deer with no eyes? No idea' which I had to endure until she had exhausted her imagination on the theme and was ready to study the picture more closely.

'It certainly looks like an ear-less horse,' she said, scratching a fingernail over the place on the painting where the ears ought to have been, as if to dislodge any grime which had accumulated on the surface of the artwork over the centuries.' I think it's genuine.'

'How odd,' I said. 'I've never heard of an ear-less horse before. I wonder if Aunt knows anything about it?'

It turned out that Aunt did know something about it when we eventually took the painting up to show her.

'Yes, dear,' she said, as she held the painting at arm's length in both hands in the kitchen and moved it around so she could see it better in the light. 'That's Gilbert Craddock - a notorious 18th-century highwayman from Lee, the old fishing village to the west of Thamesmouth. He lived at Altar Pew Hall there. His horse, Meg, had no ears, as you can see. He apparently had a pair of wax horse ears made that he could put on her when he went out on his highwayman business, so she looked just like any other horse, and he took them off again when he got home. It was the perfect disguise - no-one ever reported being robbed by a highwayman with an ear-less horse. It's the only known painting of her - and him. Winnie bought it at a jumble sale or some such thing, decades ago. It's a well-executed picture. I think I'll keep it and put it up somewhere in my little cottage.'

'And what happened to Gilbert?' I asked.

'I think I read that he drowned in a pond or something. Somebody at Thamesmouth Museum would know.'

'Was there any connection between this highwayman and Miss Weston's smuggling relatives?' asked Sophie.

Aunt shrugged.

'There might have been, dear,' she said. 'There were certainly connections between the Blyth family and some smugglers in Lee. I guess they all probably knew each other, or at least knew of each other. Who was that female smuggler in Lee who Winnie used to talk about? Edna something. Little, I think.'

Sophie and I exchanged glances.

'I've got something to show you two as well,' said Aunt, putting the painting down and crossing briefly to one of the kitchen work surfaces. She returned in an instant with a gold oval-shaped locket which she opened to reveal a miniature portrait of a beautiful, twenty-something girl with long, black glossy hair and deep black eyes.' I found this in Winnie's dresser, just where she said it was in her biography. This is Adelaide Cartwright, the girl who married Reginald Blyth.'

Sophie and I examined the picture.

'She's beautiful,' said Sophie.' She also reminds me of someone.'

Aunt and I craned our necks to look more closely.

'Well,' I said,' in one way or another this house is proving to be a bit of a treasure trove and a history lesson all in one!'

'Oh yes,' laughed Aunt in reply.' Winnie was a bit of a hoarder, so who knows what else is still waiting to be discovered!'

# Stephen Varley's Journal, Thursday 19th October

4:30pm

After yet another fitful night's sleep, which was punctuated by strange, often abrupt, noises that – after some fanciful theorising about ghosts, burglars and witches' cats – we eventually attributed to the creaking of the building, Sophie and I returned this morning to more clearing out of the cellar. Our initial finds were entirely unpromising: two old vacuum cleaners, a metal bird cage which looked like it had been bashed with a hammer and the stomach-churning find of a dead, slightly decomposed rat. However, we at length came across something else of interest – an old leather-bound book with ancient, barely legible hand-writing, which had been used to prop up an empty, three-legged chest-of-drawers. This item of furniture crashed loudly to the floor in a cloud of dust when I foolishly lifted it up to take the book out from under it, without having given any thought to the potential consequences of my actions! Aunt appeared at the cellar doorway shortly after the crash, asking if we were alright.

'Yes, Aunt,' said Sophie bluntly. 'It's just Stephen being an idiot!'

I could hear Aunt shuffling off back into the house, where she was going through some of Winifred's personal papers and marking up various items that she had decided to sell.

Sophie and I propped the chest-of-drawers up again, using a loose brick from the floor as the fourth leg this time. We placed the book on top of it and opened it up. The page the book opened on

80

was ruled into two unevenly spaced columns, with large, swirly handwriting in the wider column on the left and various numbers in the narrower column on the right.

'It looks like an account book,' said Sophie.

I nodded.

'It must be a pretty old one. The leather's really aged and that style of writing looks very dated.'

Sophie placed the forefinger of her right hand at the top of the left-hand column.

'There's a date here,' she said, indicating it. 'It looks like "1789".'

I leaned a bit closer to get a better look.

'Yes,' I said. 'I think you're right. "7th August, 1789."'

Sophie moved her finger down the column, reading off entries as she did so.

'Does that say "6 kegs"?' she asked.

I looked.

'Yes, I think so. "6 kegs of brandy." And the next one says "15 yards of silk".'

'That's a lot of silk!' said Sophie.

I continued reading.

'"30 gallons of gin... 7 tea chests... 12 swords... 18 pistol flints..."'

'Look!' said Sophie, interrupting me. 'The right-hand column has got a monetary value next to each commodity.'

We looked at one another simultaneously.

'It's a smuggling inventory!' I said.

Sophie turned the page and we found that it too contained two columns of hand-written goods and their respective values.

'"12th September 1789",' I read from the date which was written at the top left.

Sophie turned another page.

'"10th October 1789". They were obviously making a smuggling run across the Channel every month.'

I nodded.

'Let's take it up into the kitchen. We can show Aunt and have a better look at it in the daylight.'

Sophie picked up the book and we ascended the cellar steps and went into the kitchen. I called out to Aunt, who was in the lounge, to come and have a look at the book.

'Hey! There are some initials in the front!' exclaimed Sophie, as Aunt entered the room.

I peered at a spot inside the front cover that Sophie was pointing to.

'"H.N."'

'I expect you'll find that stands for "Hard Nut",' said Aunt, peering over my shoulder. 'Winnie once showed me some old smuggling books that she had found in the cellar. That looks like one of them.'

'They've got quantities and values of a whole load of smuggled goods, Aunt,' said Sophie excitedly. 'There's a lot of it - silk, brandy, gin...'

Aunt nodded sagely.

'Yes, dear. I expect there is. It would seem that old William Blyth virtually ran the smuggling trade in this whole area once upon a time.'

I looked at the letters again.

'Why has it got "H.N." in the book? Surely it should say "W.B."?'

Aunt laughed.

'If a smuggler was caught with anything that

82

connected him directly to any smuggled goods, then that would be the end of it!' she explained. 'A book with the name "William Blyth" and goods like "silk" and "brandy" in it would be as good as a death warrant. I'm guessing that the Customs officers didn't know William's nickname. If that book had been found with the initials "H.N." in it, then William would have had a pretty good case for defence that it wasn't his.'

The three of us spent a good twenty minutes leafing through the book, which proved to contain page after page of accounts of smuggled goods from 1785 to 1793, before deciding it was time for an early lunch. The find of the book was fascinating to both me and Sophie and we talked non-stop about it, and about Hard Nut Blyth, while we were eating. We were both very keen to get back into the cellar to see what else we could find.

# Stephen Varley's Journal, Thursday 19th October

*4:30pm, continued*

After lunch we returned to the cellar and waded through all kinds of junk – including an old bicycle with a missing front wheel and a hat stand that had scratch marks up it like a stretching cat might make – before finding what we presumed was another smuggling relic. Hidden under a tatty-looking, thick grey blanket that had about three inches of dust on top of it was an old wooden, iron-bound barrel, standing on one end, with the words 'four gallons' written on the top of it.

'Four gallons of what?' wondered Sophie, aloud.

'Brandy, I hope!' I said.

Sophie pushed me away playfully as she threw the blanket into a corner. More clouds of dust duly arose. Dave's dust masks were proving to be a Godsend.

'You wish!'

I laughed.

'It could well be an old smuggling barrel though,' I said, with more seriousness. Aunt said Winifred found one down here. It looks pretty old. Look how dark the wood is. And there are some scuff marks on it where it has been rolled along the ground or something.'

I crouched down and ran my hands over the marks on the curving timbers and could feel their great age under my fingers. I got a faint whiff of alcohol as I did so and leant closer to the wood to smell it properly.

'That's brandy,' I said. 'Have a sniff.'

Sophie crouched down next to me and touched the barrel with her hand, sniffing at it tentatively as she did so too.

'Nice dead spider there!' she said, distracted.

I frowned.

'Ignore the dead spider. Smell the barrel!'

Sophie took her dust mask off briefly, sniffed the barrel and wrinkled her pretty little nose, before putting the mask back on again.

'I think you're right,' she said. 'There is definitely a lingering smell of alcohol around it. I guess the brandy or gin or whatever the contents were was the saleable commodity. No doubt the barrel was left behind once its contents had been sold, probably to The Smugglers' Rest!'

I laughed.

'Yes, you're probably right about that! Let's roll it over to the stairs and take it up to show Aunt.'

We both stood up, Sophie stepped back and I pushed the top of the barrel to make it fall over, so I could roll it towards the stairs. It barely moved.

'It's heavier than I was expecting,' I said.

'Push it harder, you wuss!' chided Sophie.

I pushed the barrel harder and managed to topple it, but no sooner had it fallen onto its side than it rolled away from us of its own accord, over the crumpled grey blanket that Sophie had discarded and then slaloming slowly onwards, left-right-left like a drunken duck, as it made its way across the uneven cellar floor. After two or three rolls it came to rest as it lost momentum and a protruding cork bung that had been hidden out of sight at the back of the barrel when it had been standing upright brought it to a standstill and stopped it from rolling any further.

'Did you hear it sloshing?' asked Sophie, after the barrel had come to a standstill.

I looked at her, bemused.

'No,' I said, 'I can't say that I did.'

'I think there is still some of the contents left inside it.'

We made our way over to the barrel and rolled it half a turn so that the bung was facing upwards.

'I see what you mean about the weight,' said Sophie.' It is pretty heavy.'

I nodded, rocking the barrel slightly to see if anything sloshed around inside it.

'You're right,' I said. 'There is definitely some liquid in there. That would account for the weight and also why it rolled about so much when I tipped it over. I might get a tot of brandy from it after all!'

I held the barrel in place with the bung at the top and Sophie attempted to pull the bung out.

'It's stuck fast!' she said, making no impact on it at all on loosening it.

I laughed.

'Now who's the weakling?'

Sophie cuffed me playfully around the head.

'Well,' I said, 'let's think about this. If this is an original smuggling barrel and at least some of the original contents are still inside it, then that bung may well not have been removed for about two hundred years!'

Sophie looked around for something she could use to get the bung out with.

'What about that rope?' I said, indicating with my head a coiled length of dirty old rope that lay on the floor by the south wall. 'You could loop it round the bung and pull it out with that.'

Sophie picked up the rope and did as I suggested. Initially, the bung still wouldn't move, but after a lot of pulling it finally came free and Sophie toppled over backwards onto the dusty grey blanket, sending yet more clouds of dust into the air. I stifled a laugh.

'Nice work,' I said. 'Now go and get the bung – it landed over there behind that fire guard thing.'

Sophie glared at me but stood up and went to retrieve the bung before coming back to peer into the hole in the top of the barrel that I was still holding.

'Christ!' she said. 'It's almost full! And that is definitely brandy sloshing around in there – I can really smell it now, even with this mask on! We'll never get it up the stairs. Let me go and get Aunt to come and have a look.'

Sophie plugged the bung back in and we rolled the resealed barrel to the bottom of the stairs, where between us we eventually managed to stand it upright. Sophie climbed up the stairs and reappeared a few moments later at the top of them with Aunt.

'Look, Aunt!' I called up to her. 'An original brandy barrel!'

'Oh my goodness gracious me!' Aunt exclaimed. 'I didn't know there was one of those down there. It looks just like the one that Winnie found.'

'It's still got brandy in it,' said Sophie. 'Quite a lot of brandy too.'

'I know someone who collects brandy,' said Aunt, after a moment's thought.' He'd probably give me a good price for that if it's genuine.'

'Don't we have to declare it to Customs or something?' said Sophie, turning to face her.

'Oh, I don't think we need to bother with that, dear,' Aunt interrupted, with a gleam in her eye. 'What those people don't know won't hurt them.'

# Stephen Varley's Journal, Friday 20th October

*7:15pm*

The find of the old brandy barrel yesterday proved to be a Godsend to Aunt. She spoke to her friend, the brandy collector, on the phone in the evening and he was so excited by the news that he offered her a £1,000 non-refundable deposit for it there and then in return for his getting exclusive viewing of it over the weekend! He's travelling down from Norfolk, so he must be keen. Aunt reckons he will pay a lot more than that for it once he's seen it, so that's a nice little earner for her. She can put it towards doing up the house.

This morning, Sophie and I continued to explore the cellar. Winifred's cat - Satan! - spent some of the morning down there with us, albeit at what he evidently considered to be a safe distance away from us.

'I'm glad he's alright,' said Sophie.

We were both now completely focussed on locating any other smuggling booty that might be residing there and were stepping over things like broken flowerpots and moving abandoned writing desks aside as we were hot on the scent of more brandy and the like.

'You know we're supposed to be clearing the cellar out,' I said to Sophie at one point, 'not just moving things around?'

Sophie laughed.

'Don't be an old wet blanket,' she said. 'There might be a chest full of silk down here.'

Now it was my turn to laugh.

'Oh, I see!' I said. 'I thought you were looking for stuff that we could sell for Aunt, not material to make a load of new dresses out of!'

'I'll pay her for it!' said Sophie. 'That find of the brandy barrel has really whetted my appetite for other potentially hidden treasure. Who knows what else we might find down here?'

We pressed on with our search and in due course I noticed something sticking out of a cavity in the south cellar wall, towards the western end, where some of the mortar between the bricks had fallen away. It looked like a small cardboard tube. I went up to the wall and saw that it was actually a piece of rolled up paper. I called Sophie over.

'Look at this!' I said. 'I'm going to try to get it out.'

The paper was yellowed with age and covered in dust and spiders' webs, but it was remarkably robust, as it was quite thick, like parchment. I eased it out a bit at a time until I had the whole thing in my hands. I unrolled it to look at it. It was about eight inches long on each side, roughly square but with rough, torn edges. However, my dexterity was not what it could have been, and the paper rolled itself up again and fell out of my hands onto the floor. Decades of white-grey mortar-infused dust wafted delicately out of the rolled-up tube, like slowly, softly-falling snow.

'Butterfingers!' said Sophie.

'It must have been rolled up like that for ages,' I said.

I bent down and picked it up, and rolled it out more carefully the second time. It had the faded but still legible outline of some kind of drawing on it.

'Let's take it over there,' said Sophie, pointing to a wide shelf of about 12 inches depth that was protruding from the south wall near its junction with the west wall at about waist height not far from where we were standing. We duly went over to it, moved a couple of small, empty cardboard boxes from the shelf onto the floor and dusted off both the shelf and the parchment before rolling the latter out as best we could onto the shelf. The parchment wanted to curl up again, having been stored in that position for an as-yet indeterminate length of time.

'We need some things to hold its corners down with,' I said, trying to hold it open as best I could, but with no hope of ever fully doing so successfully.

'Wait here,' said Sophie.

She went off and rummaged around in the junk pile for a few moments and returned with some bronze weights that presumably once belonged to an as-yet undiscovered set of scales. I held the parchment open and Sophie carefully placed a weight on each corner. They were different sizes, due to their different weights, but they were nonetheless effective for our purposes.

'Brilliant!' I said.

We spread the parchment out with the weights as best we could and then began to examine it. On its surface was a hand-drawn diagram containing a number of lines of different lengths, each emanating from a central rectangle.

'What do you think this is then?' I asked.

Sophie frowned.

'I think it's a treasure map, Capt'n,' she said.

I could feel my eyebrows rising in surprise.

'A treasure map?' I repeated incredulously. 'Yeah, right!'

Sophie moved her head from side to side, craning her neck to orient herself in relation to the parchment.

'Well,' she said, with laughter in her voice initially, but becoming increasingly serious as she went on, 'what if that central rectangle is a representation of this cellar? That small block just to the right of the centre of the rectangle would be where the cellar stairs are and those hatched lines inside the block could be the cellar stairs. Those two smaller blocks abutting the left- and right-hand vertical ends of the rectangle would be the fireplaces at the west and east ends of the house respectively. This one at the left-hand end would be the one the cat went down.'

I studied the drawing more closely. I could see where she was coming from. It did bear some resemblance to the layout of the cellar - if one interpreted it that way.

'OK,' I said, 'that's plausible, but then what are these sets of parallel lines radiating out from the edges of the rectangle at various points? They would be protruding from the outsides of the cellar walls?'

Sophie shrugged.

'It could be drainage,' she said.

I wasn't convinced.

'Drainage?'

Sophie held her hands up, palms uppermost. Her

eyes seemed in the strip-light-illuminated semi-darkness to enlarge a little at the same time.

'The top left-hand lines end in a circle; that could be a pond? I think we need to go and have a look around the grounds of the building. There could well be ditches or ponds or something nearby? There's the river down below and there's Crouch Hill Pond in the village, though that is a pretty long way off from here, to be honest.'

I shrugged.

'Alright,' I said, 'let's go and have a look up top, but we'd better not be long or Aunt will be nagging us and asking what we're doing. Don't forget, we're still supposed to be clearing the cellar out!'

We took the weights off the corners of the parchment and it rolled up automatically into a tube again. I stuffed it down the front of my shirt and we set off up the steep cellar stairway into the garden in search of hidden ditches and ponds.

- - -

I've reproduced the drawing that we found as faithfully as I can below.

The 'map' found in the cellar at Home Farm

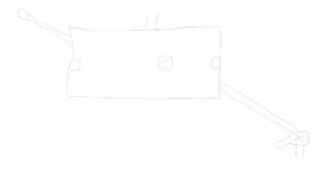

93

Assuming that the drawing was a map, as Sophie had suggested, and that we had correctly identified the cellar, the cellar stairs and the fireplaces, it had to be oriented in the way I've drawn it because of the slightly offset position of the stairs, something I've captured earlier in this journal in the plans of the ground and first floors of the house. That in turn would mean that the various sets of lines extending out from it went in north-westerly, northern and south-easterly directions respectively.

We decided to start with the north-westerly lines, expecting that the circle at the end of those lines represented a pond. We consequently spent about half an hour hacking down the undergrowth around the north-western corner of the farmhouse between the building and the old hollow oak tree, without any success, until Aunt suddenly appeared at the back door and called out to us.

'I've been watching you two from the kitchen window for the last 10 minutes, dears,' she said. 'What on Earth are you doing?'

Sophie and I looked at each other a bit sheepishly.

'We're looking for a ditch,' I said.

Aunt looked bewildered.

'A ditch?' she repeated. 'I don't think there's one there, dear. There used to be one somewhere over that way years ago, but it's been dried out for decades. Why do you want a ditch?'

'According to a piece of parchment that we found in the cellar,' said Sophie, almost interrupting before Aunt had finished, 'there are a number of ditches leading to - or from - the farmhouse. At least we think that they're ditches.'

Aunt held her hand out expectantly.

'Show me,' she said.

I dropped the sickle that I had again been using to hack away at the undergrowth and Sophie and I made our way over to the back door where Aunt stood. I took the rolled up parchment out of the front of my shirt and held it out for Aunt to take. She rolled it out carefully and with more dexterity than I had had, holding it up in front of her, with one side of it in each of her hands, and scrutinised the picture closely before rolling it up and giving it back to me.

'Well?' said Sophie. 'What do you think it is? We think it's the cellar and some ditches.'

Aunt acted a little suspiciously, like a criminal under investigation who was stringing the police along by not giving out information unless it was specifically asked for.

'I reckon that's the cellar alright, dear,' she said, 'but those aren't ditches. I would think that they are much more likely to be tunnels.'

And with that she turned her back on us and went into the house, leaving Sophie and me momentarily perplexed and looking at each other for answers. We had no option but to follow her into the kitchen.

# Stephen Varley's Journal, Friday 20<sup>th</sup> October

*7:15pm, continued*

'Tunnels?!' we both said in unison, when we caught up with Aunt in the kitchen.

'Oh yes!' she said, once we were all ensconced there and sharing a pot of tea and a plate of biscuits. 'Winnie was always going on about smugglers' tunnels connected with the farmhouse. She read about it in one of her books. The lines on the diagram look like passageways to me, and if that is the cellar, and to be honest I agree with you that it probably is, then they must be underground passageways, and underground passageways are usually called tunnels.'

Aunt's response came across sarcastically, but I don't think it was meant to.

'Did Winifred ever find any tunnels?' asked Sophie, helping herself to a biscuit.

Aunt screwed up her face.

'Not that I know of, dear,' she replied, 'but she did once try to. I always thought she was looking for them more in hope than in expectation. She was digging around in the floor of the lock-up in the High Street once when I came out of my little cottage opposite - it never used to be kept locked in those days - and another time she was tapping the cellar wall beneath the lounge in this building with a trowel. If only she had seen that map you've got - it might have helped her to target her search a bit better. Assuming she was right, of course.'

I spread out the parchment on the kitchen work surface and the three of us held out the four corners between us to keep it rolled open. Aunt put some empty cups from one of the cupboards and the plate of biscuits on the four corners to hold it down, just like Sophie and I had done with the weights in the cellar. We all stared at it intently, each taking in the faded, hand-drawn lines that were laid out in front of us.

'OK,' I said, tracing my index finger along the line of the rectangle in the centre of the diagram. 'That <u>could</u> be the cellar. These minor indentations just inside the vertical sides of the rectangle, east and west, <u>could</u> be the fireplaces. And these short repeated horizontal lines in this block in the centre here <u>could</u> be the cellar stairs and stairwell...'

Sophie interrupted my musings by suddenly clapping her hands.

'...So we can use this map to help us find the tunnels!' she said.

I looked at her in mock surprise.

'Slow down, Usain Bolt!' I said. 'There are a lot of ifs and buts to get through yet.'

Now it was Sophie's turn to screw up her face.

'I don't think there are, Stephen,' she said, with an air of sincerity. 'It's just dawned on me that this "pond" at the end of the north-westerly lines is not actually a pond at all. We found nothing at all between the house and the old hollow oak tree and we were so intent on looking for ditches there that we didn't notice what was right in front of us. This circle does not represent a pond - it represents the oak tree!'

I could feel my eyebrows rising, but Aunt nodded, as if in agreement with her.

97

'I don't know about that,' I said.' I stood inside that tree and it had roots everywhere and was very damp and muddy inside it. Why would anyone want to dig out a tunnel between the house and the tree?'

'Well,' said Aunt, developing Sophie's line of argument, 'you remember that book about Hard Nut Blyth that Winnie pasted a copy of into her journal? Remember how it mentioned a hollow oak tree used for storing smuggled goods in on land at Home Farm? Well, I've always thought that that was probably the tree and if the smugglers also stored goods in the cellar - which we know they did, from your and Winnie's finds of the brandy barrels - then it's plausible that they connected the two storage spaces with a tunnel.'

I could tell I was looking blankly at her, while I was trying to comprehend the concept.

'But why?' I said again.' Why connect the two storage places when they were both on site here?'

'Perhaps they wanted to move things around unseen by prying eyes,' continued Aunt.' The church is only next door. Anyone could have been in the churchyard, observing what was going on here. Suppose the revenue men were in the village? The movement of goods underground during daylight hours would have been a way to prevent them being seen.'

I still wasn't totally convinced and could feel myself becoming a bit irritated.

'Ok, then,' I said.' Why does this other "tunnel" from the north wall stop suddenly then? Explain that one!'

Sophie cleared her throat.

'Well, where would it have gone?' she said,

musing aloud. 'It's heading in the direction of the river, which would have been sensible if they were smuggling goods in by boat, but that's a long old way down the hill from here. Maybe they made a start on it but realised it was too much of a challenge and didn't complete it?'

'Or maybe they got a certain distance and it flooded?' offered Aunt.

I had to acknowledge that there was some logic to this idea.

'OK,' I said, pointing to the tunnel which extended in a south-easterly direction from the east wall. 'What about this one?'

'That's an easy one,' said Aunt, with mischief in her voice. 'That's heading into the village and Hard Nut's grocery shop!'

Sophie laughed.

'Well, why not?' said Aunt, her eyes sparkling with life.

I could feel myself frowning.

'OK,' I said, 'that's plausible, but what's the significance of the box with the "X" in it at the bottom right-hand corner of the diagram?'

'That would be Hard Nut's shop,' said Aunt, definitively, 'and the lines emanating from there represent his distribution network.'

'Ooh!' said Sophie, suddenly. 'I know what it is! "X marks the spot"! That's where the smugglers' treasure is!'

I laughed.

'Really?' I said. 'You think it's that easy?'

'There's one way to find out,' replied Sophie. 'Let's go downstairs and open up some tunnels!'

99

# Stephen Varley's Journal, Saturday 21st October

*9pm*

Sophie and I hardly slept a wink last night. We had hoped to make a start on our tunnel investigations yesterday evening, but the brandy collector from Norfolk arrived unexpectedly a day early because he was so excited about our barrel find that he couldn't wait until today, and dealing with him took up the rest of the day. He could bore for England about brandy and droned on for hours about Cognacs, Armagnacs and Almanacs until we were all heartily sick of the stuff! Needless to say, he was delighted with the find and paid Aunt a handsome sum for it. I helped him roll the barrel up from the cellar, through the house and into his van, using the old ' KEEP OUT!' board that was still in the farmyard as a ramp, and by the time I'd managed to get a word in and send him on his way I was completely drained. I returned to the lounge to find Aunt and Sophie flaked out on the armchairs, looking as exhausted as I felt.

' I thought he would never shut up!' said Sophie.

' I nearly punched him at one point!' I said, flopping down into an armchair myself.

' I think you should put off looking for the tunnels until tomorrow, dears,' said Aunt after a lengthy pause.' We could all do with a good night's sleep after that, I think.'

We duly abandoned our tunnel exploration project until today, but yet again we didn't get a great night's sleep. It absolutely tipped it down with rain all night, so what with that and our nervous excitement about smuggling we never stood a chance really. Sophie and I discussed smugglers' tunnels well into the small hours, musing about whether indeed there were any, and if there were, where they might lead and why. I didn't think we were ever going to get to sleep, until we popped down to the lounge and had four or five rounds of Aunt's best sherry and the next thing I knew I woke up this morning with a slight headache and a very dry throat! Sophie has looked better, bless her! Ooh, I mustn't put things like that in here, in case she reads it!

Anyway, obviously the priority for the day was to try to locate a tunnel, so after wolfing down some toast and some mugs of tea we bounded down the stairs into the cellar again and began to theorise about where best to start.

I favoured starting in the north-western corner, so that I could put the idea of the tunnel leading to the tree to bed early on.

Sophie nodded.

'Challenge accepted,' she said, with confidence.

'OK,' I said. 'Where precisely do you think we should start?'

Sophie wrinkled her nose. We heard Aunt calling 'Cooee!' down the stairs and acknowledged her greeting.

'I hope you two slept better than I did,' she said.

I looked at Sophie. She looked as tired as I felt.

'Get the map out again,' she said.

'You mean the parchment?' I said.

We rolled it out on the same shelf as the day

101

before and weighted it down with the redundant scales weights again.

'We need to do some measuring,' said Sophie.

'I saw a tape measure over there,' I said, pointing to a battered old chest-of-drawers with one of the drawers sticking out.' I think it's on the top of that.'

I walked over and returned forthwith with a large circular tape measure, about six inches in diameter, in a brown leather case, with a brass wind-up handle on the top.

Sophie laughed.

'That looks like it's out of the Ark!' she said.

'Hey, don't knock it! We need a long one and this looks like it will be ideal for the job!'

Sophie nodded sagely.

'Indeed,' she said. 'You're not wrong.'

We pored over the map again. While we were doing so, I suddenly became aware that Satan was in the cellar with us and quietly drew Sophie's attention to him.

'I wonder how long he's been down here this time,' mused Sophie, aloud.' He could have been watching us since we arrived?'

I shrugged.

'You know what cats are like,' I said.' Great at seeing in the dark.'

I absentmindedly picked up a broom that was lying at the foot of the junk pile and used it to brush aside a load of cobwebs that were dangling down from the ceiling above us and illuminated in the light.

'I propose that we measure the full length of

the west wall,' I said, looking about me as I did so,' and write the measurement on the map. There's a pencil over there that we can use. That pair of parallel lines emanating from the top left-hand end of the rectangle looks about a quarter of the way down from the top, so we can then just divide our measurement by four and start from there.'

Sophie nodded in agreement.

'Sounds like a plan, Holmes,' she said, 'but we need to move that chest-of-drawers first.'

We made our way over to the Jacobean chest-of-drawers that we had first seen from the bottom of the stairs. It was in OK condition, but not spectacular.

'We might be able to get a few bob for Aunt for this,' I said.

Sophie pulled open the drawers and closed them again one-by-one.

'At least it's empty,' she observed. 'We should be able to manage it.'

We both adopted a crouching position, knees bent, backs straight, one either side of the unit.

'After three,' I said. 'One, two, three!'

We lifted the item fairly easily between us and carried it a safe distance away from the wall. Once we had done that, we duly set about measuring the wall, Sophie crouching down in the south-western corner of the cellar and me reeling out the tape measure to the north-western corner as I walked over to it away from her. More and more tape came out of its circular casing until hardly any of it was left in there.

'That was lucky!' I said, crouching down myself.

103

'I've just noticed that it says "65 feet max." on the case. We've measured out sixty feet exactly!'

'Blimey!' said Sophie. 'That's more than I was expecting.'

We left our respective ends of the tape measure where they were and stood up and walked back to the map.

'So,' I said, moving my index finger along the lines on the map as I did so, 'if we measure 15 feet in from my end, then we should be roughly on the money.'

Sophie nodded and went back into the south-western corner and picked up her end of the tape. I returned to the north-western corner and began reeling in 15 feet of the tape, walking slowly southwards along the west wall towards her with it as I did so until the tape showed exactly 45 feet.

'It should be about here,' I said.

'Find something to mark it with,' said Sophie, excitedly.

I looked around and picked up a shard of broken red brick from the floor.

'We can use this,' I said, holding it up.

Sophie let her end of the tape measure fall and walked over to me. She took the red-brick shard from me and scratched it in an approximately vertical line down the white-painted wall where I was holding the measure at the 45 feet mark. Once she had done that we both stepped back and admired our handiwork. I reeled in the tape measure.

'Right,' said Sophie, 'now we just need to find something to dig out the wall with.'

I paused.

'Hold on!' I said. 'Something's just occurred to me. Is it going to be wise to knock the cellar wall out when there's a massive great farmhouse standing on top of us, complete with Aunt inside it?'

Sophie frowned.

'Hmmm,' she said, buying herself some time to muse over the various possibilities. 'Well... if there isn't a tunnel here, then it won't matter, because we'll soon discover just brickwork and earth and we can stop before we go too far with it. On the other hand, if there _is_ a tunnel here, then somebody else will have broken through the wall already and it would be safe to assume that they have propped it up in some way, so it shouldn't matter if we do it again. Of course, if there _is_ a tunnel and they _haven't_ propped it up, then yes, it could be an issue!'

We looked at the white-painted brickwork of the cellar walls. From what I had noticed of them so far they were quite uneven in places, with rough, raised or indented surfaces. How much of this was due to the quality of the original Tudor brickwork, the weight of time/the Victorian farmhouse on top of it, or them having been bashed about in the cellar's undoubted role as a storage space over the centuries, I had no idea. I was keen to find out for definite whether or not there were any tunnels though, so I decided on the spot that I was prepared to take the risk.

'Alright,' I said. 'How about we start gently and scratch away at this surface paint coating to see what is revealed. That won't bring the house down and it will give us a better understanding of what

105

condition the underlying brickwork is in.'

Sophie nodded.

'I'll make an archaeologist out of you yet,' she said. 'I'll go and have a look in Dad's tool bag and see if there's anything in that that we can use.'

She returned a couple of minutes later with Dave's tool bag in hand and put it on the ground next to us. She took out two different-sized chisels from it, and a large screwdriver and a wallpaper scraper.

'Are these any good?'

I laughed.

'Yep,' I said, 'they look ideal. We're going to need those gloves in there as well.'

We began to scratch away at the wall, one of us either side of the roughly vertical line that Sophie had marked. The white surface paint came off quite easily, revealing the red Tudor brickwork behind it. Wherever we scratched the paintwork off though, there was nothing but brick behind it; there was no sign of an entrance to a tunnel.

'Brick,' said Sophie, echoing my thoughts. 'Just brick.'

We redoubled our efforts, scratching high up on the wall and low down by our feet, but there was brick everywhere we looked. We then scraped away in various places at random with similar results. It was challenging, frustrating work.

'Maybe there isn't a tunnel after all?' I said, at length. 'Perhaps you were right the first time and it's actually a drawing of Tudor drains? Maybe there's a pond the other side of the oak tree in the field?'

Sophie flashed an angry look at me.

'There <u>has</u> to be a tunnel!' she said, passionately. 'We've literally only just scratched the surface. There's a lot more wall to go yet. We haven't looked hard enough. It's got to be here somewhere!'

We both stepped back and wiped some sweat from our foreheads. I looked at Sophie and could see that she was getting annoyed.

'We don't know for definite that that piece of paper is a map,' I said, trying to calm her down.' We might be jumping to conclusions.'

She glared at me again.

'This house has smuggling ancestry, we've found a smuggler's brandy barrel and Aunt caught Winifred looking for tunnels, including down here in the cellar. There has to be a tunnel here!'

I was about to offer some additional words of comfort when Sophie stepped backwards in a huff and fell over a rusting red fire extinguisher that neither of us had noticed until that point because it was covered up by a dusty, threadbare grey towel. She landed flat on her back on the floor.

I choked back a laugh that was gathering in my throat.

'And I've had enough of all this rubbish down here!' she shouted, jumping to her feet and picking up the fire extinguisher with more than her usual strength as she did so. 'How much crap can one person have kept?'

She threw the fire extinguisher away from her in anger and it crashed with a hollow sound into the wall, waist-height, about three feet to her left, before falling to the floor. An uneven, straggling crack appeared in the whitewash as a result. I caught sight out of the corner of my eye of Satan disappearing up the cellar stairs.

'Hold on!' I said.' Look at that!'

We went over to the wall where the extinguisher had hit it and looked at the damage. Sophie petulantly kicked the fallen extinguisher out of the way to give us access. It rolled over a couple of times and came to a standstill on a protruding section of the brick floor. I could see that she was calming down a bit due to the physical exertion.

To my astonishment, there was a piece of flint sticking out through the crack in the wall.

'That isn't brick!' I said.' Let me get the tools.'

I picked up the bigger of the two chisels and began to scratch away at the whitewash to the right of the protruding flint.

'There are stones in here as well,' I said.' Look!'

Sophie craned her neck to look more closely. A broad smile began to appear on her face and she visibly relaxed.

'That's rubble infill,' she said.' This part of the wall has been patched up.'

She went to get the other chisel and started scraping away furiously alongside me. Bits of stone and hard-packed earth began to fall out of the wall and make little piles of rubble on the floor. We soon made light work of creating an indentation in the wall.

'You measured it wrongly!' said Sophie, grinning at me.' The tunnel entrance is here!'

I let the good-natured criticism ride and carried on scraping until we reached a point where I thought what remained of the wall at the spot we had been scraping could be forced through.

'Stand back,' I said.' Let me have a go with this.'

Sophie did as instructed and I picked up the fallen fire extinguisher and used the base of it as a battering ram to knock the wall through. I hit the wall three times with it and on the third attempt what rubble infill that was left tumbled away from me into a dark recess beyond. A gust of damp, foul air came flooding out. I dropped the fire extinguisher onto the cellar floor.

'Bingo!' said Sophie.

Before I could reply I heard Aunt's voice behind me, calling across to us from the cellar stairs.

'What on Earth is all that racket, Stephen?!' she said.

# Stephen Varley's Journal, Saturday 21st October

*9pm, continued*

'We've found a tunnel!' said Sophie, full of enthusiasm. 'At the northern end of the west wall – just like it showed on the map!'

Aunt, who was standing halfway down the stairs, looked shocked.

'A tunnel? Really? Are you pulling my leg, dear?'

'Well, we think it's a tunnel,' I said, trying to temper Sophie's exuberance. 'It's roughly where the lines on the map on that side go, though we were initially slightly out with our measurements. We've knocked a bit of the wall through and there is definitely some kind of cavity behind it.'

'I should think you did knock the wall through!' said Aunt. 'I'm surprised they didn't hear you in Pockingham!'

I looked at Sophie and felt a bit sheepish.

'Sorry, Aunt,' I said. 'We were hot on the tunnel trail and didn't want to give up until we'd got something to report.'

'It's my fault,' said Sophie, apologetically. 'I was so determined to find one. All those smuggling tales and finds have really whetted my appetite for it.'

Aunt smiled kindly.

'I don't have a problem with that, dear,' she said. 'I was just a bit worried that you might be knocking the house down from under me.'

With that, Aunt began gingerly to descend the rest of the steep wooden steps into the cellar. It was the first time I had seen her attempt it since

Sophie and I had been at the farmhouse.

'Careful Aunt!' I said, running over to steady her as she descended. 'The stairs are bit steep!'

'It's a while since I have been down here,' she replied. 'I'm not as young as I used to be.'

I held her arm until she reached the safety of the cellar floor.

'Where's this tunnel then, Stephen?' she said, looking me directly in the eye. I could tell from the brightness of her eyes that despite her advanced years she still had a lot of life left in her yet.

'It's over here, Aunt!' called Sophie, excitedly. 'Come and have a look!'

Aunt and I walked over to where Sophie was standing and Sophie and I both stood back so that Aunt could inspect our handiwork. She leaned forward to peer through the hole made by the fire extinguisher.

'Well, I'm blowed!' she said. 'It does look like there is a cavity behind the wall here. But how far does it go? It smells a bit damp.'

She put her hand up to the opening that we had created and almost caressed the edges of the hole with her fingers.

'Maybe dear old Winnie was right after all and there are tunnels down here. Well, well, well – who would have thought it? What a shame she didn't have that map.'

There was the briefest of pauses.

'Well, Aunt,' I said reassuringly, 'we can explore them in Winifred's name.'

Aunt turned to face me and gently pressed her hand on my arm. Her eyes were wet but smiling.

'If you look closely at the construction of the cellar wall here,' said Sophie, who had clearly been inspecting it while I had been assisting Aunt with her descent of the cellar stairs, 'you can see that this stretch of it is not smooth like the rest of the wall, but has a very uneven surface. It looks from what we have excavated so far like it has been broken through at some point and back-filled with rubble.'

I looked at Aunt with a wry smile on my face.

'This is what it's like living with an archaeologist,' I said.

Sophie prodded me good-naturedly with the chisel she was still holding and ignored the interruption.

'I think if we keep chipping away at this we will unveil an opening about six feet high and four feet wide, if the lines between the rough and smooth parts of the cellar wall are anything to go by.'

'How very exciting, dear!' replied Aunt, clapping her hands with genuine excitement and wiping the back of her hand across her eyes.

Sophie and I looked at one another.

'Shall we continue to remove the rubble infill then, Aunt?' I asked.

'Oh yes, dear,' Aunt replied. 'I want to know what's behind it as much as you do. As long as you can assure me that the house won't fall down!'

'Oh, I guarantee that it won't!' replied Sophie, rather more definitively than I would have done. 'If this _is_ a smuggling tunnel then it's going to be at least 200 years old. The top four or five courses of the original brickwork over the opening into the tunnel are still firmly in place - it doesn't look like

112

they've ever been moved. And, in any case, the tunnel itself will be outside the house beneath the garden; this is just the entrance to it.'

Aunt looked vaguely, though not entirely, reassured. So did I.

'Why don't you take a seat on the cellar stairs and watch us from there, Aunt?' I said, keen to get on with it. 'Sophie and I are both getting a bit dusty and grimy doing this.'

Sophie stretched out her jumper to show that small shards of white paint and red brick were spread all over it.

'Alright dear,' said Aunt. 'I'll do just that.'

Sophie and I returned to our work, and with Aunt fully onside and sitting safely away from us on the cellar stairs we now began to chip away excitedly without inhibition at the opening we had made. I briefly left the scene to get two pairs of protective plastic goggles from Dave's tool bag; one pair was so new that it was still in its cellophane wrapping. Once we had those on we became less delicate in our chipping and began to hack at the wall like my dad does when he is 'pruning' a rosebush.

After several minutes work the wall began to weaken and larger and larger pieces of it began to fall out, either onto our feet, so that we had quickly to lift the latter up out of the way from time to time, to avoid getting painful toes, or out into the dark damp space that lay beyond. Eventually we had created such a big hole and the rubble infill that was left between the bricks was so loose that I motioned to Sophie to step back. I gave the remaining rubble infill an almighty big kick and some

113

of it fell away from me into the void. Two more big kicks and a bit more hacking later and we were left with an opening that we could easily step through. Aunt stood up and came over and Sophie and I peered into the dark space behind the wall as she arrived behind us.

I could feel the excitement emanating from Sophie as she stood next to me.

'I'll get the torch!' she said.

Sophie returned with the torch from Dave's tool bag that we had used to look for the cat in the bedroom and shone it into the opening beyond the wall. It was indeed the beginnings of a tunnel and we looked at one another with great excitement.

'I'm going through!' said Sophie, impulsively, and before I could stop her she was through the wall and standing on the other side of it, her torso - the only part of her that was visible as the top and bottom of the wall were still largely in place and therefore obscured her head and feet - blocking my view.

'Be careful, dear,' said Aunt, over my shoulder. 'You don't want the roof caving in on you.'

Sophie laughed.

'I think I'll be alright, Aunt,' she said.' It's lined with brick in here. Not the red Tudor brick, nor the yellow Victorian brick mind, but Georgian brick. You can always tell it: it's much darker, like Handel's House in London. The difference is even noticeable in the torchlight.'

Sophie's voice sounded curiously deadened by the walls around her as she spoke, as if she was both nearby and far away at the same time.

114

'I've never been there, dear,' said Aunt, matter-of-factly.

'Anyway,' continued Sophie, clearly in her element, 'I have first-hand experience of tunnelling. My dad worked on the Bell Common Tunnel on the M25 near Epping in 1984 and he took me there two or three times. I was only three at the time. It was fascinating! I think it's that that gave me my interest in archaeology.'

'She can bore you to death with this for hours, Aunt,' I said, winking.

'I heard that!' said Sophie, continuing with her sermon. 'It's thought that tunnels were first dug by prehistoric people enlarging their caves. There was a 3,000-feet long tunnel built under the River Euphrates in Babylon in about 2100BC I think, so I should imagine that resourceful 18th-century smugglers would have found it comparatively easy!'

I thought about what Sophie was saying.

'If this is a smuggling tunnel,' I said, 'I suppose it would have been dug out by hand, would it? I hadn't really given it a thought.'

'Oh yes,' said Sophie, enthusiastically. 'All tunnels before about the late 17th century were dug by hand. The use of gunpowder in tunnel construction only came in around then, and dynamite wasn't available until about the mid-19th century. I can't see them using any explosives here though – explosives are more likely to be used for tunnelling through rock. Clay is comparatively easy to dig through and, given that a smuggling tunnel – if that's what this is – would have been secret, and gunpowder would have alerted the whole neighbourhood, it just wouldn't have been either a sensible or a practical approach.'

Aunt looked mildly frightened and mouthed the word ' Explosives?' at me.

'It's best to let her just get on with it,' I whispered.

'A lot of old tunnels are supported by wooden pit props,' continued Sophie, her bodiless voice coming to us a little spookily through the hole in the wall,' not least the ones that appear in <u>Scooby Doo</u> cartoons! I think there's surviving evidence of oak timbers being used for that purpose in some parts of the world from about the 1450s. Sitka spruce was preferred in the 1960s. Timber props need to be replaced every two or three years though. They use steel props nowadays.'

'It's just as well that this tunnel is brick-lined, then,' I said, trying to move the conversation along. 'Are the walls and ceiling both brick?'

'Yes,' said Sophie. 'The tunnel's actually arched with brick. It's nicely done, too. Whoever constructed it certainly knew what they were doing.'

Sophie crouched down so we could see her face through the opening.

'Do you want to come in as well then, Stephen? Let's see where it goes.'

I looked at Aunt, who nodded encouragingly, and bent down and stepped through the hole. It was like climbing through a five-bar gate which had the middle bar missing, stepping over the bottom part and trying to duck under the top part.

When I was inside the space with Sophie I stood up.

The tunnel was indeed about four feet in width,

as Sophie has predicted. The combination of arched roof and narrowness made me feel a little claustrophobic.

Sophie shone the torch away into the darkness. There were tree roots coming through the brickwork of the roof at various points and it all smelt very damp and unpleasant.

I took a moment to examine the tunnel brickwork, running my hand over its surface to try to feel the age of the structure. It was damp and uneven to the touch. The floor too was damp, made of clay, also uneven, but generally flat. Some large flat stones, like stepping stones, had been laid down on it to make walking easier and there was water lying in places between them.

My thoughts were broken by Sophie's voice.

'I can't see the end,' she said, pointing her torch as far into the blackness as she could. 'It looks pretty wet on the floor up there though.'

'What's happening in there?' I heard Aunt say from the cellar behind us. Her voice sounded curiously distant, amplified and deadened, as it entered the space around us.

'There's definitely a tunnel here, Aunt,' I said.

I was about to say something about Sophie when I realised that she was no longer crouching next to me but had stood up and gone further into the tunnel about 10 feet ahead of me. I could see her hunched silhouette in the torchlight.

'Be careful, darling!' I said, involuntarily.

Sophie turned her head towards me. Tree roots of varying thicknesses hung down in a clump between us, obscuring part of her face, but as

117

the fluorescent light from the cellar filtered into the tunnel and picked out the rest of her shadowy features, I could see that she was smiling.

'This is amazing!' she said, excitedly. 'We could be the first people to have been down here in 200 years.'

'Which is why,' I said, suddenly putting a 'Health & Safety' hat on, 'we need to check that it's safe to do so.'

Sophie laughed.

'Come on,' she said, encouragingly. 'Just a little bit further. It can't be too far to the tree.'

She waited for me to join her as I made my way in an uncomfortable, stooping-cum-crouching gait that reminded me of the actor Roddy McDowell's character, Cornelius, in the original film version of 'The Planet of The Apes'. Just as I reached Sophie, she grabbed my arm so suddenly that it made me jump. She pointed to something that was lying on the ground about three feet in front of her.

'What's that?' she said, focussing her torch onto it.

'What's what?' I said, unnerved, trying to focus my eyes in the semi-darkness.

She moved the torch beam rapidly from side-to-side over the object, giving it a 3D effect that made it easier for us to pick it out in the darkness.

'It looks like a piece of paper,' I said.

Sophie edge forward a couple of steps, keeping her torch on the object, and leant forward to pick it up.

'It's a label,' she said.

I moved forward to join her and she stood up

as best she could to show me the find. It was a torn black piece of paper, like a label from a bottle, with the word 'brandy' written on it in gold letters. There was also a gold-lettered date on it in slightly smaller font: '1793'.

'Another smuggling relic?' I said, rhetorically.

Sophie nodded.

'Let's see what else is in here,' she said.

We edged further into the tunnel a foot at a time, Sophie shining her torch around on the floor, walls and ceiling in front of us as we did so, looking for anything that stood out from its surroundings.

'The floor's very wet here,' said Sophie, shining the torch down to show how it was reflecting off some lying water. 'It's getting wetter with every step.'

We edged further forward a few more feet until the torch picked out another item lying on the floor in the distance, half-submerged with water.

'What's that?' she said.

I squinted as I tried to focus on the object in the darkness.

'It looks like a shovel,' I said.

We approached the object until we were close enough to see what it was. Sophie focussed the torch beam fully onto it.

'It's not a shovel,' I said, with some surprise and a sudden realisation, 'it's an oar!'

Sure enough it was indeed an oar. The paddle end was nearest to us, with the handle disappearing away from us into a puddle of water.

'An oar?' repeated Sophie, incredulous.

We edged right up to it until we were standing

119

over it, just on the edge of the puddle. Sophie shone her torch into the blackness beyond, but all we could see from this point onwards was water on the ground and tree roots coming out of the ceiling.

'Wow!' I said. 'I thought this was just a puddle, but it looks like the whole tunnel is flooded.'

Sophie nodded.

'This is as far as we go,' she said.

I bent down to pick the oar up. The wood was slimy and rotten and part of it fell away in my hands as I lifted it up.

'You know what,' I said. 'This is the side of the house where the track leads down to the river. The smugglers would have used the river to bring in their booty. I reckon this oar came from an old boat that the smugglers used.'

Sophie nodded.

'I think that's highly likely,' she said.

'I suppose,' I continued, trying to picture myself in the 18th century, 'that a couple of hundred years ago all the local people in all the local communities along the river here – smugglers and law-abiding citizens alike – would have used the river for transportation.'

Sophie nodded again.

'Yes,' she said, 'it would have been essential for everyone. I know that until about the 1920s the island of Foulness, which is a few miles away to the east of us had no roads on it at all. All the farmsteads on the island were dotted around the coast and accessed solely by boat. The families that were settled on the island mostly married into families in Marnham on the other side of the River

Crouch. That seems a bit odd if you look at the map, because Marnham is miles away by road, but it's easy by boat. Boat transport via the rivers, creeks and tributaries around here would have been the normal way of life for the islanders, as well as for the inhabitants of mainland villages like Cannow's End and Pockingham.'

While Sophie was talking, something else caught my eye on the floor of the tunnel.

'Look!' I said. 'There's another oar over there, with a load of old twigs on it.'

Sophie went over to the object and picked it up.

'It's not an oar!' she said, holding it up for me to see. 'It's a broomstick! The "old twigs" are part of it - the sweeping end!'

I was a little taken aback.

'Oh!' I said. 'I wasn't expecting that.'

Sophie looked the broomstick over.

'Let's go back and show Aunt what we've found,' she said. 'I'll take the label and the broomstick; you bring the oar.'

- - -

When we were safely back in the cellar we showed Aunt, who was waiting patiently for us, the broomstick and the remains of both the label and the oar.

Sophie looked radiant, despite the dust and grime on her hands, face and clothes. She was always in her element digging around for the past in dusty, dirty places and she looked so beautiful when she smiled.

'Goodness me!' said Aunt, looking at the finds we showed her.

'The tunnel is flooded at the far end, Aunt,' said Sophie, gently. 'I reckon that dried-out ditch you told us about gave way at some point and the water now collects in the tunnel instead.'

She held out the label to show Aunt; it was really wet.

'We'll put it on the radiator, dear,' said Aunt. 'That will dry it out a bit.'

We all made our way up the cellar stairs and into the kitchen, where Sophie carefully spread the label out on the top of the radiator. The writing on the label stood out more clearly in the natural light: it was definitely from a brandy bottle from 1793.

'Well,' said Aunt, 'that _is_ a find!'

She turned to look at the other discovery that Sophie was carrying.

'And what's this?' she asked. 'A broomstick?'

'Yes,' said Sophie, holding it out for Aunt to take. 'It's still in pretty good condition.'

Aunt turned it round in her hands.

'It certainly is, dear,' she said, laying it down on the kitchen table.

'We also found this!' I said, holding the remains of the oar out for her inspection.

'What on Earth is that?' she asked. 'It looks a bit like my grandad's shovel!'

I laughed and I put it down on the kitchen table next to the broomstick.

'I think it's an oar, Aunt,' I said. 'The blade of it is narrower and more curving than a shovel's.'

Aunt leant over the table to inspect it.

'Hmm,' she said. 'I think you're probably right. Where's the rest of it?'

Sophie laughed.

'That's all there is of it, Aunt,' she said. 'The rest of the shaft has evidently rotted away. I would think it was originally quite a bit longer.'

And so our day exploring the north-west tunnel ended. It was too wet and tree-rooty to go any further into it and we were both really tired from all the physical exertion, but at least we had a couple more finds to show for our efforts. With the barrel and the brandy label we knew for definite that smuggled goods had been in the old farmhouse's cellar at some point, and the oar seemed to give a clue to the method of transportation. We weren't sure how the broomstick fitted in; maybe it had been used on one of the smugglers' boats, or perhaps it had simply been used for sweeping out the cellar.

We had a talkative dinner, said our goodnights to Aunt and I wrote this entry up in my journal. I look forward to venturing back into the cellar again tomorrow to see what else awaits discovery!

# Stephen Varley's Journal, Sunday 22nd October

*8pm*

Sophie and I were both exhausted when we went to bed last night and for once we fell asleep straightaway and slept all through the night. Even another heavy shower of overnight rain that neither of us heard, but Aunt soon told us about when she looked in on us before she went to the morning church service, did not interrupt our sleep.

Our task for today was to see what else, if anything, we could find in the north-west tunnel and then see if we could locate the northern one. After getting dressed and having breakfast we went eagerly down into the cellar once more, followed at a discreet distance by Satan.

'I think he's getting used to us,' said Sophie.

We soon found, however, that the north-west tunnel was impassable beyond the point we reached yesterday, as the overnight rain had flooded it even further.

'I think the ditch system in this area has completely collapsed,' said Sophie, panning the torch around when we were back inside the tunnel again. 'It could be something to do with the tree roots – look how much they have invaded the space. It's even worse down the back there, the closer it gets to the tree. I think we'll have to give up on this one.'

With some disappointment I reluctantly agreed with her.

'One thing that's been bothering me about all this tunnel business,' I said, 'is where on Earth – if

124

you'll pardon the pun – did the smugglers put the earth that was dug out of them? I don't see any piles of clay lying around.'

Sophie snorted.

'Well, how hard have you looked, Stephen?' she said, dismissively. 'The clay could easily have been used to build up the sea wall, or to make some bricks. It could even have been used to line a pond, or maybe it was simply spread thinly over the surrounding fields to decrease the chances of detection? It _was_ over 200 years ago. There are plenty of possible uses for it, but I shouldn't think we'll ever know where it went for certain.'

I pulled a face.

'Yeah,' I said, 'I suppose you're right.'

Leaving the north-west tunnel to the tree roots and the water we turned our attention to locating the northern tunnel.

'Ok,' said Sophie, authoritatively. 'You know the drill: move the Jacobean chest-of-drawers, get the tape measure and measure out the wall.'

I went to get the tape measure but halfway there an idea suddenly occurred to me and I stopped in my tracks.

'What is it?' asked Sophie, mildly alarmed.

'I've had an idea!' I said.

I walked back to Sophie, took her hand and led her across to the Jacobean chest-of-drawers which was standing against the north wall.

'These two chests-of drawers are a pair, right?' I said.

Sophie followed my gaze across to the one we had moved away from the west wall and then she looked back at the one by the north wall right in front of us.

'Yes,' she said, 'they look like it to me.'

I nodded.

'And where was the one by the west wall standing before we moved it?'

'Right over there,' she said, pointing. 'Right over there – in front of the tunnel entrance.'

'Exactly!' I said. 'So what's the betting that the tunnel entrance on this wall is right behind this chest-of-drawers?'

Sophie beamed a lovely broad smile at me.

'I think you're right!' she said, with excitement in her voice. 'Let's move it!'

We duly moved the second, equally empty, Jacobean chest-of-drawers away from the wall and marked another red-brick-shard vertical line on the flaky white paint behind where it had previously stood.

'Let's get cracking!' said Sophie.

We began to chip away at the north wall, just like we had done with the west one, until we had reached the point where we needed to break through it.

'We'd better let Aunt know that we're going to knock the wall through,' I said. 'She's bound to be back from church by now and I don't want her having a heart attack again when we do!'

I went up to get Aunt and returned with her in tow. I helped her down the stairs again until she stood next to me at the bottom, peering out into the semi-darkness where Sophie was still gently chipping away at the wall.

'I wanted to be here for the breakthrough,' said Aunt to Sophie, by way of explanation. 'I'll wait here though and you can call across to me and tell me what you find.'

I collected the old fire extinguisher from where we'd left it and re-joined Sophie with it at the north wall. When we were ready I banged the extinguisher hard against the wall like before. Unfortunately this time the wall remained solid and the extinguisher broke instead! The top snapped off of it and the watery contents went all over the place, spraying into my face and over Sophie as well.

'You idiot!' spluttered Sophie through mouthfuls of water. 'Turn it off!'

I looked for a suitable knob or lever but could not find one.

'I don't know how to,' I said.

Sophie grabbed the extinguisher off me and threw it away towards the west wall, where it landed with a thud and continued to spray its contents in the vicinity for a few moments until it had emptied itself. I caught sight out of the corner of my eye of Aunt trying to stifle a laugh.

'It's not funny, Aunt,' I said.

Sophie looked rather wet, but undeterred.

'Thanks for that,' she said.

It took a visit to the shed in the back garden of the farmhouse and the retrieving of a sledgehammer – which weighed a ton – from it before we had anything reliable and sturdy enough to hand to break through the wall with.

'I'm going to stand back,' said Sophie, when I returned with it. 'Be careful where you're aiming that!'

The sledgehammer proved more up to the task

than the fire extinguisher had been and I successful broke through the wall after only two strikes. Between us, Sophie and I cleared the rubble away. Once again some foul damp air seeped through into the cellar from the cavity beyond.

'Bingo!' said Sophie, under her breath. 'Let's get in there!'

I turned back to call over to Aunt to give her an update.

'There's definitely another space here,' I said. 'We're going to go in and have a look round.'

Sophie, of course, stepped through the space first, but before she was barely in she let out an exclamation of disappointment.

'What's up, darling?' I asked her, crouching down to look into the space myself.

Sophie likewise crouched down on her side of the gap, so that I could see her face, and pointed the torch into the darkness ahead of her. I craned my neck to get a proper look.

'If this _was_ a tunnel, it's blocked up now,' she said. 'It's only about six feet long.'

I could see from the beam of Sophie's torch that the tunnel was not brick-lined like the previous one. The walls, roof and floor were all made of clay.

Aunt came over from the stairs to see what was going on.

'I think what's happened with this tunnel,' explained Sophie to both of us, the archaeologist inside her beginning to kick in again,' is that it caved in early on while they were still digging it and it was just abandoned. Look at these shovel marks on the walls...'

128

She panned her torch to highlight the spot indicated.

'I think there was a natural collapse of the clay and whoever was digging it just gave up. I don't think they can ever have completed the excavation as originally planned.'

She shone her torch on the back wall, so we could see. Aunt shuffled uneasily next to me.

'Very disappointing, dear,' she said, in a rather casual manner, and began to head back to the stairs. 'I'll go and put the kettle on.'

I held my hand out to Sophie through the gap in the wall. She looked crestfallen.

'Come on, darling,' I said. 'Back to the drawing board.'

# Stephen Varley's Journal, Sunday 22nd October

*8pm, continued*

We followed Aunt upstairs and had a cup of tea and some biscuits in the kitchen. I mused on how that room was becoming our HQ for our adventures. Satan appeared at the kitchen doorway, having evidently followed us, and sat down on the threshold.

'I think he's beginning to like us,' I said.

Sophie smiled.

'Is there no hope of finding a tunnel there?' asked Aunt, the disappointment of our findings evident in her voice.

'I'm afraid not, Aunt,' said Sophie, examining a biscuit.

'You don't think it was ever accessible by boat from the river? It's pointing in the right direction. A tunnel leading to the farmhouse from the river would have been a great way for those smugglers to access the building!'

Sophie shook her head.

'No,' she said. 'The tunnel definitely caved in before it got very far, but, even if it hadn't done, I would think that the engineering required for it would have been far too challenging. I don't know why they started digging it in the first place, to be honest; a tunnel from here to the river would have been a mammoth undertaking. Maybe it was just going to be a storage space or something?'

I mused for a moment about the possibility of a tunnel to the river.

'We could always go down to the river to see if there are any clues there to a tunnel opening at that end?' I said. 'They might have started at the other end instead when this one collapsed.'

Sophie screwed up her face.

'I think you're clutching at straws, Stephen,' she said, 'but I'm happy to go and investigate it with you if you fancy it.'

Aunt seemed enthused by the idea.

'Why don't you two go for a walk down to the river then and let me know how you get on? It'll do you good to get out of the house for a bit. I'm making good progress with clearing out Winnie's things. I'll carry on with that.'

Sophie and I eventually decided that this was a good idea, and after a suitable period of rest and recuperation, encouraged by sandwiches, more biscuits and some tea, we duly set off to walk down to the river. Stout walking boots and waterproofs were the order of the day, as the ground was pretty wet after all the recent rain. It was a beautiful, bright autumn day though, and the river below us sparkled in the sunshine.

When we were about halfway down the track to Crouchside Farm I stopped by a tree and unfolded a modern Ordnance Survey map of the area which Aunt had handed to me as we left the farmhouse.

'A tunnel from the river to the farmhouse would have been very useful,' I said, indicating the map with a nod of my forehead. 'The Crouch looks like a significant river, with a lot of tributaries and creeks that the smugglers could have moved about in. Even today we can see about a dozen or so pleasure craft moving along it. It looks from this map like it's a bit like a main highway, with a few smaller

" B-road" tributaries leading off of it!'

Sophie nodded.

'Yes,' she said, 'but I still think it's too big a task to have carried out, certainly without raising awareness of what you were doing.'

We carried on walking down the track until it reached the sea wall. We turned right (east) there and walked along the sea wall until we were roughly level with Home Farm. We could only see the roof of the farmhouse because the house itself was obscured by the curve of the hill up from the river and the hedgerow and trees on its northern boundary, but we could position ourselves roughly in the middle of the north wall by using the roof as a landmark.

I looked at the OS map again.

'About here, do you think?'

'Yes,' said Sophie, 'somewhere here.'

There was a small stretch of plant-filled water inside the modern sea wall in front of us and I realised in that instant looking down at it that the original shoreline would have been much lower than the current one.

'A freshwater lagoon,' said Sophie, following my gaze. 'See the bulrushes growing up there? This could feasibly have been a creek entrance years ago. See that indentation in the field? That could possibly mark the line of a long-lost creek, but it's all a bit speculative without proper research.'

We visually scoured the field in the vicinity of the lagoon where we hoped a tunnel entrance might once have been, but could see nothing.

'I think the tunnellers were over-ambitious if

they thought they could put a tunnel in from here,' said Sophie, looking up the hill at the farmhouse again. 'This would have been a long tunnel and if they got too far into the water table or flood plain then it would easily have collapsed. I suppose they could have envisaged constructing a short tunnel accessed by boat with a docking point of some kind inside of it – like you see in the Bond films where they smuggle a stolen submarine into some megalomaniac's subterranean hide-out or something – but they would have to have disembarked from the boat and then carried their goods via a pretty steep and long tunnel up the hillside. I just can't see it being plausible.'

I had to agree.

I took a few photos of the area on my phone to show Aunt and then we returned to the farmhouse to think over our next plan of action.

# Stephen Varley's Journal, Monday 23<sup>rd</sup> October

8pm

In the end we left off the topic of tunnels for the rest of day because it was tiring work looking for them and we were all a bit cheesed off that the north tunnel had proved to be such a let-down. We instead returned to tidying up the rest of the house and looking for items that Aunt could sell. Aunt herself found two solid silver brooches and a nineteenth-century clock that we all thought might raise a bit of money. She also told us that one of her friends in the village had promised to help her sell some of Winnie's stuff. I found a torch, which was very handy as it meant that Sophie and I now had one each.

After a decent night's rest we went down into the cellar again this morning to have a go at locating the south-eastern tunnel, while Aunt went across to All Saints church to try to locate some gloves that she had apparently left there during yesterday's service. I was now sure that what we thought was a map of some tunnels was indeed a map of some tunnels – it had been accurate with two-out-of-two of the sets of parallel lines so far, so I was confident that we would strike lucky with the third tunnel as well. Satan evidently shared our optimism, for he followed us more closely than ever and sat down only a few feet away from us.

The map seemed to suggest that this was the longest and potentially the most interesting of the three tunnels, though we were both still a bit perplexed by the box with a cross in it that

134

was marked on it towards the bottom right of the diagram.

Sophie and I duly made our way over to the eastern wall of the cellar, dust masks, gloves, chisels and torches at the ready. As we had seen on the first day that we had been down into the cellar, there was a huge, dark wardrobe, about seven feet tall, standing against the east wall near the south-eastern corner.

'You know where the tunnel entrance is going to be, don't you?' said Sophie, sizing up the wardrobe in front of us.

I breathed a heavy sigh.

'We're never going to shift that!' I said.

The wardrobe had two vertical hinged doors which opened outwards from the centre of the unit in classic fashion. The doors had brass door handles which were joined together by some ancient cobwebs. I brushed the cobwebs aside and pulled the handles, expecting the doors to open, but they remained tightly shut. I tried a second time, more firmly this time, but with the same result. The whole unit shook as I made this manoeuvre.

'It's locked,' I said.

Sophie exhaled heavily and rolled her eyes.

'You don't say!' she said. 'And where, pray tell, is the key?'

We looked around in the immediate vicinity in the vain hope of finding one. I was aware of the cat pacing around in the semi-darkness behind us.

I was starting to muse about breaking the doors open with an old brass candlestick that I spotted lying in the junk pile along the south wall, when I suddenly had a brainwave.

'Ooh!' I said.' An old uncle of my dad's used to keep the key to his wardrobe on top of it. I wonder if Winifred did the same.'

I reached up onto the top of the wardrobe, standing on tiptoe as I did so, and felt around with my fingers. They fell upon some kind of gooey substance.

'Yuk!' I said.' I don't know what that was. Some kind of gooey substance.'

Sophie looked unimpressed.

'Could be mould,' she said nonchalantly. 'Try a bit further along.'

I did as I was instructed and groped around in the darkness on top of the wardrobe for a few moments until my fingers alighted on a small metal cylinder about 5mm in diameter. I picked it up between my thumb and forefinger and lifted it down for us both to look at.

'Voila!' I said, triumphantly.' A key!'

Sophie looked surprised.

'Two keys actually,' she said. 'There's another one dangling from the keyring that's attached to it.'

I looked down at my find.

'So there is,' I said.

The cat came over and rubbed its body against my leg. I shook it off, a bit unnerved by its suddenly close presence.

'I have to say,' said Sophie,' I thought you were making the whole dad's uncle story up. Why on Earth would anyone keep a key to a locked wardrobe on top of the wardrobe? It's the first place you thought to look; surely anyone wanting to get at what's inside it would have done the same?'

'In my dad's uncle's case it was because we children were often round there,' I said. 'He put the key up high so that we couldn't get it. I've got no idea why Winifred did the same — maybe she was used to having kids round as well?'

'I doubt it!' said Sophie, clearly losing interest. 'Anyway, try the keys in the lock.'

I again did as I was instructed. The first key I tried fitted into the lock but would not turn it. The second key also fitted, but this one turned, and I could physically feel the lock undoing through the barrel of the key.

'Perfect fit!' I said.

I stepped back from the wardrobe and pulled the doors open towards me as I did so. It was jam-packed with old junk and one of the larger items in there — an ironing board which had been stacked vertically and somewhat precariously like a deliberate booby-trap — came flying out and landed on my foot.

'Ow!' I said, letting go of the doors and reaching down to my foot instead. 'I've never known anyone to store as much junk as this anywhere!'

# Stephen Varley's Journal, Monday 23rd October

*8pm, continued*

It took us a while to move the wardrobe. It was full of old junk and was bloody heavy. We had to empty all the junk out to make it more manageable to move. There was tons of crap in there: half a dozen old ornaments (some broken); numerous musty old blankets; several rolls of wallpaper; a big bunch of iron keys; twelve hats (between them representing most of the leading fashions of the 20th century); a ridiculously large paperweight with a model of the Houses of Parliament inside it; and a couple of piles of dusty old books, primarily sporting plain red and green covers. All these items had been seemingly just thrown in on top of one another over the decades and had been lost to posterity until we came along. Collectively they really weighed the old wardrobe down. Not that that needed doing anyway, because it was solidly built - what Aunt might have described as 'properly made, like things were in the old days' - and consequently weighed a ton in its own right.

'This is a pain,' I said. 'We're going to have to empty this and move it before we can even start looking for the tunnel!'

It took us well over an hour to clear all the junk out and take it upstairs into the kitchen, where we could make a cursory evaluation of the merits of its constituent components. Satan continued to pace up-and-down around us as we removed items from the wardrobe. It was heavy, thirsty work and, once we had brought the last lot of junk up, we

138

sat for a few minutes at the kitchen table, drinking a refreshing glass of lemonade each. Satan followed us up the cellar stairs and sat down at the kitchen doorway again, flicking his tail from side-to-side.

'I think that cat's taken a shine to you,' said Sophie, mockingly.

I was just about to ask where Aunt was, as she had been conspicuous by her absence, when at that very moment I heard the front door opening, followed by the recognisable sound of Aunt's footsteps hurrying enthusiastically up the hallway. She almost ran into the kitchen, causing Satan to move aside temporarily, before he resumed his original place. I looked at my watch. She had been well over an hour retrieving her lost gloves from the church.

She was full of excitement and brimming with news.

'I've just been telling Brian about the smuggling tunnels!' she said enthusiastically. 'Isn't it exciting?!'

I wasn't as impressed as she had hoped.

'Who's Brian?' I asked.

'Reverend Brian Grant,' she said, in a tone that suggested I ought to have known that,' the rector of All Saints.'

I rolled my eyes.

'Oh Aunt! Why have you told _anyone_ about them? We're going to get all the local busy bodies coming up for a look now, and maybe even the press!'

Aunt looked a bit sheepish, but was instantly dismissive of my concerns.

'Oh, I shouldn't worry about that, dear,' she

said, slightly deflated but still undeterred. 'All the old residents in the village have known about the tunnel stories for decades. Why on Earth would anyone want to come round here bothering us about it?'

Just as she finished speaking, the doorbell rang. Sophie and I exchanged glances.

'I'll get it,' said Sophie.

Aunt and I spent a few tense, silent moments together in the kitchen until Sophie returned with a visitor. I deduced from the white collar he was wearing that it was Reverend Grant.

'I was really fascinated to hear about the tunnels just now, Amelia,' he said, with similar levels of enthusiasm to her own. 'I wonder, is there any chance that I could have a look at them?'

I covered my face with my hands. Reverend Grant looked at me and then back at Aunt.

'Have I said something wrong?' he asked.

'No, Brian,' said Aunt, quite curtly. 'This is my great nephew, Stephen Varley, and his wife, Sophie, that I was telling you about. Stephen was just berating me for letting the cat out of the bag about the tunnels.'

'I wasn't berating you, Aunt!' I protested. 'I was just questioning the wisdom of telling everyone about them while we are still exploring. We don't know what we'll find, if anything, yet.'

'Well you've already found that brandy barrel, dear, and the brandy label and the oar. That's enough evidence to say that smuggling has been going on here, I would think!'

'Yes,' I said, 'but you know what archaeologists

are like' – I glanced at Sophie – 'we don't want "experts" descending on the house and getting in the way while we are trying to clear it out for you.'

'I think I should go,' said Reverend Grant, clearly sensing that he had arrived at a bad time.

'No, no, no,' said Aunt. 'I won't hear of it! It's my house and they're my tunnels and if I want to tell my friends about them I will!

'Stephen, can you take Reverend Grant down into the cellar and show him what you've found so far please!'

I was about to protest when I felt Sophie's hand on my arm.

'This way, Reverend Grant,' she said, intervening.

The three of us – and the cat – left the kitchen and headed into the hallway and down the cellar stairs.

'Well, well,' said Reverend Grant as we descended them in single file, Sophie in front, then him, then me and then Satan, 'this is exciting!'

I resisted the urge to push the Reverend headfirst down the stairs and dutifully followed the trained archaeologist and our visitor into the underground space. Sophie, who was an angel, bless her, first took him to see the north-west tunnel, with me and Satan in tow a few paces behind, and explained about how we had moved the Jacobean chest-of-drawers, broken through the wall and found the brandy label and the oar, and then took him across to the north tunnel where we all expressed our disappointment about it being evidently unfinished. She then led him across to the wardrobe in front of where we were expecting the south-east tunnel opening to be.

'You haven't moved the furniture out of the way for this one yet then, I see,' said the rector, almost to himself.

'That's because we were interrupted,' I whispered to Sophie.

She kicked me, unseen by the Reverend.

'Well,' he said at length, so politely that I wished I hadn't been quite so hard on him.' I'll leave you to it then. I'm sure you'll be wanting to get on. Thank you for showing me around. Nice to meet you both.'

He shook hands with us warmly and Sophie led him to the stairs. Once he had disappeared up them Sophie returned and began to remonstrate with me.

'What was all that about, Stephen? You were quite rude to him and Aunt just now!'

I sighed.

'It's just... Well... Are we supposed to be down here doing this? I don't know what the rules are about digging tunnels, especially this one, which looks like it's heading off into the village somewhere. Should we be telling the authorities or something? Now that Aunt has told half the village it's just made me a bit jumpy, that's all.'

'I don't think she's told half the village!' said Sophie, trying to reassure me.' Anyway, as Aunt said earlier, it is her house and they are her tunnels. We haven't left her property yet in this subterranean world. If this tunnel goes beyond the boundary of her garden, we'll worry about it then, but to be honest, if they've been here all these years, I don't think anyone's going to worry too much if we're just exploring them. Who knows, there may be other

142

people in the village exploring their own cellars and tunnels even as we speak!'

I laughed.

'There will be now!' I said, semi-seriously. 'Now that Aunt has told everyone.'

'What you need,' said Sophie, 'is some physical exercise to work off your anger.'

I could feel my eyes brightening at the prospect and looked knowingly at Sophie.

'No,' she said, handing me some gloves, 'not that kind of exercise! We need to move this wardrobe!'

# Stephen Varley's Journal, Monday 23rd October

*8pm, continued*

We stood one either side of the wardrobe to weigh up the size of the task before us.

'It's going to be heavy!' warned Sophie.

I looked her straight in the eyes.

'Bend your knees and keep your back straight,' I said. 'We can do it.'

We braced ourselves for the necessary effort and Sophie started a methodical countdown out loud.

'On the count of three!' she said. 'One... two... three!'

We tensed our muscles in unison, gripping the wardrobe tightly and straightening our knees as we lifted it off the floor and away from the wall. We only managed to raise it about three inches because it was still heavy even though it was empty. It was also a little top-heavy and at one point I thought it was going to fall on top of us.

'To you!' I said. 'Quickly!'

Sophie backed up slightly and I advanced towards her, and between us we managed to carry the wardrobe about three feet along the wall to the north, where we were glad to be able to place it down on the ground again.

'That *was* heavy!' said Sophie, stating the obvious.

Once we had put the wardrobe down we 'walked' it another couple of feet in the same direction, so it was clear of what we assumed would be the tunnel entrance. Sophie came round and stood next to me when we'd finished and we both turned to look at the wall behind where the wardrobe had stood. There

144

was of course nothing there – it was just a wall. Satan moved to within a few inches of us.

'I was hoping the entrance to this tunnel might have been open,' said Sophie. 'At least that would have been a small reward for moving the wardrobe!'

I laughed.

'Wouldn't that have been good?!'

Sophie approached the wall and ran her hands over it. I shooed Satan away.

'Yep, just like the other ones,' she said. 'This wall has been patched up...'

'Here we go again, then,' I said. 'You get the chisels and screwdrivers and I'll get the sledgehammer.'

Once again we began to scratch away at the wall, removing the white surface paint until we revealed a gap in the wall that had been back-filled with rubble. Sophie winked at me as if to say 'I knew it!'. This time, though, the rubble infill was surprisingly thin – a 'front' layer to whatever lay behind. It fell away quite easily as a result, gradually revealing some vertical planks of dust-covered wood behind it. We looked at one another quizzically.

'Interesting,' I said. 'Let's keep going.'

Aunt came down at this point to see how we were getting on and I apologised to her for my rudeness earlier.

'I was just worried that people might come round poking their noses in,' I said, by way of explanation.

'It's a small village, dear,' said Aunt, magnanimously brushing aside any offence that I might have caused her, 'they do that all the time!'

The three of us laughed and it helped break the tension.

'I think you do need to go and apologise to Reverend Grant though, Stephen,' said Sophie, after our laughter had died down. 'You were quite rude to him.'

I looked at Aunt to gauge her expression. She looked like she agreed with Sophie.

'OK,' I said. 'I'll do it now. "Strike while the iron's hot" and all that.'

I left the farmhouse and went to the church where I found Reverend Grant laying out some hymn books on the pews. He looked up at me as I entered the building and came over and shook my hand. I felt like a prize idiot.

'I'm really sorry for my rudeness earlier, Reverend Grant,' I said. 'I don't know what came over me. It was quite out of character.'

'Call me "Brian",' replied the Reverend, as magnanimous as Aunt had been. 'It's quite alright. I was interrupting you. I shouldn't have just shown up like that.'

'Even so,' I said, 'I was out of order. I was just concerned about Aunt spreading the news of what we were doing. I'm not sure of the legality of exploring tunnels like the ones we've found and I just got a bit jumpy. It's nothing personal. I would have been the same with anyone.'

'Your secret is safe with me,' replied Reverend Grant, tapping the side of his nose with his index finger and clearly over the whole affair. 'I'm used to hearing people's confessions.'

I adopted a wry smile.

'Thank you,' I said. 'You've been very kind.'

There was a brief pause.

'Would you join us for lunch?' I said. 'Sophie and I are just taking a break anyway.'

The Reverend nodded in acquiescence.

'Thank you,' he said. 'I'd be delighted.'

I returned to the farmhouse with Reverend Grant and the four of us consumed a light lunch and a pleasingly congenial chat in the farmhouse kitchen, watched all the time from the doorway by Satan. When Brian left we all parted on the best of terms.

Sophie kissed me while Aunt was showing him out.

'Well done,' she said.

Having taken our leave of Aunt and Brian, Sophie and I returned to the task in hand, followed of course by Satan.

We scraped away more and more of the cellar wall until it became apparent that the vertical planks were joined together. We soon discovered, in fact, that they weren't just vertical planks, they were a door!

'Blimey!' said Sophie. 'I wasn't expecting that!'

We scraped the rest of the wall-covering away and soon revealed a small door handle as well. Sophie grabbed the handle and tried to push the door away from her, but it didn't move, though it did rattle.

'It's locked,' she said.

I could feel myself beaming as I took out the keys I had found on top of the wardrobe.

'Do you think the other key fits it?' I asked.

Sophie clapped her hands excitedly.

'Give it a go!' she said, stepping back to give me clearance.

I inserted the key into the lock and turned it. The

mechanism was rather stiff and I had to 'shimmy' the key around a bit in the lock, but it did eventually turn it and the door creaked slowly open away from us into the darkness beyond. I gave it a push to get it fully open. A waft of stale, damp air blew into my face as I did so, revealing yet another brick-lined tunnel approximately six feet high and four feet wide. I picked up one of the torches and shone it into the cavity.

'Hey Presto!' I said.' We've found our tunnel!'

Before either of us could say or do anything else, Satan ran past us like a thing possessed and jumped through the opening into the tunnel and disappeared into the darkness.

Sophie picked up the other torch and joined me at the opening. We both peered inside.

'Bloody cat!' I said.' It's been getting under our feet all day and now it's gone in there!'

I panned my torch up and down the space, then shone it as far as I could into the void but Satan had vanished.

'I'd leave him,' said Sophie, panning her torch around as well.' He knows the layout of the place much better than we do. He's obviously gone exploring.'

I shrugged my shoulders.

'The tunnel smells a bit damp,' I said, edging slightly closer to the entrance and shining my torch on the ground,' but at least the floor is dry in this one.'

'I can't believe it had a door on it!' said Sophie. 'We must be the first people to have opened it in years.'

We both craned our necks to see inside the space that had been revealed to us. Sophie inclined her head slightly towards me, but continued to look down the tunnel as she did so.

'It's deathly quiet in there,' she said.

I nodded.

'It also looks like it bends round to the right a bit.'

I shone my torch along the right-hand wall to illustrate my point. The torch beam soon ran out of wall and crossed a dark void before transferring itself onto the left-hand wall beyond it.

There was the briefest of pauses before Sophie - as was becoming traditional - stepped through the opening without warning and entered the tunnel. She looked back briefly at me as she did so.

'Come on!' she said, excitedly, brandishing her torch. 'We need to go exploring as well!'

# Stephen Varley's Journal, Monday 23<sup>rd</sup> October

*8pm, continued*

I followed Sophie into the darkness, torch in hand. We made our way cautiously through the first few feet or so of it. It was darker than the flooded tunnel and I felt a bit nervous.

'This is a much longer tunnel than the tree one,' I observed, trying to buy myself some time.

Sophie laughed, her voice deadened by the brickwork.

'Come on!' she said. 'It'll be an adventure!'

I turned to look at Sophie as she was speaking and I accidentally shone my torch in her face. She moved it away with her free hand and deliberately shone her torch into my eyes in retaliation. I was momentarily blinded, just as she had evidently been.

'Not so clever now, Mister, is it?' she said.

'Sorry,' I said. 'It's a tight space in here again.'

We both took a few moments to get our sight back and once we had done so we shone our torches in unison into the depths of the tunnel again. We jumped out of our skins as we did so, for our torch beams lit up a creature in the tunnel, just this side of the bend.

'It's Satan!' said Sophie.

Satan meowed very loudly, as if recognising that he was being referred to, and we both stood momentarily transfixed as we looked at him. He was sitting on the clay tunnel floor, almost staring at the pair of us, slowly wagging his tail from side-to-side with an air of impatience or annoyance. His eyes were shining in a weird manner in the torchlight and I involuntarily lowered my torch to reduce the effect.

I turned back to Sophie.

'Let's get on with it,' I said.

As if understanding my words, Satan stood up and turned on his heels and disappeared round the bend.

We made our way gingerly forwards until we were perhaps 25 yards into the tunnel, by which time we had started to follow the bend. It was pitch black beyond that point because the light from the cellar couldn't reach it. I shone my torch along the arched roof in front of us and could see the line of brickwork disappearing round the corner out of sight. I looked down at the floor to see if there was any sign of Satan and, in doing so, I suddenly noticed some kind of flat, rectangular wooden object propped up on the floor on the inside of the bend. It seemed to be made of the same wooden planks as the tunnel door and measured about 18 inches by 12 inches in size.

'Hold on!' I said, grabbing Sophie's arm and shining my torch onto my discovery. 'Look at this!'

I made my way over to the object and crouched down to examine it more closely. Sophie duly followed me and crouched down next to me and shone her torch on it as well.

'There's some writing on it,' she said.

She shone her torch left-to-right along each line of the crudely handwritten and faded words that were just about discernible there and read them aloud as she did so.

'" There be... no cursin'... beyond... this point".'

151

We looked at one another, bemused.

'What?!' I said.

Sophie picked the object up, shaking some loose dirt off of it as she did so. We both stood up and gathered round it as she held it out with one hand in front of her, focussing our torches on it so we could study it more closely.

'Look!' she said, tilting the object backwards and forwards slightly to ascertain the best angle at which the writing became clearest. 'It's definitely a notice of some kind. Take a picture of it.'

I got my mobile phone out and took a photo. The flash, which went off automatically, momentarily blinded us and lit up the whole tunnel for an instant. Here's a print of the photo I took.

'What do you think it means?' Sophie wondered aloud.

'I've got no idea,' I said, 'but the English is rubbish!'

Sophie laughed.

'It's the same wood as the door,' she said, running her fingers over it. 'It's got to be the smugglers'. We could get it dendrochronologically dated to prove that it's 18ᵗʰ century.'

I obviously looked a bit vacant.

'I mean,' she said, elaborating, 'that we can get the wood dated using proven dating techniques.'

I looked back at the tunnel entrance; part of it was obscured by the bend in the tunnel wall and the entrance to the cellar seemed a long way off behind us.

'I don't think we should go any further at the moment,' I said. 'It's dark beyond the bend and we don't know how much further it goes. We've come quite a way in as it is and Aunt's up in the house somewhere, well out of earshot. If anything happens to us and we need any assistance, we'll be in big trouble!'

Sophie looked doleful and started to do that thing she does with her eyes when she wants to get me to do something I'm not keen on.

'No,' I said. 'Seriously. I think we should go back and at the very least tell Aunt where we are.'

I could tell from Sophie's expression that she knew it was the sensible thing to do.

'Alright,' she said, reluctantly.

We made our way cautiously back to the tunnel entrance, taking the curious notice with us.

# Stephen Varley's Journal, Monday 23rd October

*8pm, continued*

'Witchcraft!' said Aunt, very definitively, when we were up in the kitchen again with her, collectively looking at the sign that we had found. 'It has to be!'

I was already beginning to fear since the sign's discovery that she may well be right. Smugglers I could cope with; witches were another matter altogether.

'What makes you so sure, Aunt?' I asked tentatively.

'"No cursin'",' she said. 'It can't mean "no swearing" - why would there be a notice up for that? It must mean "no invoking a curse" or "no using a curse against anybody".'

'We did find that broomstick in the north-west tunnel, Stephen,' said Sophie, speaking her thoughts aloud.

I frowned, and paused before responding, a pause which allowed Aunt to continue with her previous point.

'What other type of cursing is there?' she said.

She disappeared into the lounge and returned with a dictionary and flicked through the pages until she reached the place she was looking for.

'"Curse - to put a curse on or afflict with great evil, to utter offensive words in anger or annoyance, to blaspheme",' she read aloud.

'Blaspheming is possible!' I said quickly, hoping to put the witchcraft theory to bed before it had even got up. 'The church is only next door and the tunnel leads vaguely in that direction.'

Aunt nodded sagely.

Sophie changed tack slightly.

'I've been wondering about Satan,' she said. 'A black cat, descended from one that was supposedly created out of thin air by some magic trick performed by Miss Weston, a lady with known witchcraft ancestry, which has been following us about a lot downstairs of late and which has now rushed headlong into a tunnel where a sign was found saying " No Cursin'"?'

Aunt looked momentarily horrified.

'You let Winnie's cat go into the tunnel?!' she exclaimed.

'We didn't have much choice, Aunt,' I said. 'It was in and gone before you could say "Jack Robinson".'

'I'm sure he'll come back out again of his own accord,' said Sophie, calmly, back-tracking from the point she was apparently making. 'You said yourself that he comes and goes as he pleases.'

Aunt looked vaguely reassured.

'Do go on, dear,' she said.

Sophie swallowed hard while collecting her thoughts.

'Well,' she said. 'Satan has become more active around us since we have been exploring the tunnels. I'm sorry, Stephen, but I can't help feeling that there is some witchcraft connection with the one he's just disappeared into.'

I sighed heavily, temporarily lost for words. Aunt broke the silence.

'I'd go and find out now, if I was you,' she said,

encouragingly.' It's better to know one way or the other and it's always better to tackle things head on and get them over and done with rather than dwelling on them for ages. It can give you a headache.'

I knew what she meant.

' If you don't come back in half an hour,' she continued,' I can always send out a search party!'

So, Sophie and I duly returned to the tunnel, albeit very reluctantly on my part at least. Satan was sitting at the tunnel entrance when we arrived, seemingly waiting for us. He scampered off into the darkness again when he saw us.

We took with us a table lamp (minus lampshade) from the lounge and a 50m extension lead that I found in the shed, so that we could shine a bit more artificial light further into the tunnel and round beyond the bend. By the time we had plugged the extension lead into a socket in the farmhouse hallway though, and trailed it down the cellar stairs, across the cellar and into the tunnel, it just about reached the point where we had found the notice.

' It's better than nothing,' said Sophie, correctly reading the evident disappointment on my face.' It is throwing more light beyond the bend here. I think I can make out the end of the tunnel now. We must be about half way.'

So, with the lamp in place, throwing our shadows onto the walls and arched roof in front of us as we made our way deeper into the tunnel, we continued our journey until I spotted something else lying on the floor. It looked at first glance like another wooden oar. We both shone our torches on it and quickly made our way over to the item. We quickly discovered that although it did indeed look like a wooden oar, with one end flattened and the other end shaped into a pole, it was actually made of rusting iron.

'It looks like the remains of a shovel,' said Sophie.

I bent down and picked it up. It had the flat blade of a shovel and the remains of a circular handle, only about a foot of which was left.

'Look,' said Sophie, pointing to the jagged end of the handle. 'It looks like it snapped off. The top part of the handle is missing. I don't reckon it was up to the job.'

'It's pretty heavy,' I said, holding the object out in front of me and weighing it up in both hands. 'You'd have thought it would be quite sturdy.'

'Yes, but by the looks of it this is an $18^{th}$-century shovel. We had a look at some old tools on my archaeology course and this looks very similar to one that I saw on that. Shovels from that period were not made in the same way as they are now. The local blacksmith probably put this together.'

'What's it made of then?' I asked.

'It's going to be wrought iron, I would think,' replied Sophie. 'And what probably happened here – because it's a method that was used extensively elsewhere – was that two men were involved in the excavation process: one would have chipped away at the clay with a mattock – a tool that looks a bit like a pick axe – and the second would have shovelled the fallen clay out into the cellar. If this is one of Hard Nut Blyth's shovels – and it's the right period I think – then he probably had a gang of men in the

157

cellar shovelling the clay over to the stairs and then up out into the garden.

'Ooh!' I said. 'A bit like you see in films when people form a chain and pass buckets of water along to each other to put a fire out!'

'Yes,' said Sophie, 'something like that.'

We spent the rest of the day edging further into the tunnel until we eventually reached the end of it, which was about another 25 yards from the middle of the bend. To our astonishment, there was a second door at the end of the tunnel that looked exactly like the one at the beginning, except that this one had a plank wedged horizontally across it at about waist height, like a defensive bar on the inside of the gates of a castle - a 'draw bar', I think it's called. Some additional oak timbers had also been propped up against the door, as if to prevent it from being opened from the other side. Satan was sitting impatiently facing the door, flicking his tail angrily from side-to-side. He stood up and turned round to face us when we reached him, his yellow eyes shining unnaturally in our torch beams.

There was another wooden sign resting against the planks that were propping the door closed, into which someone had scratched the words 'Do not open'. There was a fourth word below this which was harder to read, but after shooing Satan out of the way - with some difficulty because he was extremely reluctant to move - we scrutinised it more closely and eventually worked it out that the word was 'ever'.

'"Do not open ever"?' read Sophie aloud. 'Why on Earth not?'

158

Satan meowed loudly from between our feet, so that we both jumped.

I could feel my heart sinking.

'Witchcraft,' I said, feeling slightly nauseous as I spoke the word.

Satan meowed again, as if reading my thoughts.

Sophie put her hand on my shoulder as if to reassure me. I could see from the slight brightening of her eyes in the torchlight that she knew that I had hit the nail on the head.

'It's alright, Stephen,' she said.

There was a short pause, until she eventually added: 'You do know that we have to open it though?'

I did know, of course, but it didn't make it any easier. I had had enough dealings with witches during my previous time in Cannow's End to last a lifetime, but we'd come so far and discovered so much in this underground world that I was reluctant to turn back.

'Damn witches!' I said, half to myself and half aloud.

Satan meowed for a third time and we both jumped again.

'Get lost!' I said, kicking out at him repeatedly until he had retreated to a safe distance.

Sophie put her arm round me.

'Let's leave it for today,' she said, 'and come back in the morning. It'll take a bit of time to clear all that wood away anyway, and I think we've done enough for today.'

I nodded.

'Alright, darling,' I said. 'I think that's a good decision.'

We left the door as it was, switched off the lamp and returned to the cellar. Satan followed us to the tunnel entrance, meowing loudly with our every step. When we reached the bottom of the cellar stairs, I turned back to look at him and could see the silhouette of his tail flicking angrily in the shadows.

# Stephen Varley's Journal, Wednesday 25th October

<u>2:30pm</u>

The following morning we went down very early – sometime around six-ish – and made our way into the tunnel. I had had real trouble sleeping after discussing the potential witchcraft connections with Sophie and I had resolved overnight to go through with it, come what may.

Satan was sitting impatiently at the tunnel entrance again when we got there. He looked like he had been there all night! I felt a nervous excitement about the day ahead, a bit like when you get up early in the morning to go on holiday to somewhere that's a long drive away, maybe to Cornwall from London, or something like that. You don't want to leave home, but you can't wait to get going.

Satan disappeared into the tunnel ahead of us again and when we reached the second door, having switched on the lamp again, he began to prowl around our feet, flicking his tail slowly from side-to-side again as he did so. I gently tried to ease him out of the way with my foot, but he just ignored me and simply circled around in another direction.

'Ignore the cat!' said Sophie, impatiently, and with some surprisingly uncharacteristic trepidation in her voice. 'Let's just get on with it!'

We removed the oak props and the horizontal bar, stacking them all side-by-side along the left-hand wall of the tunnel. I got the keys out of my pocket but was fumbling around so much for the right one that I dropped them. Satan immediately pounced on them and briefly sniffed them, before backing off again.

'Butterfingers!' said Sophie. 'You're like one of those women in a murder mystery who is being chased by a stranger in the shadows and can't open the door to her apartment in time!'

I looked a bit sheepish and actually felt a little scared. Sophie looked worried.

'Come on,' she said, gently. 'We agreed we'd do it. It'll be over in no time.'

She bent down to pick up the keys and looked momentarily puzzled.

'But which one of these keys is going to work though?' she said.

I thought for a moment.

'It's unlikely to be the one for the wardrobe,' I said. 'Let's hope it's the one that opened the tunnel door and that both tunnel doors have the same key.'

Sophie moved to the door and inserted the appropriate key in the lock, wriggling it a little as she did so.

'It fits,' she said, 'but it's stiff. We need some WD40.'

I went back down the tunnel into the cellar and returned in an instant with a can of the required lubricant which I had previously noticed in Dave's tool bag. Sophie took the can from me and sprayed it into the keyhole, before giving it back to me. She then tried the key again and it slowly turned until there was a loud 'clunk'.

'Bingo!' she said.

The door opened slowly away from us and Satan immediately went through it. We shone our torches

162

into the space beyond, as the door creaked open to its full extent. It wasn't another tunnel as such, as we had been expecting, but a small underground room, about eight feet by five feet, with three more doors leading off it, one each to the left, the right and straight ahead.

'Some kind of storage room?' said Sophie, stepping into the space. I followed her in.

We entered the room from the narrower end, so it was slightly longer than wide from our perspective. It had brick walls and a clay floor like the tunnels, but the roof was flat and made of substantial oak beams. I shone my torch on them to get a closer look.

'Ships' timbers,' said Sophie, following my gaze. 'Probably 15$^{th}$ or 16$^{th}$ century, I should think. I expect they came from Thamesmouth or Lee – both were important maritime ports in the medieval period.'

'Do you think it's safe to stand under them?' I asked. 'They look a bit rotten in places to me.'

Sophie inspected the nearest beam to her a bit more closely.

'They probably are,' she said, reaching up to touch it, 'but this space is quite dry, so they've lasted pretty well in the circumstances.'

We panned our torches around the room, looking for anything of interest, but it was empty.

'You know what?' said Sophie, musing aloud as we stood there. 'The square on the map with the cross in it must represent this room. It's roughly in the right location.'

I nodded.

'I think you're right,' I said. 'I wonder where we

163

are on the ground level above.'

Sophie pulled a face.

'We could go upstairs and have a look?'

Keen to take any excuse to put off the inevitable opening of the additional doors, I instantly agreed. Satan, who was sitting facing the door on the left, flicking his tail slowly from side-to-side in by now classic fashion, clearly didn't, as he meowed really loudly as if to take issue with my decision. His impatience with us was palpable.

'We'll be back in a jiffy, Satan,' said Sophie, trying to reassure him.' We want to know what's behind that door as much as you do.'

'Speak for yourself!' I said, semi-seriously.

Satan meowed again.

'Come on, Stephen,' said Sophie. 'Let's go upstairs and check where we are, just so we know what we're getting ourselves into.'

I exhaled heavily.

'Ok,' I said.' We know that we're about fifty yards south-east of the farmhouse...'

'...Starting predominantly eastwards and then curving predominantly southwards around the halfway point...' added Sophie, getting into specifics.

I nodded.

'So, let's go back upstairs, grab the map and measure out the route on the ground and see where we end up.'

'Deal,' said Sophie.' And then we can come back down here and decide which door to open first!'

I looked at Satan, sitting impatiently in front of the left-hand door.

'I think it's going to be that one,' I said.

# Stephen Varley's Journal, Wednesday 25<sup>th</sup> October

*2:30pm, continued*

We returned to the farmhouse, collected the map and went out of the front door into the south-facing garden.

'It must start round here,' I said, turning immediately left and leading Sophie round the south-eastern corner of the building to the east wall. I walked on a few more paces. 'I reckon the tunnel entrance from the cellar is below us about here.'

Sophie nodded.

'Yeah, that looks about right,' she said.

I held the map out carefully in both hands in front of me, so that we could consult it without it folding up suddenly like last time.

'That's odd,' I said. 'I've just realised that the map shows the tunnel being straight, but we know that in reality it bends. Why do you think that is?'

Sophie shrugged.

'It is a very basic map,' she said.

I nodded and moved on.

'OK,' I said, 'we know that it's about 25 yards from the tunnel entrance to the apex of the bend and another 25 yards or so from there to the room, so all we've got to do is head in a vaguely south-easterly direction, slightly more easterly than southerly to begin with, and then bend our walk a bit so that we are going slightly more southerly than easterly. Does that make sense?'

'Yes,' said Sophie, 'but I can already see one problem: we're going to be leaving the farmhouse boundary pretty soon because we're very close to that hedgerow already.' She indicated a hedgerow boundary which lay beyond the farmyard and separated the eastern part of the farmhouse garden from the churchyard.

'Ok,' I said, 'what we'll have to do is measure out what distance we can on this side of the hedge and then go round the other side into the churchyard and measure the rest of it out from there.'

'Agreed,' said Sophie. 'You pace it out here and I'll go round into the churchyard.'

I looked at the ground in front of me and then back at the map.

'So I guess if I pace it out with large strides then each large stride should equate to about a yard?'

Sophie nodded.

'Go for it. You stop where you get to and I'll go round into the churchyard and mark the spot and then you come round and join me.'

I let the map roll itself up and held it in my right hand and set off in I guess what someone with a compass might have called a vaguely east-south-easterly direction. Sophie hurried out of the farmhouse garden, through the farmyard and round the other side of the hedge into the churchyard. I had to make an effort to stride one yard at a time because the length of the stride felt unnatural. It required concentration to keep my balance over the first two or three yards and I counted the distance aloud so that I wouldn't forget it. By the time I had 'walked' 19 yards I had already reached the hedgerow. There weren't many leaves on it, but it was about a yard wide and quite a bit taller than me, so it was difficult to see through it and impossible to see over it.

'Nineteen' I said aloud, with finality, as I reached it, so that Sophie could hear me.

She moved into position on the other side of the hedge and I went round to join her so that we were ultimately both standing on the churchyard side of it.

'Right,' I said, 'I did 19 yards on that side. There's about a yard from that side of the hedge to this, making 20 so far. That means there is about another 30 yards to go, and I think I should probably start bending my route in a slightly more southerly direction now.'

'Yes,' said Sophie, in agreement. 'You need to head south-south-east rather than east-south-east. Mind you, I can already see why there is a bend in the tunnel: you're going to be skirting the north-east corner of the churchyard – it's like whoever built the tunnel wanted to avoid going directly under the churchyard, probably because of the graves.'

I nodded.

'Yes,' I said, 'I think you're right.'

I set off again, striding across the churchyard grass in a slightly southerly-curving direction, until I had covered another 10 yards and run out of room because I had reached the eastern hedge of the churchyard; I had effectively cut off the north-eastern corner of the churchyard as Sophie had suggested I would.

'Ok,' she said, coming over to join me, 'call it

167

another yard for this hedge, that leaves 19 yards on the other side.'

I looked over the hedge, which was only about five feet in height on this side, in the direction of the proposed route.

'I don't think we can go round there,' I said. 'It's somebody's front garden.'

Sophie came over and stood looking over the hedge alongside me. We could see a house set back to our left with a long front garden between it and the road.

'Hmm,' she said thoughtfully, looking along the hedge to the right on the other side.' I don't think we need to go round there, Stephen,' she said. 'I think we can tell from here where the tunnel is leading. Look!'

Sophie pointed in the direction where our route was leading. All I could see about 20 yards away was a small shed.

I looked at Sophie.

'Do you mean that the tunnel leads to this person's shed?' I asked, incredulous.

'No, Stephen,' said Sophie, dismissively. 'That building isn't somebody's shed. It's the village lock-up!'

I rolled out the map and we both looked at it.

'Blimey!' I said.' I think you're right! That means that the subterranean room - which is marked by the box with the cross in it on the map - must be directly beneath the lock-up!'

Sophie nodded.

'What better way to smuggle things in and out unseen!' she said.' The smugglers must have stored things in the underground room and then moved them either into the farmhouse or out into the village, depending on what they were doing at any one point. Let's go and have a look at the lock-up and see if there are any smuggling clues there.'

For completeness, I paced out the remaining 20 yards as best as I could on the churchyard side of the hedge, to avoid having to go into the private garden. Sure enough, it was about the right distance to the lock-up, which stood at the road end of the garden on the public highway. We left the churchyard via the gate into Cannow's End High Street, to have a proper look at the lock-up, which was the first property on the left.

I have reproduced our route below for future reference.

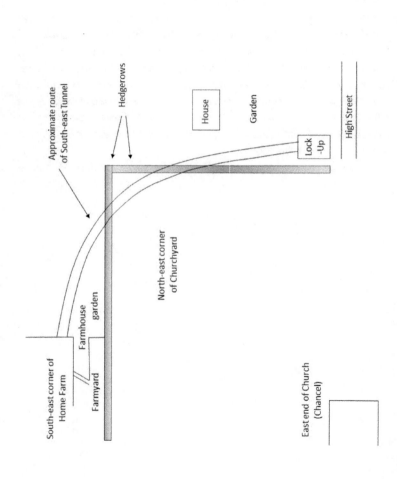

The lock-up was a small wooden building that looked exactly like a garden shed. It had a red-tiled roof and a wooden door that was criss-crossed from top to bottom with bands of iron. There was a sign above the door which read: 'Cannow's End Parish Council - Village Lock-up & Stocks 1773'.

'That's not a 1773 shed!' I said, laughing. 'It's a lot more modern than that!'

'I agree,' said Sophie, 'but that doesn't mean there wasn't a similar building on the site before this one.'

We had a look round the outside of the building, or at least what we could see of it from the road, but we struggled to see inside it because there didn't seem to be any windows. Eventually we spotted a small, barred opening on the western (churchyard) side, which we made our way over to and peered through side-by-side.

'It's dark in there,' I said. 'It's difficult to see anything.'

'We should have brought our torches,' said Sophie.

Nevertheless, after a few moments spent staring into the darkness our eyes became accustomed to the dark and we could gradually make out, standing diagonally on the floor in the middle of the shed, a pair of wooden planks which were placed on their narrowest sides, one on top of the other, each about eight inches in height and eight feet in length. The planks had a row of circular holes cut into them, with one semi-circle of each hole in each of the two planks, so that a completely circular hole was made when they were fitted together. The planks were joined together at one end by an iron hinge and at the other end by what looked like some kind of fastening.

'Oh,' said Sophie, as the shape of the object gradually became clearer to us,' it's a set of stocks. It's an old form of punishment where wrongdoers had to sit on a bench with their feet through the holes in the planks. See how the planks hinge open and those holes are cut out for their legs to go through? They were locked there for hours at a time so that they could be made an example of.'

I pulled a face.

'That sounds a bit unpleasant,' I said.

Sophie laughed.

'And that wouldn't have been all,' she continued. 'Passers-by could have hurled abuse at them, or rotting fruit, or spat at them, or anything.'

'Indeed,' I said, musing on the possibilities.

With our eyes now more accustomed to the dark, we pressed our faces closer to the iron bars on the small window opening and looked around the space to see what else was inside the shed. We could not, however, see anything. The stocks were on their own.

'No sign of any smuggling activity,' I said, stepping back from the window, disappointed.

'No,' said Sophie, copying my movements. 'The stocks was usually an outdoor punishment. I wouldn't have expected to see them inside a building. I reckon they have been moved there for safekeeping, now that they no longer have an active role to play in the modern judicial system! The shed itself was probably a local prison cell for putting criminals in who warranted a sterner punishment.'

I thought about what she had said.

'Presumably then, at one stage whatever building was here had a false bottom in it, so that the room beneath it could be directly accessed from the lock-up? In which case, any members of the smuggling gang who were imprisoned here could easily have escaped underground under the cover of night to enjoy a night of comfort in the farmhouse or something and then returned here in the morning before their absence was noted.'

Sophie laughed at the idea.

'It's possible!' she said.

We spent a few more moments looking round the outside of the lock-up and then back across the churchyard towards the farmhouse to take in our location. We could see the roof and upper storey of Home Farm on the other side of the hedgerow.

'Well,' said Sophie. 'There might not have been any more smuggling clues out here, but at least we have got our bearings. I propose we return to the underground room and start opening some doors!'

# Stephen Varley's Journal, Wednesday 25th October

*2:30pm, continued*

We made our way back to the farmhouse and went down into the cellar and into the south-eastern tunnel. Once we had reached the underground room, which we now knew was beneath the village lock-up, we stood looking at the three doors in front of us and considered our options. Satan was still in place in front of the left-hand door.

'I feel like Alice in Wonderland,' I said. 'Didn't she end up in an underground room that had doors leading off it? How did she know which one to pick?'

Sophie looked pensive for a moment.

'We have to start with Satan's door,' she said. 'I can't bear the thought of making him wait while we explore the other two! In any case, the village is in that direction and we can follow up Aunt's theory that this tunnel led to Hard Nut's grocery shop!'

I laughed.

'Ok,' I said. 'We've got to start somewhere. Let's go for it!'

We moved over to the door on the left. Satan obligingly stood up and stepped aside to enable us to access it. The door handle was an iron ring, like you might find on a quayside, slightly out of proportion in size to the rest of the door. I could see that it opened outwards. Sophie used it to try to pull the door open, but the door was locked. We got out the keys but they were too small. We tried all three doors with them, but the locks were the wrong size.

'We need some more keys,' said Sophie, half to herself.

A lightbulb went on in my head.

'There were some old keys in that big wardrobe,' I said. 'I wonder if those will fit.'

Sophie looked excited.

'Go get them!' she said.

I disappeared upstairs into the farmhouse and found the keys in the kitchen where we had left them. I hadn't paid them much attention before, but I now saw that there were three keys on the keyring, which I hoped meant that there was one for each of the doors in the room. I bounded downstairs again with excitement.

'I've sprayed some WD40 into all three keyholes,' said Sophie, when I got back.

I handed her the bunch of keys and she selected one and wriggled the key around in the lock. After a bit of wriggling it clunked the lock open and Sophie pulled on the door handle to reveal what was behind the door.

'First time lucky!' I said.

The door, which was hinged on the right, slowly opened towards us, and, as Sophie gently pulled it open no more than a couple of inches, a ghastly putrid stench of foul air - much worse than from any of the tunnels to date - assaulted our nostrils. Even Satan, who had been patiently waiting for us to gain access to whatever was beyond, seemed to take an involuntary step or two backwards, like our neighbour's cat did once when her very young daughter made it sniff a bottle of smelling salts.

'Jesus!' I said. 'What the Hell is that smell?'

Sophie motioned me to back off down the tunnel and we both briefly returned to the cellar to let the horrible smell dissipate. When we returned, wearing our dust masks as smell defenders, we found Satan sitting outside the slightly ajar door, trying to use one of his paws to open it further. The door was far too heavy for him though and he was making no progress. He meowed pathetically at us when we returned to the spot, as if asking for our help.

I looked at Sophie.

'I'll open the door,' I said, struggling to get the words out from behind my dust mask, 'and you shine your torch into the void. I don't want anything taking us by surprise.'

Sophie nodded.

She switched on her torch and stood above and behind the cat, as best she could in the available space, ready to point the beam into the darkness that lay beyond.

I pulled at the door using the iron ring. The door was incredibly heavy, certainly a lot heavier than the door at the entrance to the tunnel. I pulled it towards me, very slowly at first because of the effort required, then gradually faster as it gained momentum. The long-unused hinges creaked eerily as the door opened, picking up speed the further it did so, until the weight of it made me lose control and it swung open with force and hit me, knocking me backwards onto the damp earthen floor. The door itself opened so wide that the wood sounded like it was splintering as it reached the limit of its hinges. The table lamp in the tunnel went out and a rush of ice-cold air passed over us.

176

Sophie gasped in horror and put her hand to her mouth as her torch beam settled on whatever it was behind the door. Satan, who had been poised to enter the opening as soon as it became wide enough, also recoiled in abhorrence at what lay beyond. The two of them stood stock still in the eerie, shadowy light caused by our torches.

'What is it?!' I said.

Both Sophie and Satan stood motionless, Sophie in an almost cinematographic horror pose, Satan with his back arched and his hackles up.

I jumped to my feet and scrambled over to stand beside them. I shone my own torch into the space.

There, behind the door, was a niche about two feet in depth, the full height and width of the door, a bit like we'd opened a large cupboard. In the niche/cupboard, handcuffed and feetcuffed by rusting iron manacles to two vertical wooden beams that looked like the ships' timbers of the main room's roof, and pierced through with a rusting cutlass, was the remains of a human skeleton, the mouth of the skull hanging open like a horror tableau on a ghost train ride at a fairground. The skull still had a full head of greying hair, which fell down over most of the face. The skeleton was attired in the remnants of a long, white, tattered dress. At the feet of the skeleton lay a combination of those of its bones which the gory supports had not been able to keep in place as the flesh had decomposed, and the skull and bones of another creature, a small mammal which I thought, having memorably been frightened by one in a museum once when I was very young, to be that of a cat. Behind the bones of

177

both I could make out another wooden sign, just like the other ones, which read 'Welcome to Hell!'.

I felt sick to the pit of my stomach.

As the three of us stood there in shock, the bones of the cat that lay at the human skeleton's feet seemed to dissolve into thin air and disappear right in front of our eyes. There was a deathly silence, the only sign of life being Sophie and my torches playing on the eyeless face of the bony remains, their whiteness reflecting a faint glow back at us. I could hear my heart beating in my head and, because of the dust mask, my breath was coming in short, hollow rasping pants, just like Darth Vader's in 'Star Wars'.

It must have been the first time in centuries that the door had been opened. I felt a horrible sickly wave of nausea pass over me.

'Oh my God!' said Sophie, terrified. 'It's an immurement.'

Her voice cut through the silence like a knife and shocked me back into reality.

'And worse than that,' she continued, her voice faltering as she spoke, 'it's the figure I saw in the farmhouse window!'

I put my arm around her. She was really cold and physically shivering. I looked at her and she turned to face me until our eyes met.

'We need to go,' I said, silently blinking to myself in the semi-darkness, not really comprehending what was going on.

# Stephen Varley's Journal, Wednesday 25<sup>th</sup> October

*2:30pm, continued*

Before I had a chance to ask Sophie what an immurement was, we were chilled to the core by a piercing scream coming from somewhere in the house above us.

'It's Aunt!' I said.

We ran out of the tunnel into the cellar and bounded smartly up the stairs into the hallway and on into the kitchen. In the latter we found Aunt, looking as white as a sheet, holding the old oar we had found in both hands as if she was about to strike us with it.

'What is it, Aunt?' I cried, stopping abruptly as I entered the kitchen, with Sophie barely a pace behind me.

Aunt was shaking and unable to speak. To answer me, she pointed through the doorway from the kitchen across the hallway and into the bathroom. I turned to look in that direction myself. There, to my astonishment, stood what I can only describe as a 'Skeleton Cat' – just like the one we had seen in the newly discovered room downstairs, but in animated, apparently alive, form. Its back was arched and its tail was flicking from side to side like Satan's had been. Its eyeless skull looked horribly menacing and it was clearly angry.

'Jesus!' said Sophie, moving to a position of relative safety behind me and instinctively grabbing my shoulders.

Without really thinking properly I grabbed the old wooden oar out of Aunt's hands and crossed to the bathroom, where I swung it round through the doorway like a cricket bat to try to smack the cat away from us. I made perfect contact, catching it – and myself – by surprise with the speed of my movement.

As the oar made contact with the Skeleton Cat, the latter smashed into a million pieces, like a balloon full of water exploding on impact with a wall. Barely had it done that, however, than all the pieces instantly reformed themselves into the Skeleton Cat again!

'You've got to be kidding me!' I said, aloud.

I heard a thud behind me and turned to see Sophie catching Aunt as the latter fainted against the kitchen table. I looked back quickly at where the cat had been, but it had taken the opportunity provided by my momentary distraction to rush past me out of the bathroom and down the hallway. I gripped the oar more tightly and rushed into the hallway in pursuit. The cat ran into the old dining room (our bedroom) and by the time I arrived there too I was just in time to see it disappearing into the chimney. I cursed my ill luck and returned to the kitchen to find Aunt propped on a stool, looking fairly groggy, and Sophie trying to bring her round with some smelling salts and a glass of water.

I put down the oar and knelt in front of Aunt, holding her knees and looking her straight in the eyes.

'What happened, Aunt?' I asked.

She opened and closed her eyes lazily. I could tell that she wasn't completely with it.

'It just appeared,' she said,' out of nowhere, like an apport.'

## Stephen Varley's Journal, Wednesday 25th October

2:30pm, continued

'What's an apport?' asked Sophie, after Aunt had had sufficient time to gain her composure once more.

'It's the appearance of something out of nowhere,' said Aunt, her voice still a little shaky, 'like how Winnie said she made her first cat, Magic, appear out of thin air all those years ago.'

'It's a paranormal phenomenon,' I added helpfully. 'I did some research into it once for an article I wrote for <u>London Ghosts & Hauntings</u> magazine. Objects can appear suddenly at séances, for example. Things like precious stones or flowers have been recorded as appearing in mid-air above a séance table and dropping onto the table in front of the astonished attendees. There was a big experiment about it in the 1990s - the Scole Experiment, it was called.'

Sophie looked bemused.

'But how can things just appear out of thin air?' she said.

I turned the palms of my hands upwards and shrugged my shoulders.

'It's still unexplained, I think, but there is a lot of evidence that it happens.'

Sophie looked at Aunt.

'So that "thing" just appeared out of nowhere?' she asked.

Aunt nodded.

'Yes, dear, it did.'

'Could it have come in through the back door?' asked Sophie.

'No, dear,' replied Aunt, quite firmly. 'I saw it materialise in front of me out of nothing, like Captain Kirk and Mr Spock in those Star Trek programmes, teleporting in from another planet.'

Sophie looked at me.

'Where did it go?' she asked.

'Into the chimney in our bedroom.'

There was a pause while we all mused about what had happened. Eventually, I broke the silence.

'We found a room downstairs, Aunt,' I said, 'at the end of the south-east tunnel. There were two skeletons in it – a human one handcuffed to the wall and a cat one lying at her feet. The cat skeleton disappeared in front of our eyes. It evidently reappeared here.'

Aunt looked at me blankly, like she was struggling to take everything in.

'You said "her",' she said, half-statement, half-question.

'The human skeleton was dressed like the woman I saw in the upstairs window the first day that we came here,' said Sophie.

Aunt began to wail.

'Do you think it's a witch and a witch's cat?' she asked.

I did, and I was feeling really sick about it myself inside.

'I don't know,' I replied, looking at Sophie for support.

She grimaced.

'We need to find the Skeleton Cat, Stephen,' she said.

'Hold on a minute,' I replied, sensing that she

was preparing to go in search of the creature in question.' Let's not do anything rash.'

Sophie laughed out loud.

' It's a bit late for that, don't you think?!'

I rolled my eyes and looked at Aunt.

' I'll be fine, Stephen,' she said, as if reading my thoughts.' I'll just rest here for a bit. At least if it reappears I know what to expect this time. You go and look for it. I'll be alright.'

Sophie and I left the room and headed, with some trepidation, back into the cellar for another trip into the south-east tunnel.

# Stephen Varley's Journal, Wednesday 25<sup>th</sup> October

*2:30pm, continued*

'You used the word "immurement" earlier,' I said to Sophie, as we made our way back nervously through the cellar and across to the tunnel. 'I'm guessing that's got something to do with the French for "wall"?'

Sophie nodded.

'Yes,' she said. 'We went to visit Corfe Castle in Dorset while I was studying and there was a famous case of it there where a woman was what they called "walled up" behind bricks on the orders of King John. It stuck in my mind – what a horrible way to die.'

I grimaced.

'So this woman was literally imprisoned... what, not behind a wall in this case but in a locked room handcuffed to the wall, with no means of escape and no food or drink? She must have starved to death?'

'Yes,' said Sophie, 'or dehydrated. It would have been pitch black in there as well, of course. Imagine if you suffered from claustrophobia. It must have been dreadful.'

'Very ghoulish,' I said. 'They had some horrible punishments in the old days.'

The table lamp in the tunnel was still off, but the switch for it was still on, so I flicked it off and on again in the hope of sparking it back into life and sure enough it did light up.

'Curious,' I said.

'The thing about our victim,' said Sophie, musing

185

aloud, 'was that she was not only "walled up" – or "doored up" to be more precise – but she was handcuffed and pierced with a cutlass as well. There was no way she was ever going to get out of there in that state.'

'Are you sure it's a woman?' I asked.

'Yes,' said Sophie. 'I saw enough of the pelvis through that tattered dress to tell that. And it was definitely the woman I saw in the window.'

We made our way down the tunnel to the door, which was still swung wide open, as we had left it. Satan was nowhere to be seen. We stood there looking at the gruesome remains of the imprisoned woman and the space where the Skeleton Cat had lain among the remaining human bones there.

'This house has certainly got some skeletons in the cupboard,' I said aloud, trying to raise my morale and grinning to myself in the half-darkness of the table lamp and torchlight.

'Stephen!' said Sophie, mildly annoyed. 'This is no time for jokes!'

# Stephen Varley's Journal, Wednesday 25<sup>th</sup> October

*2:30pm, continued*

As neither Satan nor the Skeleton Cat were anywhere to be seen and the witch skeleton wasn't going anywhere – hopefully! – we decided to close the door to the 'cupboard'. We stood for an instant, looking at the human skeleton again before we did so. The skull in particular was horrible: it hung down slightly to left, as if it had fallen onto the victim's chest, and the mouth was lolling open in a way that would have been impossible if the victim had been alive, as the jaw bone had become detached at one end and was flapping loose like a washing line that had become untied from one of its posts.

It took an age to close the door, due largely to its weight, but also it seemed due to some unseen force which appeared to be trying to hold it open against our attempts to close it.

Sophie and I exchanged glances.

'Push it harder!' I said, anxiously.

Once the door was closed, I locked it securely and tested it two or three times to make sure.

'It is locked, Stephen,' said Sophie, firmly.

'I know,' I said. 'I just wanted to make sure. Bloody witches!'

There was no sign of either Satan or the Skeleton Cat in the cellar either, so we decided to go back upstairs to check on Aunt. As we were exiting the cellar we encountered her coming to meet us in the hallway.

'The Skeleton Cat is back!' she said, all in a tizzy. 'It's gone upstairs. It's knocking things over!'

I gently ushered Aunt aside and hurried to the foot of the stairs and then up them in hot pursuit, with Sophie right behind me. On the landing at the top of the stairs we found that the table with the dead plant on it which I'd noticed the first time I'd been up there had been knocked over and the porcelain pot which the plant was in was lying smashed on the floor. The earth and the plant had both spilled out of it onto the carpet.

A noise from the south-west bedroom alerted us and we went into that to see what was happening. There we found the cat running round and round the vertical walls and over the doorway above us as we entered, like a Wall of Death motorcycle act from days gone by at Thamesmouth fairground. The room was largely empty now, as we had cleared most of it out, but what items there still were in there were crashing to the floor in a whirlwind of speed and bones!

The cat was initially oblivious to our arrival, until I shouted at it and it suddenly took notice. Before we could do anything, however, it completed one final circuit of the walls and then disappeared straight up the chimney. We could hear it going up into the attic.

We rushed out onto the landing again and I reached up to grab the string with the toggle on it that was hanging down from the loft hatch and lowered the hatch with it as quickly as I could.

'There's a retractable ladder up there,' called Aunt helpfully from the bottom of the stairs. 'I remember seeing Winnie use it two or three times.'

I found the ladder, pulled it down quickly and

climbed up it like a shot until my head and shoulders were in the attic while the rest of me remained on the ladder. However, because it was so dark the first sensation I had was not one of seeing anything but one of feeling something rushing round me in circles like a whirlwind.

'It's doing the same up here!' I shouted over my shoulder to Sophie.

Every couple of seconds or so, at regular intervals, I felt a rush of wind pass by me as the cat completed another circuit.

'What are we going to do?' shouted Sophie from behind me.

'Go and get the oar!' I said. 'I'll hit it with that next time it comes round.'

Sophie did as she was bidden and returned with the implement. I twisted round on the ladder so that she could pass it up to me. I then found myself moving my head around in circles as I mimicked the movements of the manic Skeleton Cat, trying to anticipate when it would next fly past me. I moved further up the ladder until the whole of my top half was in the attic, the bottom half still remaining in the landing space on the ladder. I manoeuvred the oar around until I had a good grip of it and monitored the circling cat two or three more times, waiting for my moment to strike, like someone playing the 'bat the rat' game at an amusement arcade.

Sure enough, the cat came round as envisaged and I whacked it hard with one short, sharp bat of the oar.

'Bingo!' I said, having evidently picked up that catchphrase from Sophie. 'I got it first time!'

However, as had happened the first time in the bathroom, the cat shattered into its component bones, which then individually began to circle around me until after a couple of circuits they reformed into the whole cat again and it suddenly disappeared. Everything in the house went deathly silent.

I looked around in the darkness, straining my eyes to see where it was hiding.

'It's gone back down the chimney!' shouted Sophie. 'I heard it passing through the fireplace in the south-west bedroom.'

I descended the ladder as quickly as I could, oar still in hand, and we both dashed down to the ground floor and into the former dining room to see if had emerged there.

Aunt had moved into that room from her position at the bottom of the stairs when she heard Sophie's shout and she turned immediately to see us as we entered.

'It's gone down into the cellar!' she said. 'I heard it rattling against the brickwork as it went through.'

'We have to shut the cellar door!' said Sophie, quickly, 'and trap it down there!'

I threw the oar onto the floor and we both ran into the hallway. We could hear the Skeleton Cat whirling around below us in the cellar.

I shut the door firmly and leant against it to keep it closed. Aunt fetched the key and I locked the door with it.

'Now back to the chimney!' I said.

Back in the old dining room I grabbed the oar off the floor and shoved it into the fireplace, working it up and over the brickwork into the chimney cavity beyond.

'Am I right in thinking that this is the only open chimney in the house?' I asked Aunt, as the three of us stood panting in the room.

'Yes,' she said. 'The others are blocked up. It won't be able to get out of any of those.'

'OK', I said. 'The oar should block the cat's exit for the moment!'

We all took a few moments to catch our breath.

'So,' said Sophie at length, 'it's trapped in the cellar at least, but what on Earth are we going to do about it next?'

I thought for a moment.

'I think the first thing to do,' I said, 'is to find out who the woman in the cupboard was. Once we've done that we may get a better idea of who and what we are dealing with.'

We decamped to the lounge and Aunt took down another book off Winifred's shelves and handed it to us for our perusal. I looked at the cover: it was entitled _Notable Witch Country Witches_.

'You remember how this area was once known as "The Witching Village", Stephen?' said Aunt, as she handed it to me.

I nodded, swallowing back the unpleasant remembrance of my last time here.

'This book is a biographical compendium of notable witches and wise men in the area. I never knew it existed until yesterday, when I was tidying up in here and it fell out of the bookshelves. Hopefully it will help you find out who the woman is downstairs.'

191

I turned the book over in my hands, looking first at the front cover and then at the back.

'It's another book by Eric Sycamore,' I said, immediately recognising the name. 'The bloke who wrote <u>Witchcraft World</u> that I told you about. He obviously specialised in this kind of thing.'

'Let me have a look,' said Sophie, correctly detecting a reluctance on my part to open it.

She took the book from me and flicked through the first couple of pages to the Contents.

'Blimey!' she said. 'There are biographies of at least 30 women in here. Oh, and three or four men. This could take some time!'

There was a pause during which all we could hear was the sound of the whirling cat in the cellar below.

'I hate witches,' I said, definitively.

Sophie put her hand on my arm.

'We'll sort this out, Stephen,' she said. 'We just need to find out what to do.'

Sophie read through the book in silence for about twenty minutes. I could feel myself gripping the arms of the armchair I was sitting in ever tighter with each passing minute and I consciously made myself relax to ease off my grip. I could hear the Skeleton Cat still whipping up a whirlwind below us as it circled the cellar walls like it had done in the south-west bedroom and the attic. Occasionally there was a loud crash as some item of junk which was caught up in the whirlwind was thrown by the vortex against the wall in another part of the space. On one occasion there was a tremendous thud as what we took to be the wardrobe that Sophie and

I had had such difficulty in shifting was toppled from its upright position and thrown forward face-first, as it were, onto the floor.

'We need to do something about this soon!' I said impatiently. 'We can't have this going on for ever. Is there anything in that book that looks like it might help us?'

Sophie looked up from the book.

'Yes,' she said, speaking in my direction, but with her eyes still focussed on the pages. 'I think I've found our victim.'

'Go on, then,' I said, keen to get it over with. 'Who do you think it is?'

Sophie took a deep breath.

'There's only one possibility, Stephen: Miss Weston's ancestor - Old Mother Cartwright!'

# Stephen Varley's Journal, Wednesday 25<sup>th</sup> October

*2:30pm, continued*

Of course it was Old Mother Cartwright. It had to be! The more I thought about it, the more obvious it was. She was a noted witchcraft ancestor of Winifred's and had presumably lived right here at Home Farm. She had been subject to a court case in 1759 for, what was it, 'bewitching men and cattle with very many strange and diverse afflictions'. She was known to make potions from local herbs. But when had she been walled up in the cellar? And by whom?

'What does it say in the book, Sophie?' I asked.

Sophie looked first at me and then at the pages that lay open in from of her.

'"Old Mother, or Goodwife, Cartwright",' read Sophie aloud, '"whose real name was Grace, was a noted witch in Cannow's End in the mid-to-late 18<sup>th</sup> century. She is recorded as having cast spells on a number of villagers, especially local fishermen, with whom she seems to have had a long-running feud. She also bewitched 12 of the Lord of the Manor of Cannow's End's best horses, one of which was seriously being considered for a career as a racehorse, to be based at a now-lost racecourse at Galleywood near Chelmsford. This incident took place in 1787. She was indicted for this, but the outcome is not recorded.

'"In 1790 she was indicted again, this time for putting a spell on three-year-old Cecily Miles, daughter of a Thamesmouth sailor, who fell ill for a month after being bewitched. She was tried, but found not guilty of the charges.

'"In 1791 she is said to have bewitched a man named Joshua Meddle, following an argument she had with him as he was unloading fish from his boat down on the River Crouch near Crouchside Farm. It is thought that she wanted some of his fish but he refused to give her any. Meddle was taken ill the same day and spent the next six weeks in bed.

'"Then, in 1792, there was William Blyth, skipper of a Cannow's End fishing vessel, who was bewitched by the Goodwife and went into a stupor, breaking out into a sweat and rolling his eyes before collapsing and falling overboard in front of his crew. He was saved from drowning by a fellow sailor and was bedridden for three weeks until he agreed to buy off the Goodwife with his entire catch of fish the next time his boat went out."'

'William Blyth!' I said, excitedly. 'As in Hard Nut Blyth?'

Sophie pulled a face.

'It must be, dear,' interrupted Aunt.' Blyth would have been, what, 39 in 1792, according to Winnie's book. We know that the Goodwife's son, William, was born in 1768 and although there's some confusion in the records about her age, the Goodwife and Hard Nut could easily have been contemporaries. She'd have been an old woman by the 1790s.'

I looked over Sophie's shoulder at the book and paraphrased aloud what I was reading from it in my head.

'It says here that Old Mother Cartwright's other activities allegedly included making one of her neighbours sick and lame " with such violent fits that the informant conceived her sickness to be something more than merely natural". She is also said to have admitted that she had had "carnal copulation with the Devil" over a number of years and that he visited her three or four times a week, " in the likeness of a gentleman"'.

Aunt snorted with derision.

'Some gentleman!' she said.

Sophie looked slightly pained by the whole thing.

'Can't we call her " Grace"?' she said.' It sounds a bit more personal. I think modern research has shown that a lot of these so-called witches were simply vulnerable old women who were targeted by people who were looking for scapegoats for bad things that happened to them. Their only crime was to be old and friendless.'

Aunt nodded sagely.

'Yes, dear,' she said, with real warmth in her voice.' Let's do that.'

'Didn't Hard Nut's older brother's grandson, Reginald, marry Adelaide Cartwright, Grace's granddaughter?' I asked, moving the conversation on slightly.

'Yes, dear,' said Aunt, ' in 1820, I think, from memory.'

' Maybe that marriage of the grandchildren was designed to patch up the feud of the grandparents?'

Aunt looked pensive for a moment.

' It's possible, dear,' she said.' The name " Meddle" rings a bell, too. I think that family was involved in the smuggling trade as well.'

I looked at Sophie.

'What else does the book say?'

Sophie consulted the pages in front of her again.

'It says that in 1795 Grace was accused of bewitching a man called George Matthews, a Cannow's End resident who farmed oysters from the creeks around the neighbouring village of Pockingham. He was taken ill and died within 24 hours. She was found guilty of his murder and was jailed in Thamesmouth. However, she somehow escaped from her cell overnight. She was in it when the gaoler locked her up in the evening but gone when he opened up in the morning. The door was still locked and there was no visible means of escape and no sign of where she went or how she got out.'

'Blimey!' I said. 'That sounds like real magic. What else does it say about her?'

Sophie re-consulted the book and screwed up her face.

'It says that Grace had some "familiars" or "imps",' she said, 'which were "animal-shaped supernatural spirits or demons which were said in the old days to serve witches and help them cast spells on innocent civilians".'

Aunt and I exchanged glances.

'"Familiars",' continued Sophie, reading directly from the book, '"were believed to be the alter-ego of the witch, remaining closely linked to her metaphysically but sometimes taking on an independent life of their own. In Goodwife Cartwright's case these familiars always took the form of black cats."'

'Black cats?!' I said, interrupting. 'Black cats like Satan perhaps?!'

Sophie looked at me blankly, then returned to the book.

'"Some of these cats",' she continued, '"were fairly harmless, mischievously spilling a drinker's ale in the local inn or appearing suddenly out of thin air simply to scare the wits out of Cannow's End locals such as fishermen and farmers. Others were much more malicious, allegedly killing young children or valuable livestock, seemingly on a whim."

'"The most notable of...", I'm going to say "Grace's...", "familiars was 'Vinegar Tom', who was at least a hundred years old and had protected her from harm since she was a child. It was said that..." Grace... "was prepared to 'fight up to the knees in blood' to protect this creature."'

'"Vinegar Tom?",' I said. 'What kind of name is that?'

'I've heard about witch's familiars before,' said Aunt. 'They often had bizarre names, for some reason. I think there was once one called Grizzly Greediguts or something.'

I laughed. Sophie continued to read from the book.

'"Vinegar Tom is described in contemporary documents as being 'a large black cat'. He was recorded as having got up to a whole load of tricks over a long period, mostly controlled by..." Grace... "but sometimes acting on his own. His activities included the killing of several local pigs, at least two cows, a horse, and two greyhounds. At least two witnesses said that they had seen..." Grace... "'smack her mouth and beckon with her hand and Vinegar Tom would appear out of thin air'. One witness even said that she had seen Vinegar Tom speaking to..." Grace...!

'"In both the Blyth and Matthews cases' a large black cat' was seen with..." Grace..." just moments before the victims were stricken by illness. During the altercation with Matthews..." Grace... "was alleged to have said that if they did her any ill she would rain Hell down upon them in return and if a tragic end befell her before she could do that, then Vinegar Tom would seek recompense from the perpetrators in her place."'

Sophie slammed the book suddenly, making both me and Aunt jump.

'Do you think there was a battle?' she said. 'Between Grace and the smugglers? Right here, in this farmhouse? Blyth and Meddle were in the smuggling trade. Matthews may well have been too. He would certainly have known the creeks round here pretty well? We've found smuggling and witchcraft artefacts in the tunnels. There must be a connection between them, surely?!'

I felt a shiver run down my spine as I contemplated the possibility.

'Well,' I said tentatively, 'I suppose it is possible...'

Aunt nodded.

'That notice you found about" No cursing beyond this point",' she said. 'It could perhaps have been written by the smugglers, warning Grace off? No cursing: no magic tricks?'

Aunt stood up and left the room, apparently heading for the bathroom.

I could feel Sophie warming to the idea.

'Yes!' she said, enthusiastically, turning to explore it further with me.' Maybe they got fed up with her interfering in their business and tried to warn her off with notices, but in the end they had to come together and fight it out!'

I envisaged the likely scene. It was certainly possible.

'You think the smugglers captured her and walled her up below?' I asked.

'Why not?' said Sophie. 'There was a cutlass in her ribs and the dates in this book are about right for the smuggling activity that we know about. I reckon the smugglers had enough of her and managed to catch her somehow and locked her up in that room. Maybe they were in the middle of constructing a tunnel there when they caught her and they simply sealed her up in it and left her there to die! We know from this book that she escaped from Thamesmouth Gaol. Perhaps that's why they handcuffed her, so she couldn't use her magic to escape again?'

I winced.

'What a horrible thought,' I said. 'And what a waste of a good tunnel.'

'Indeed,' said Sophie, agreeing with me. 'They didn't have much luck, did they? One tunnel flooded, another collapsed and that one off the room had to be abandoned as a prison for a witch.'

There was a pause as we both considered what we'd learned.

'Grace's cat - the Skeleton Cat - has got to be Vinegar Tom,' I said at length,' but surely he should have died with his owner. I wonder what caused him to come alive.'

200

'It's got to be some sort of final spell,' said Sophie, 'maybe made with her dying breath. She had her hands and feet bound and had been stabbed with the cutlass. She couldn't move or escape, in the way that she had escaped from Thamesmouth Gaol, to seek her revenge on the smugglers, but the cat wasn't bound at all. It must have just curled up at her feet like a loyal pet and been locked up with her. The book says that she would use Vinegar Tom to seek recompense if she met a tragic end. My guess is that she cast a spell that would see Tom come to life and able to seek revenge vicariously if he ever got out, probably on the first person who opened the door!'

I grimaced.

'We let him out! Do you think he thinks that it was us who locked him up in there?'

Sophie nodded.

'Yes, probably,' she said. 'I suppose Grace would have been expecting smugglers to open it, but unfortunately it was us. And of course the cat has been sealed up in there so long now that it's turned into a skeleton in the meantime. Judging from its unfocussed whirling behaviour downstairs and elsewhere I bet it has gone completely mad in the meantime because its restless spirit has been cooped up in that cupboard in a state of spiritual purgatory for centuries.'

'The Curse of the Skeleton Cat!' I said, thinking aloud. 'It sounds like one of Enid Blyton's Famous Five mysteries!'

'Yes, Stephen,' said Sophie, slightly crossly, 'except this isn't a story - it's real!'

I exhaled heavily.

'I'm painfully aware of that!' I said. 'I can't believe we've got to go through all this once more! I hate this bloody village. I'm getting déjà vu all over again.'

Sophie frowned.

'You know what we've got to do next?' she said. 'Work out how to end the curse.'

I was just about to ask how when there was a sudden shriek from the hallway, as Aunt was returning from the bathroom.

'What is it Aunt?' I called through the lounge doorway, jumping up and moving towards it as I did so.

'The cat is back!' came the reply.

# Stephen Varley's Journal, Wednesday 25ᵗʰ October

*2:30pm, continued*

Luckily, when we reached a panic-stricken-looking Aunt Amelia, who was standing frozen like a statue in the hallway, her hands clasped to her mouth, we discovered that the cat that was back was actually Satan, not the Skeleton Cat.

'Aunt!' I said, admonishingly. 'I thought you meant the Skeleton Cat!'

Aunt looked me straight in the eyes, as if confirming subconsciously that it was me, before she visibly relaxed and let her arms fall down by her sides.

'I'm sorry, Stephen,' she said. 'I just caught sight of him out of the corner of my eye. I thought for a moment it was the Skeleton Cat again.'

Sophie put a hand on Aunt's arm.

'At least we know that Satan is OK,' she said. 'We haven't seen him for a while.'

We all looked at Satan, who was sitting in the hallway by the door to the kitchen. He seemed to be fine.

'Where do you think he's been?' asked Sophie. 'We last saw him in the tunnel when we opened the door and found Grace and Tom, but we've locked the cellar door now. How do you think he got out?'

I spoke before I could stop myself.

'He must have used a skeleton key!' I said, laughing at my own joke.

Sophie and Aunt both glared at me.

'Sorry,' I said, 'but I'm finding this whole witchcraft thing very trying. I thought I'd try to lighten the mood with some humour.'

'I prefer to lighten the mood with some sherry, dear,' said Aunt, smiling at me.' Shall we go in the kitchen and have a glass?'

'I've just had a thought,' said Sophie, sticking with the previous subject. 'There is a way that Satan could have got out of the cellar – that gap in the wall that he squeezed through when we were first down there!'

She looked at me as she spoke and I nodded in agreement.

'It's very possible,' I said. 'In which case we need to block that up in case the Skeleton Cat takes the same route!'

'You two go and do that, dear, and I'll pour us out some drinks,' said Aunt, heading to the kitchen.

Sophie and I went out of the back door and made our way over to the shed. There, we found three empty, if dusty, light-brown hessian sacks.

'These will do,' I said. 'We can roll them up and stuff them in the hole.'

We made our way round to the south-western corner of the building and after a bit of trial and error rooting about in the vegetation there we managed to locate the hole.

'I don't know how Satan can squeeze through there,' I said, kneeling down and bending forward to peer into the hole.' It's very narrow.'

It was dark at the other end of the hole, but the sound of the Skeleton Cat kept coming and going as it continued its whirling behaviour in the cellar and got closer to the opening and then further away again.

204

'Pass me the sacks one-at-a-time and I'll roll them up and wedge them in.'

In due course I had successfully wedged the three rolled-up sacks into the hole, one after the other, like three train carriages disappearing into a tunnel.

'Not only does that stop the Skeleton Cat from escaping,' said Sophie, as we jointly stood up to head back to the kitchen,' it also means that Satan won't be able to go down there again for the time being, which is no bad thing.'

We returned to the kitchen and found Aunt already one glass of sherry ahead of us.

'I needed to calm my nerves, dear,' she said, before I could make any comment.

Sophie and I joined her, and after two or three more glasses each, with the three of us sitting around the kitchen table, I began to feel quite merry. We could hear the Skeleton Cat rushing round in the cellar, clattering into objects and occasionally knocking something over. It was like some kind of weird lift music, always there in the background but not really contributing anything to the situation. At length, Sophie broke the mood of quiet revelry by returning directly to the topic in hand.

'Do you think that Satan and the Skeleton Cat are connected in some way?' she asked. 'The Skeleton Cat is probably a witch's cat and Miss Weston apparently conjured one of Satan's ancestors out of thin air?'

'It's possible, dear,' I could hear Aunt replying, through the fog and blur of too many sherries.

I tried to snap myself back into sobriety so that

205

I could partake in the discussion without saying anything stupid.

'We need to find out more about the curse,' I said, half to myself.

'Grace Cartwright evidently put a spell on Hard Nut Blyth and his gang,' said Sophie, pondering aloud. 'We deduced when you were in the bathroom that this may have triggered a feud between her and the smugglers, which led to them incarcerating her in the cellar.'

'Along with her cat,' I added.

'Stephen and I think it likely, Aunt, that, as Grace could never get free herself – because, unlike when she was in jail, her hands and feet were bound – she put some kind of spell on her cat so that it would wreak vengeance on whoever opened the door next.'

'She would have expected it to be the smugglers,' I added.

Aunt nodded sagely.

'The Curse of the Skeleton Cat,' she mused.

'Exactly!' I said, triumphantly, glancing at Sophie to try to get a reaction from her.

'So...' said Sophie, ignoring me and drawing the threads of our narrative together in order to summarise the situation, 'we need to find out more about Grace Cartwright, more about her cat and more about spells cast on living animals that have the power to bring them to life after they've died. Then, once we've done that, we need to learn how to reverse the spell.'

I tried to grasp the significance of that last point through my alcohol-befuddled brain.

'Piece of cake!' I said, sarcastically.

Aunt looked at me with rather glazed eyes.

'No thank you, dear,' she said.

I laughed.

'No, Aunt,' I said. 'I didn't mean...'

At which point Sophie, who was evidently the most sober of the three of us, prodded me under the table and glared at me.

'Focus, Stephen!' she said.

I thought for a moment.

'What we need now is to work out how we end the curse and get Vinegar Tom out of this purgatory.'

'Ah well,' said Aunt, knowingly. 'I've got a book of spells, if you remember? There should be something in there that will help us with that. Let's go to my little cottage and I'll dig it out for you.'

# Stephen Varley's Journal, Wednesday 25th October

*2:30pm, continued*

Somehow I managed to stagger from the farmhouse, round the churchyard and into Aunt's cottage. Aunt was in front of me on the journey and I could see that she was swaying as drunkenly as I was. Only Sophie looked relatively sober.

Once we were all safely inside Aunt's cottage, she ushered us into her cosy little living room and got the book down from a shelf in there for me and Sophie to look at.

'You look at it, Sophie,' I said, leaving her to take it from Aunt.

She duly took the book and began leafing through it. Aunt retired briefly to the kitchen to make us some strong black coffees.

At length Sophie announced that she had located a section in the book about ending curses.

'Go on, then, darling,' I said. 'What have we got to do?'

Sophie read aloud to me from the pages.

'" On the night of a full moon, gather the following items: a black tablecloth, one tablespoon of powdered dill, one tablespoon of powdered St John's wort, one tablespoon of powdered ginger, a candle, some matches, some paper, a pen which writes in black ink, a black cloth bag and a length of string that has been knotted nine times. Lay out all the items on the black tablecloth. On the paper, write the full name of the entity that has cursed you and put it in the bag. Then put the plant extracts in the bag, one at a time, in reverse alphabetical order. Light the candle and drip nine drops of wax into the bag, on top of the plant extracts and the paper. Visualise the entity that has cursed you and say their name aloud nine times while tying the bag closed with the knotted string. When this has been done, bury the bag and its contents on the property of the entity that has cursed you, chanting the following while you do so:

'" Buried bag and buried curse

Decrease to nothing with this verse.

Now my words aloud are spoken

Will this deadly curse be broken!"

'" Leave the bag and its contents buried and undisturbed overnight, then dig it up and burn it. The curse will end and any malevolent spirits that have been causing harm will be eradicated forthwith."'

There was a lot to take in in that, so I had to think for a moment.

'It sounds like a bit of an old wives' tale,' I said at length. 'Do you think it will work?'

Sophie consulted the book.

'There are some testimonies at the bottom of the section from various individuals, stating that it worked for them, a bit like book reviews on the Amazon website. One of them is a rector, another one a baronet.'

Aunt re-entered the room with a tray containing three cups and saucers and a plate of biscuits.

'How are you getting on, dears?' she asked.

'We've found a spell, Aunt,' said Sophie. 'We're just discussing whether it will work.'

Aunt put the tray down on a small coffee table in front of us and became suddenly serious.

'The spells in that book always work,' she said,

firmly. 'That book has proven providence and power. There is no need to doubt it on this occasion.'

Sophie and I exchanged glances.

'We have to cast the spell at full moon, Aunt,' I said. 'When's the next one?'

'How should I know, dear?' replied Aunt, a little impatiently. 'I'll get my diary. It will say in there.'

She left the room for a moment and I took the opportunity to speak to Sophie alone again.

'If there's no full moon for a month, we've had it!' I said. 'How on EARTH are we going to keep the Skeleton Cat contained all that time?'

Sophie shook her head.

'It's definitely a lot closer than that,' she said. 'I remember looking out of the window one night recently when I couldn't sleep and it was getting really big and bright then. It must be approaching full moon pretty soon. We can't have more than a week until the next one.'

'Seven days exactly, dear,' said Aunt, returning while we were in mid-conversation and holding up an open, blue-covered, A5 diary in triumph. 'Today's the 24$^{th}$ and the next full moon is on the 31$^{st}$. Seven days to keep the Skeleton Cat under lock and key.'

'Seven days?!' I said. 'You mean we've got to put up with it whirling around in the cellar until then?'

'It could be worse, Stephen,' said Sophie. 'It could have been three weeks!'

'I don't think I can bear being in the farmhouse all that time with it making all that noise,' I said. 'And what if anyone else hears it?'

Aunt shook her head.

'That farmhouse has some pretty thick walls,

210

Stephen,' she said, ' and there aren't any houses near enough really. There's only the church, and that will be empty most of the time. My little cottage and the house over the road behind the lock-up are the next closest and we can't hear it from here.'

We all automatically stopped what we were doing and listened in unison for any sound emanating from the farmhouse. All we could hear were a couple of birds twittering immediately outside the front room window.

'Ok,' I said, ' but can we just triple-check that it's really secure in the cellar please? We don't want that cat getting out before we have time to stop the curse!'

# Stephen Varley's Journal, Wednesday 25th October

2:30pm, continued

Thankfully, when we got back to the farmhouse the Skeleton Cat was still in the cellar. We could hear it whizzing round and round, knocking objects over, or, more likely, whirling them around in the vortex it had whipped up, as we approached the cellar door in the hallway. It was handy that, as Aunt had pointed out, there were no other houses nearby, otherwise the neighbours might have thought we had kidnapped somebody!

'Do you think the approaching full moon is contributing to its odd behaviour?' asked Sophie, rhetorically, trying the door and confirming that it was locked.

'I tell you what else is approaching,' I said. 'Bloody Halloween!'

Sophie looked at me briefly. I could tell from her eyes that she was counting forward the days in her head.

'Oh, so it is,' she said. 'The full moon is actually on Halloween, isn't it? The combination of both events must be particularly powerful.'

We found Satan sitting bold as brass on the kitchen table, flicking his tale ferociously from side-to-side and staring at us with his bright, yellow, piercing eyes. Sophie and I both hesitated at the threshold, but Aunt seemed oblivious.

'Get off the table, Satan!' she said, crossing the kitchen towards the angry-looking animal and shooing him off of it onto the floor. He looked angrily back at the three of us before disappearing sulkily past

Sophie and me into the hallway.

'Well, your Skeleton Cat is still in the cellar, Stephen,' said Aunt, reassuringly.

'<u>My</u> Skeleton Cat?' I said. 'I don't want anything more to do with it than I have to!'

Sophie and I left Aunt pottering about in the kitchen and set off on a tour of the house, checking especially the chimney entrances and the hole we'd blocked up in the garden; all were secure. We knew that all three tunnels we had found were impassable – two were blocked and, although the one ending in the room had two as-yet unopened doors in it, we knew from Sophie's oiling of the locks and trying of the door handles while I was in the kitchen collecting the bunch of iron keys, that they were as securely locked as Grace's and Tom's door had been.

Having satisfied ourselves that everything was sufficiently secure, we returned to the kitchen where we found Aunt cooking a meal for us all. I had lost all track of time but deduced from this activity that it must be somewhere around early evening. We could hear the Skeleton Cat whizzing round in the cellar beneath us. Satan did not reappear.

'Sherry, dear?' said Aunt, as I entered the kitchen, with Sophie right behind me.

She pointed to a bottle and some glasses which were standing on the table.

'I don't think so, thanks,' I said. 'My head's a bit foggy as it is.'

'Nonsense, dear,' said Aunt, leaving the cooking to itself for the moment and pouring some liquid out into the glasses. 'It's been a challenging day and sherry is good for the constitution.'

Sophie squeezed my arm.

'Come on, Stephen,' she said. 'Let's have a toast to the success of our venture.'

We all picked up our glasses.

'To ending the Curse of the Skeleton Cat!' said Aunt, a sparkle of mild inebriation lighting up her eyes.

'To ending the Curse!' said Sophie.

We all clinked our glasses together.

'The sooner the better,' I said.

We ate a hearty meal of beef and potatoes, washed down by yet more sherry. The more we had the more it blocked the sound of the cat out, so I soon got into the swing of filling everyone's glasses until we had emptied the bottle. I mused for a moment on how I might be in danger of turning into an alcoholic if I stayed in the farmhouse much longer.

'Aunt,' I said at length, having mused as long as I dared, 'could Sophie and I stay with you for the next few days please? I'm not sure I can cope with the constant drone of the cat if we have to stay here.'

'Of course, dear,' said Aunt, rather loudly, clinking her sherry glass unexpectedly against mine while I was taking a final swig from it. Some of the contents spilled out and ran down my chin. I picked up a napkin to dab on the spillage. 'You are both welcome at mine any time.'

'I think we should all stay here tonight, Stephen,' said Sophie, who was evidently still in a slightly more sober state that either me or Aunt.

'Great idea, Sophie!' said Aunt enthusiastically,

rising to her feet and crossing to a cupboard. 'The night is still young!'

She got another sherry bottle out of the cupboard and began pouring its contents into our glasses. I wondered momentarily how many bottles she had got stashed away in the place and when she had brought them in. I tried putting my hand over my glass, as I had a pounding headache as it was.

'Nonsense, dear,' said Aunt, batting my hand out of the way and spilling sherry onto the table as she tried to give me a refill. 'There's plenty more where that came from!'

Sophie intervened, standing up and taking the bottle out of Aunt's hand.

'Let me do the refills, Aunt. You go into the lounge. We can continue the party in there and do the washing up in the morning.'

'Wonderful idea, darling!' said Aunt, moving unsteadily towards the hallway, a full sherry glass in her hand as she did so. 'See you in the lounge for part two!'

Sophie shook her head and topped up our glasses.

'Come on, Stephen,' she said. 'One night letting our hair down will do us all good. We know the cat is secure.'

I could feel my head beginning to fog up. The constant drone from the cellar was certainly beginning to dim.

'Alright,' I said, rising to my feet. 'What the Hell?!'

We made our way into the lounge, flopped down onto the comfy chairs and carried on drinking until midnight.

# Stephen Varley's Journal, Wednesday 25th October

7:35pm

Needless to say, I woke up with an alcohol-induced headache, having somehow evidently made it to bed last night. I thought I could hear some kind of bizarre alarm clock going off this morning: it was whiny and interminable and grew louder the more I came to. I eventually looked about me in a half-dazed state, trying to work out where it was coming from so that I could switch it off, when I suddenly realised that it was the noise of the Skeleton Cat in the cellar. It must have the energy of a hundred dogs! As far as I knew, it had not stopped continuously whizzing round the cellar since we had locked it in there.

'We've got to get out of here,' I said to Sophie, who was gradually waking up beside me. 'That cat will drive me mad if we have to stay here until the 31st.'

Sophie looked at me blankly, her eyes glazing over. 'Stop shouting,' she said, and pulled the covers over her face.

By the time Sophie and I had got up and got ready it was nearly mid-day. We found Aunt sitting in the kitchen, wearing the same clothes that she had had on the day before. I wasn't sure if she had gone home overnight and just worn the same outfit two days on the trot, or whether she had slept somewhere in the farmhouse, but I didn't really like to ask.

'Did you enjoy last night, Aunt?' I said, taking some headache tablets out of Sophie's handbag and washing them down with two glasses of water.

'I can't remember much about it, dear,' she replied, rather sheepishly.

It took me until about 2:30pm this afternoon to start feeling relatively sober again. I have already written up since then a number of entries in this journal about what happened yesterday, so I have now reached the point where I can write up today's activities.

I've basically spent most of the afternoon nursing a dull headache and sitting in a stupor. I checked with Aunt around 4pm or so that she was still OK for us to stay with her for a few days, to get us out of earshot of the whirling dervish in the cellar. She couldn't remember having agreed to it, which was slightly embarrassing, but of course she said 'Yes'.

I was pleased to be leaving the farmhouse for Aunt's 'little cottage', as a lot had happened there since our arrival. First there was Satan in the south-west bedroom chimney, then there was the discovery of the tunnels and finally there was the witch skeleton and the Skeleton Cat. Cannow's End is the strangest village in the world, and yet, I was also becoming quite fond of it again. It had been great spending time there with Aunt and Sophie. The rural, backwater nature of the place really appealed to me. Northumbria, where Sophie and I now lived, was lovely, but it was a long way off from our roots in Essex and Suffolk respectively. I could certainly see us moving back here at some point.

It was a relief to get to Aunt's cottage and decant into the bedroom upstairs at the front.

Sophie and I haven't left the room since we arrived and Aunt has spent most of that time snoring gently in the room next to us.

'That was some night,' said Sophie, at one point, when we were lying next to one another on the bed.

'It was indeed,' I said.

There were long pauses in our conversations. I knew Sophie must be suffering from a sherry-induced headache as well.

'Do you think that cat will be alright while we're here?' I asked, after a few minutes' silence had passed.

Sophie laughed.

'You make it sound like it's a real one and we've temporarily put it into a cattery!' she said.

I smiled to myself in response.

'You know what I mean, though,' I continued. 'If it gets out, we're done for. Even worse if it gets out and leaves the farm and rampages around the neighbourhood: it will create a local scandal!'

Sophie sat bolt upright, but then appeared to regret it, reaching a tentative hand to her evidently pounding forehead. She exhaled heavily.

'Maybe we should check up on it from time to time?' she said. 'Morning and night? To make sure it's still in there?'

'Ok, but not tonight, darling,' I replied. 'First thing tomorrow, eh?'

Sophie nodded and slowly laid back down on the bed.

There was silence between us and the next thing I knew it was dark and I was waking up in the room having evidently fallen asleep. The faint yellow light from the nearest streetlamp was illuminating a mirror near the window in the darkness. I looked at the clock: 7:35pm. I got up and sat by the window, and I'm now writing up this journal in the light of the streetlamp.

# Stephen Varley's Journal, Tuesday 31st October

11:50pm

As soon as Sophie and I were up and dressed the following morning we went to the farmhouse together to check on the Skeleton Cat. Satan was sitting on the front door step when we arrived and he stood up as if to greet us when we got there. The Skeleton Cat was still evidently whizzing round in the cellar, so we breathed a sigh of relief and left it to it. Satan followed us around all the time and when we locked up we left him sitting on the door step where he had been when we arrived.

'Even Satan is unnerving me now,' I said.

Sophie touched my arm.

'Stick with it, Stephen. It's only a few days now,' she said.

We paid twice daily visits to the farmhouse on Thursday to Monday and each time we heard the Skeleton Cat whizzing round the cellar and found Satan awaiting our arrival and watching our departure. We took some food for the latter each time, but he barely seemed to touch it.

This morning it suddenly occurred to me that we had not done anything about the ingredients for the spell, which were absolutely critical to ending the Skeleton Cat phenomenon! I went to find Sophie to discuss it with her.

'Aunt may already have some of them in stock,' she said. 'Let's see what she's got and we can always go into Thamesmouth to get the things that we're short of.'

We checked with Aunt and she did indeed have

most of the ingredients we needed, but we did have to
drive into Thamesmouth to find a black tablecloth, a
black cloth bag and some St John's wort.

The black tablecloth was easy: we got it from
Watkinson's, in the main shopping centre. The black
cloth bag was slightly harder. We eventually got
one from a handbag shop on the edge of town,
after a quick search on the internet for potential
nearby stockists. The St John's wort was almost
impossible. We had both heard of it, but neither
of us knew what it was, other than a plant of
some kind, so we had to Google that as well. We
learned that it was a well-used plant in the medical
community, for treating such diverse things as
depression, birth control and blood clotting.

'How bizarre!' I said, as Sophie read the details
to me from the screen of her smartphone. 'What's
any of that got to do with whirling cats?'

'Hey,' said Sophie, 'remember what Aunt said!
Let's just go with it!'

We did go with it, but do you think we could
get any from anywhere? We looked in supermarkets,
chemists and small corner shops, but all to no
avail. Some shop assistants said they stocked it but
didn't have any in at the moment; others just stared
at us blankly. Explaining why we wanted it would
have been difficult, so we just smiled politely and
went on our way.

As the afternoon ticked by and we were running
out of time Sophie suddenly remembered that there
was a spiritual health shop down on the seafront,
so we headed off there as quickly as we could.
Although it was only about 2pm, the shopkeeper

– a rather eccentric-looking, elderly lady with long black-and-mauve hair – looked like she was on the point of shutting up when we arrived. She was standing at the glass door with the 'Open' and 'Closed' sign in her hand, looking like she was in the process of turning it from the former to the latter. She turned the notice back to 'Open' when we arrived and beckoned us inside with a long index finger topped by a long black finger nail.

'Thank you,' said Sophie, as the two of us entered.

'I thought you were never coming,' replied the woman, nonchalantly.

I looked at Sophie in surprise. Had she been expecting us?

An over-powering smell of incense assaulted my nostrils as we moved further into the shop, which was packed with just about everything spiritual you could wish for: candles; statues of Buddha; incense sticks; soap; motivational posters; pictures of wolves; dream-catchers; a statue of a North American Indian chief; and various multi-coloured textiles in predominantly yellow, mauve and green. Various things hung down from the ceiling too: a rubber toy skeleton; some black and orange bunting; hair extensions; and a diagram of an all-seeing eye. We had to duck beneath them at times as we moved into the space next to the counter.

I discreetly looked the woman up and down. She must have been in her late sixties, but was trying to look younger. She had a long, mauve, velvet dress on – more like a gown really – and long black hair with a mauve streak and some mauve and black ribbons in

222

it. Her fingernails were alternately black and mauve as well. He hands looked old and stained, as if she was a habitual smoker.

'I've got what you need,' she said, as the three of us finally stood together, she behind the glass-topped counter which was full of rubber rats, bats, cats and God knows what else, and Sophie and I on the customer side. We hadn't yet told her what we needed, so I was interested to see what she was going to produce for us.

'Here it is,' she said, taking out a small bottle from under the counter as she did so. She placed it on the counter top and stood back in expectation.

I craned my neck to look at it more closely, so I could read the label.

'St John's wort,' it said.

Sophie and I stared momentarily at the bottle and then looked directly at one another in complete and utter shock.

'I told you I'd got what you needed,' said the woman, leering slightly.

'Thank you,' stammered Sophie.

The old woman looked at me.

'Skeleton Cat got your tongue?'

I swallowed to get some saliva around what I suddenly realised had become a very dry mouth. I could feel myself going very pale.

'Thank you,' I said, stammering out my words and pointing at the small bottle on the counter. 'How much is it?'

The woman screwed up her face.

'It's on the house, dear,' she said, folding her arms and becoming so still that I thought for a

223

moment that she had turned into a statue.

'Oh no, please let us pay!' said Sophie. 'You won't make any money giving things away.'

The woman glared at her so penetratingly that Sophie involuntarily stepped back a bit and lowered her gaze.

I picked up the bottle.

'Thank you again,' I said, turning towards Sophie and indicating the shop door to her with my eyes.

The woman nodded in acknowledgement.

'Make sure you mix it in the same proportion as everything else,' she said, as we turned to head for the door.

'Everything else?' said Sophie, looking first at the bottle and then at the woman.

'The dill and the ginger,' she said.

My heart missed a beat.

'Come on, Sophie,' I said, anxious to get out of there.' We need to get back.'

Sophie nodded to the lady and I forced a grimace. 'You've been most kind.'

As the door was closing behind us, we heard the woman saying:' It's the least I could do.'

# Stephen Varley's Journal, Tuesday 31st October

<u>11:50pm, continued</u>

We left the shop as quickly as possible, hurried back to the car, jumped in and slammed and locked the doors behind us.

'What the Hell was that all about?' I said, visibly shaking.

'God knows!' said Sophie. 'How did that woman know what we wanted?'

'Have you been in there before?'

'No, but I've heard about it. People said she was good!'

'No kidding!'

And so the conversation went on as we buckled up and drove back to Aunt's. I don't think we stopped talking all the way. My heart was pounding with excitement and incredulity for most of the journey. Even when we arrived at Aunt's cottage we just continued the conversation with her.

'Oh yes,' said Aunt, as we both gabbled out snippets of the story of how the woman had known what we wanted without us telling her. 'I know the shop. I've heard that Old Liz is good at her trade. I've never been in there myself, mind.'

'Old Liz?!' I repeated. 'Is that what her name is??'

'Long black hair with a mauve streak in it?' said Aunt, inquisitively.

I nodded.

'And mauve and black ribbons and fingernails too!' said Sophie, excitedly.

'Yes,' said Aunt. 'That's Liz alright. She's dressed

like that since the world began.'

'I had her down as being in her sixties,' I said, trying to be humorous.

Aunt raised her eyebrows.

'I think she's older than that, dear,' she said, impassively.

'How do you know her then, Aunt?' asked Sophie.

'I don't really _know_ her,' said Aunt.' I encountered her a couple of times in Thamesmouth in my youth. She had a bit of a reputation when we were younger for pushing the spiritual boundaries: trying out Ouija boards, that sort of thing.'

'Ouija boards are scary!' said Sophie.

'So was she!' I said.

Aunt laughed.

'She's pretty harmless,' she said.' Would either of you like a sherry?'

'No!' we chorused in unison.

Aunt looked a bit taken aback.

'No, thank you, Aunt,' said Sophie, more politely. ' We both spent the day nursing headaches last time.'

Aunt threw back her head and laughed.

'Me too!' she said, her eyes sparkling.' Did you get everything you went into town for?'

Sophie held up the black bag to show that to Aunt and then produced the black tablecloth and the bottle of St John's wort from inside it.

'We sure did,' she said.

'Good,' said Aunt.' Then we're all set for tonight.'

'It still spooks me out how Old Liz knew what we wanted,' I whispered to Sophie at a convenient moment.

'I know,' she whispered back,' but who cares?

226

We've got everything we need for tonight's spell. We need to focus on getting that right now. We'll worry about Liz later. Just take it as a good omen.'

We had dinner at Aunt's and then the three of us returned to Winnie's farmhouse. The Skeleton Cat was still wailing away when we got there.

'How has that cat not run out of energy by now?' I asked of no-one in particular.

'It must be a very powerful spell, dear,' said Aunt in reply.

'I hope our spell is powerful enough to counteract it then!' I responded.

'Of course it will be, dear,' replied Aunt, unflappably, waving her spell book that she had brought with her in front of me.' It's in this, isn't it?'

We spent an uneasy evening looking out of the kitchen window for the full moon. It was initially rather cloudy, so we struggled to see it, but as 10:30pm came around the skies began to clear and we could see the moon quite low down in the sky.

'It looks big tonight,' observed Sophie.

'Perfect,' said Aunt.' The bigger the better.'

'So when do we start doing the spell, Aunt?' I asked.

Aunt consulted her spell book.

'We need to do it before midnight,' she said,' but it doesn't say how long before – it just says "after dark". It's dark now and the full moon is visible, so I propose that we do it now.'

She removed the existing patterned table cloth from the table in the farmhouse kitchen and Sophie spread out the black one in its place. Sophie and I had already ground some measures of the three plants – the dill, the St John's wort and the ginger – into powder and placed them into three separate transparent plastic sandwich bags earlier in the evening and Sophie now fetched those, along with three saucers and some tablespoons, and placed them on the tablecloth. The three of us sat round the table and Sophie took the rest of the items out of the black cloth bag one at a time and laid them out on the tablecloth in front of us: the candle, some matches, some paper, a pen with black ink and a length of string that we had already knotted nine times in preparation. Sophie laid the black cloth bag on the tablecloth as well when she had finished emptying it.

'Who's going to perform the spell, then?' I asked, when they were all laid out.

There was a slight pause while we all individually pondered the question.

'Who opened the door to the cupboard in the tunnel?' asked Aunt, at length.

Sophie and I looked at one another.

'We kind of both did it really,' I said.

Aunt looked thoughtful.

'I think you should both perform the spell then,' she said. 'Both together, to make sure that it works.'

I looked at Sophie and we both instinctively reached forward and moved the piece of paper towards us, using our left hands to hold it down, so that it was between us. We then both picked up the pen with our right hands and held it jointly between us over the paper. It was a bit cumbersome, but we managed it.

228

'Write the full name of the entity,' said Aunt, following what we were doing, while looking up and down at us from her book.

'Grace's or Vinegar Tom's?' I asked.

Aunt looked down at the book for inspiration and then back up at us again.

'I would go for both,' she said.

Sophie and I moved the pen together, holding the paper down as we did so.

'Goodwife Grace Cartwright,' I said aloud as we wrote.

'Vinegar Tom,' said Sophie.

We briefly admired our handiwork.

'That all reads OK,' I said, 'considering that we've never written anything jointly like that before!'

Sophie nodded.

'Now put the paper with the writing on it into the black cloth bag,' said Aunt.

We jointly lifted the paper and placed it in the bag.

'What next?' I asked.

'The plants next,' replied Aunt, briefly consulting the book again, 'in reverse alphabetical order.'

Sophie placed the three empty saucers in front of her and tipped the powdered contents of each of the three sandwich bags individually onto their separate surfaces. I looked at the display lying there on the table in front of me for a few moments while I went through my reverse alphabet in my head. It looked like some plates of exotic foodstuffs in a tapas bar.

I picked up one of the spoons and scooped up the St John's wort, adjusting the spoon in my grip after I'd done so, so that Sophie could also hold the end of it with me.

229

'Remember what Old Liz said,' she said. 'Equal measures of all three items.'

Aunt picked up another spoon and used its handle to skim off the top of the contents of our spoon to make it dead level.

'A level tablespoon for each of them will be easiest to measure,' she said, putting her own spoon down.

Sophie and I tentatively manoeuvred our St John's wort-laden spoon until it was over the bag and Aunt temporarily put her book down and held the bag open so that we could tip it in. We shook off a few fine particles that had remained on the spoon so that it all went in, then slowly withdrew the spoon.

'Now the ginger,' said Sophie.

I scooped up some ginger with the spoon and Aunt again used the handle of hers to level it off. We repeated the process from before and tipped and shook the ginger into the bag. Then we did the same with the dill.

As I put the spoon down I could feel that I had sweat on my brow and I involuntarily reached up to wipe it off with the back of my sleeve.

'You're doing well,' said Aunt, encouragingly, picking up her book again.' Now light the candle and drip nine drops of wax into the bag.'

We did as we were bidden, each drop seemingly taking an age to fall. When the ninth one went in we quickly retracted the candle to avoid accidentally dropping a tenth drip in, dripped some more wax onto one of the saucers and stood the candle upright onto the wax.

'Now,' said Aunt, reading directly from the book,

'visualise the entity that has cursed you and say
their name aloud nine times while tying the bag closed
with the knotted string. I think you should both
simultaneously say both names, just to be certain.'

I picked up the knotted string and looped it around
the top of the bag, closing it tightly round it like it
was a small drawstring kit bag. Sophie and I began
to chant simultaneously.

'Goodwife Grace Cartwright. Vinegar Tom.
Goodwife Grace Cartwright. Vinegar Tom...'

When we had completed nine incantations and
were satisfied that the bag was tied firmly closed,
we both let go of it and sat back in our chairs.

'What now, Aunt?' asked Sophie.

Aunt glanced at her book again.

'You need to bury the bag. It says you have to do
that "on the property of the entity that has cursed
you". We know from Winnie's research that the
Cartwrights owned Home Farm, so it's reasonable
to assume that Grace lived here for at least part
of her life. Although we can't say for definite
that Vinegar Tom was with her, her trial records
said that he was a hundred years old and that he
protected her from an early age, so I think it's a
fair assumption that he was. I suggest you bury
it in the garden out the back, somewhere near the
shed maybe.'

I was slightly unnerved that there was not 100%
certainty in what we were about to do. If Tom had
never lived here with Grace, then the spell could fail
and we would be stuck with his wailing for another
month until the next full moon! I wasn't sure I
could take another day of the mad cat in the cellar,

231

let alone another month, but we had no option but to go with it.

'Come on, Stephen,' said Sophie, sensing my reluctance, 'let's get it over with.'

We went into the back garden, while Aunt remained at the back door, still holding her spell book. The garden was bright in the moonlight and I looked up to see the full moon shining right above us. There was, however, an unusual low mist hanging around about three feet from the ground and I felt a bit unnerved by it. Sophie stopped suddenly in her tracks and put her hand on my arm. She was staring across the garden.

'What is it?' I asked, momentarily afraid.

'I just saw Grace again,' replied Sophie, 'disappearing into the mist over there.'

She pointed.

'Oh God!' I said. 'Don't start that again! Let's just get on with it – and quickly!'

I went to the shed and got out a spade. Sophie pointed to a spot where the earth was bare and I started to dig.

'How far down do you think?' I asked after a couple of spadesful.

Aunt, who was silhouetted from where we stood against the hallway light behind her, consulted her book again.

'It doesn't say,' she said. 'Just make sure it's completely below ground level and fully covered over.'

It was cold in the garden and, in part for warmth and in part for good measure, I dug what was probably an unnecessary two feet down for a bag that was barely six inches high, but I kind of got carried away with it. I only realised how far I'd gone when I felt a gentle, loving touch on my arm. I looked up to see Sophie smiling at me, with care and concern.

'That's deep enough, Stephen,' she said. 'We can put the bag inside it now.'

I put down the spade and we both held one of the top corners of the bag.

'Remember the chant!' called Aunt from the doorway.

I glanced at Sophie.

'Remind us what it is, Aunt?' said Sophie, over her shoulder, without taking her eyes off mine.

'"Buried bag and buried curse

Decrease to nothing with this verse.

Now my words aloud are spoken

Will this deadly curse be broken!"'

Sophie nodded and she and I repeated the chant aloud as we placed the bag into the ground. We backfilled the hole with earth with our hands as we did so, until the bag was out of sight. We then stood up and I took up the spade again and filled the rest of the hole with that, patting the earth down with the blade as I did so and then stamping around on top of it to flatten it down.

'Not too much,' said Sophie, gently. 'We've got to dig it up tomorrow!'

I'd forgotten that bit.

'Ok,' I said quietly, ramming the spade blade into the ground nearby so that it would stand upright and be handily placed for us to retrieve it when we returned the next day. I also placed a loose paving slab which I found lying by the shed horizontally over the earth to ensure that it remained undisturbed.

'We don't want anything digging it up overnight!' I said.

Sophie smiled. The moonlight created enchanting shadows on her beautiful face.

'That's it for tonight, dears,' called Aunt from the doorway. 'It's just gone eleven thirty, so you've done it in plenty of time.'

Sophie reached out for my hand and we held hands as we trudged back to the warmth of the farmhouse. I got out my journal and wrote up this entry to give me something to do while we waited.

'What a beautiful moon,' said Aunt, looking up at the sky.

# Stephen Varley's Journal, Wednesday 1<sup>st</sup> November

*pm*

*Neither Sophie nor I slept at all well last night. I had a fitful sleep, dreaming about witches, Skeleton Cats, skeleton dogs and a tall woman with mauve hair! I've got no idea where the dogs came from, but the rest of it was pretty obvious!*

*I was fearful that the spell would not work, although as Aunt reminded me again when we went to bed, it was in her book and that had 'proven provenance'. I was also apprehensive about digging the bag up in the morning.*

*We both got up about six-ish in the end and made our way bleary-eyed into the kitchen, where we found Aunt, who had slept in the lounge (a clue perhaps to where she had spent the drunken sherry night), sitting at the kitchen table, blowing on a hot mug of tea which she held cupped in both hands. The wailing cat could be heard doing its thing in the cellar beneath us.*

*'Morning, dears,' she said. 'You didn't sleep either?'*

*I shook my head.*

*'I had a dream about an enormous broomstick,' said Sophie, as we took our seats at the table.*

*'Would you like a cup of tea, dear?' asked Aunt, indicating a recently-boiled kettle.*

*'In a minute thanks,' I said. 'I need to come to a bit more first.'*

*We all sat there in silence for a few moments.*

*'Your paving slab is still there,' said Aunt after a couple of swallows of tea. 'Your buried treasure*

is ready for digging up.'

I looked out into the garden through the kitchen window. It was still dark outside, but I could see the outline of the handle of the spade in the light emanating from the kitchen. I groaned at the thought of it all.

'I hope it works,' I said. 'I can't take much more of this wailing cat!'

Sophie put her hand reassuringly on my arm.

'Come on, Stephen,' she said. 'We're in the home stretch. We might as well do it now and get it over with.'

I looked down at my pyjamas and then at Sophie in hers.

'Really?' I said. 'In these clothes?'

'There's no time like the present,' said Aunt, persuasively.

We all stood wearily up from the table and Sophie and I went out into the garden just like we had done the night before. The cool, still morning air hit me suddenly as I opened the back door and I was forced to take a sharp intake of breath. I could see Sophie's breath hanging in the air in front of her face.

'Right,' I said, 'let's get this over with then.'

We crossed the back garden to the spot in question. I dragged the paving slab aside and retrieved the spade. I reflected for a moment that slippers were probably not the best footwear to go digging in, but I couldn't be bothered to go back into the house and change. I glanced briefly at Sophie and then back at Aunt, who was standing, as on the previous night, in the back door doorway, the hallway light behind her again silhouetting her diminutive frame.

'Dig it up and burn it!' she called from the doorway.

I started to dig tentatively at first, with some reluctance, but I gradually removed the earth sufficiently until I had uncovered the top of the bag.

'We'd better pull it out together,' said Sophie, 'just in case.'

I laid the spade on the ground and we both knelt down and cleared more earth away with our hands. We then took a corner of the bag each and together we lifted it up and shook it free from its earthen grave.

I was briefly unnerved to find something landing next to me suddenly. I turned round quickly to see that it was a box of matches.

'You'll need those, dear,' said Aunt, evidently having thrown them at us from where she stood.

'You made me jump, Aunt!' I said.

'Sorry, dear,' came the reply.

I gave the box of matches to Sophie.

'You light it,' I said.

Sophie opened the matchbox and struck a match along the side of it. The match burst into flame. It was a welcoming sight.

'Hold it with me,' she said.

We both had one hand on the bag and one on the match. We rested the bottom of the bag on the ground and folded the top of it over the match to protect the latter from any drafts that might arise and to provide it with something above it to burn.

The bag seemed to take ages to catch light but, just as the flame on the match was approaching our fingers and I was about to suggest blowing it out and starting again, the fire took hold. To our surprise, the whole bag caught fire at once and we both instinctively dropped it and moved backwards. Sophie was left holding the remains of the match and quickly blew it out and threw it onto the ground. The fire took hold so rapidly that the bag and its contents were transformed into a black, smouldering crisp in a matter of seconds.

A cloud of smoke from the remains of the bag rose up and floated mid-air in front of us. The distinctive ghostly figure of Grace simultaneously materialised out of thin air before our very eyes, just like the Skeleton Cat had evidently done with Aunt in the farmhouse kitchen. I could feel the hairs on the back of my neck standing on end and I heard Sophie gasp.

We exchanged brief glances and watched as Grace stepped forward to cup the puff of smoke in her white spectral hands and raise it slowly up above her head, allowing it to dissipate into the air above her. She seemed to look and nod at us as she did so, before she gradually dematerialised again.

' Blimey!' I said.

Sophie grabbed my arm.

' It was like she was saying "Goodbye",' she said. ' Like we've somehow laid her spirit to rest and she came back specially to thank us for it.'

There was a moment's silence, which became gradually longer as we were lost in our thoughts until I suddenly realised something.

238

'Listen!' I said, holding my hand up and looking first at Sophie, then at Aunt.

We listened, heads cocked to try to pick up any sound. It was deathly quiet.

'The cat has stopped wailing!' said Sophie, with evident relief.

'It's worked!' shouted Aunt excitedly from the doorway, clapping her hands together as she did so. 'I told you it would!'

I could feel a broad grin breaking out over my face and some tension that had evidently been in my body for some time draining out of it.

'Thank Heavens for that!' I said.

'Come into the warm, both of you,' said Aunt. 'I'll pour you out a cup of tea.'

# Stephen Varley's Journal, Wednesday 1st November

*1pm, continued*

By about mid-morning we were awake, dressed and energised enough to face the next challenge: going into the cellar. There had been no sound emanating from it for three or four hours and I don't know about Sophie, but I had certainly been putting off the inevitable. Eventually, Sophie said to me ' Shall we do it then?' and I knew that we had to just go for it.

I unlocked the door to the cellar, opened it a couple of inches and listened carefully. All was quiet. Then, with my heart pounding and my pulse racing, I opened the door fully and listened again. Still nothing.

I realised at that moment, as I stood looking down the cellar stairs into the space below, that Sophie and I had left the cellar lights on. Presumably the lamp was still on in the tunnel as well. The stairs seemed to disappear into the bowels of the Earth. I hesitated.

' Do you want me to go first?' asked Sophie, from over my shoulder.

' No,' I said. ' It's Ok, I'll do it.'

I put my foot on the top step and worked my way down slowly, one step at a time, until I reached the relative safety of the Tudor-brick floor. I looked all around me for any sign of movement. The junk pile that had stood against the south wall of the cellar was strewn all over the place and the big, heavy wardrobe that we had heard fall over was lying on its face some distance away to my left. It was, however, all very still and quiet. There was no sign of the Skeleton Cat.

I called up to Sophie.

'It's all clear, I think. Come down.'

Sophie made her way tentatively down the stairs and I was so pleased when she was finally standing next to me that I gave her an impromptu hug and kissed her on the nose. She kissed me on the lips in return.

'Come on,' she said.

We made our way across to the south-east tunnel, where I saw something at the tunnel entrance that made me stop in my tracks. I pointed it out to Sophie. It was the Skeleton Cat, lying, like a skeleton should, flat out on the floor. We both stood motionless ourselves for a moment, checking for certain that it was not moving, then Sophie nudged me from behind to prompt me to go forward and we both gingerly made our way over to it. I picked up an old umbrella that was lying nearby and tentatively prodded the nearest part of the skeleton, the tail, with that. I dislodged the last bone in the tail from its neat, straight row and it stayed dislodged. I then tentatively moved the next bone with the point of the umbrella and that too remained out of place.

I breathed a sigh of relief and Sophie clutched tightly hold of my arm.

'It's over,' she said.

I threw down the umbrella and we approached the skeleton.

'I think we should re-bury Tom with Grace,' I said.

Satan suddenly appeared at our feet, making me jump again, and meowed loudly as if in agreement.

'Let's get some gloves,' said Sophie.

We duly returned the skeleton of Vinegar Tom to his place at the feet of Grace Cartwright, in the skeleton cupboard in the room off the south-east tunnel. Sophie did her best to curl him up into a pose that made it look like he was sleeping there.

'That's how he was when we found him,' she said, a trace of a tear in her eye.

Satan followed our every move, taking one last wander around to sniff Tom's skeleton before heading off down the tunnel back to the cellar.

'I think he approves,' I said.

We closed and locked the door to the cupboard, leaving Grace and Tom finally resting safely inside.

'Rest in Peace, both of you,' said Sophie.

I squeezed her hand.

'We need to make sure this is never opened again,' I said. 'We don't want anyone else having to go through what we went through.'

'I'll get my dad to brick it up properly,' said Sophie, 'and re-plaster the wall.'

We also locked the door to the room and the door to the tunnel, taking the table lamp and extension back into the cellar with us.

It was mainly with relief, but also with some sadness, that we left Grace and Tom sleeping again, but we had had enough of tunnels for the time being, so when we got upstairs Sophie phoned her parents and arranged for us to stay with them for a few days. We needed a holiday – and Thamesmouth was as good a place as any to spend it.

# Stephen Varley's Journal, Sunday 12th November

*8pm*

We had a lovely break in Thamesmouth, staying there until Thursday morning. We asked Aunt to come as well, but she decided to remain in Cannow's End to look after Satan. He had become noticeably more friendly and sociable after we had laid Vinegar Tom to rest and he and Aunt appeared to be beginning to strike up a bond between them. Sophie and I needed a break though and I'm pleased to say that we got one.

We went up the pier (it was a bit chilly, to be honest!), we played on the amusements, we watched some live bands and we enjoyed some good food. It was like a home away from home. Sophie's parents loved having us. You could see there was a lot of affection between them and their daughter.

'Don't forget that Mum and I would love to have you back living nearby again,' said Dave to Sophie as we were saying our goodbyes. 'Northumberland is so far away. I miss having my Little Princess close at hand.'

Sophie blushed.

'We _will_ think seriously about it, Dad,' she said, kissing him on the cheek.

We returned to Cannow's End and went straight to Aunt's cottage to see how she was. She was waiting for us when we arrived, looking relaxed and happy.

The three of us made our way to the farmhouse, which I'm pleased to report was exactly as we had left it. Aunt unlocked the front door and Satan, who was sitting in the hallway, stood up and approached us as we entered, rubbing around our legs for attention and purring loudly as he did so.

'I'm glad they're both alright,' I whispered to Sophie, at an opportune moment.

After a pleasant evening with Aunt we left her to return to her 'little cottage' while Sophie and I slept in our usual room in the farmhouse, with Satan curled up on a cushion nearby. All three of us slept soundly all night.

Aunt came round at about 10-ish on Friday morning, by which time Sophie and I were up, refreshed and raring to go.

'Thanks for that break,' I said to Sophie when we were getting dressed. 'I really needed it.'

'Me too,' she said.

When the three of us were in the kitchen we discussed what approach to take next regarding clearing out the house. Sophie and I had been so distracted by our adventures in the cellar that we had been deflected from our original plan of helping Aunt to clear it out and patch it up. Aunt, bless her, had still been tinkering away at things during our absence, but Sophie and I decided that we would now set aside a couple of days to complete the clear-out and help Aunt with anything that she needed of us. We therefore spent all of Friday, yesterday and the early part of this morning completing the task of clearing up the farmhouse. We have filled the skip, which is still in the farmyard, to the absolute brim, so that when the driver comes to collect it tomorrow he will no doubt be giving us a bit of grief for overfilling it!

I could sense all the time that we were clearing out the farmhouse that Sophie was a little uneasy about something, so I finally asked her about it at lunchtime.

'What's the matter, darling?' I said. 'I can tell that you've got something on your mind.'

Sophie turned to face me and looked me straight in the eye.

'You know that we've got to find out where those other two doors off the underground room lead?' she said.

I grimaced. I did know, but I had been putting off mentioning it myself.

'I know,' I said, 'but the discovery of the skeletons has really made me wary. What if there are any other skeletons behind the other doors? I don't want to unwittingly unleash any other curses.'

'Take it one step at a time,' advised Aunt, when we discussed it with her. 'You know what warning signs to look out for: notices about curses or welcomes to Hell. If you encounter any of those, stop immediately!'

Sophie and I therefore duly returned to the cellar, while Aunt went off to the late morning service at All Saints church. We re-entered the south-eastern tunnel, rigging up the table lamp and extension lead and taking our torches with us as before. Dave had been back to brick up the doorway to the skeleton cupboard and plaster over the wall while we had had a day out shopping in Thamesmouth with Sophie's mum, so the first thing we noticed when we returned to the room was the bright new patch of whitewash over the new brick walling. I felt a shudder go down my spine when I saw it.

'I feel like we've trapped Grace and Tom in there again,' I said.

Sophie looked sad.

'I know what you mean,' she said, 'but they are dead and they died years ago. They've been living in some weird kind of horrible purgatory ever since, so think of it this way: we've finally laid their souls to rest and no-one else will disturb them now.'

'It seems an age since we first started doing this,' I said. 'Remember how excited we were at finding the first tunnel? It seems like a lifetime ago.'

Sophie laughed.

'It's only been about three weeks,' she said.

We looked at the two unopened doors in the room.

'Any preference?' I asked.

Sophie looked first at one, then at the other, then back again to the first one.

'This one?' she said, indifferently, pointing to the one on the right. 'It's got to lead to the church, surely?'

We made our way over to the door in question and used another of the iron keys to unlock it. It was stiff, but it opened, albeit slowly and with a grating creaking noise that set my teeth on edge. Again, the usual smell of damp air assailed our nostrils, but it was not anywhere near as unpleasant as the smell emanating from the skeleton cupboard had been when we had first opened that.

I looked at Sophie.

246

'Ladies first,' I said.

Once we were both safely through the door we shone our torches around into the space beyond it. It was, thankfully, another tunnel, its walls and ceiling again comprising an arch of un-whitewashed Georgian brick, and its floor comprising the usual clay. Unlike the other tunnels that we had encountered, however, this one had a bit of a gradient on it, descending quite steeply away from us.

'I wasn't expecting that slope,' I said.

Sophie nodded.

'I guess it's so that the tunnel goes low enough to pass under the graves in the churchyard?' she suggested.

We descended the tunnel until we reached a point where it briefly flattened out before beginning to rise again.

'It's just like the Dartford Tunnels,' said Sophie, with enthusiasm. 'They descend, flatten out and then ascend again as the tunnel makes its way under the River Thames.'

'Thank you, Sherlock!' I said, unimpressed, but I pictured myself driving through them in my mind for reference as she spoke.

As we stood on the flat section, just as we were about to start ascending the slope beyond it, I noticed something white sticking out of a broken section in the arched brick ceiling.

'What on Earth is that?' I said, pointing at it as I did so.

Sophie stooped forward to have a look.

'It's a femur,' she said.

'A what?'

'A femur,' she repeated. 'A human thigh bone.'

I felt sick to the pit of my stomach again.

'Oh God! Don't say it's another witch skeleton!'

Sophie inched closer to the object and stood underneath it so that she could examine it better. She shone her torch up and down the object and I could clearly see that it was a bone. I was taking no chances, so I remained where I was, a couple of paces behind her!

'Well?' I said, trembling slightly, as I did not really want to hear the answer.

'I think we're safe, Stephen,' she said, smiling. 'Come and look at this.'

I reluctantly and with some trepidation made my way over to where Sophie was standing.

'Look at the floor first,' she said, shining her torch onto it.

I did the same and scanned the area around our feet.

'Some loose bricks,' I said, 'some loose earth and some more bits of bone.'

Sophie nodded.

'Now look at the ceiling.'

I could see as I did so that there was a gap in the brickwork of the tunnel roof, where the loose bricks had fallen out of. The leg bone was hanging down through the gap.

'Follow the bone up to the top,' said Sophie, panning her torch slowly up it as she did so.

'There's a bigger bone there,' I said.

'Yes,' said Sophie. 'It's the bottom of a pelvis. And from what I can see of it, it's a male one.'

248

I clearly looked at her in a perplexed manner, because she didn't wait for me to say anything but just carried on.

'The bones on the floor,' she said, shining her torch over them again,' are the patella, tibia, fibular, tarsals, metatarsals and phalanges: the kneecap, lower leg bones and feet bones to you. They have clearly fallen off of the femur when the roof of the tunnel gave way at this point.'

'Ok,' I said, starting to get a little irritated.' What does that mean in English?'

Sophie smiled again.

'It means,' she said,' that this skeleton belonged to a man who was buried in the churchyard and whose remains were disturbed when the brick roof of the tunnel, which must have been cut just below his grave, gave way under the weight of the earth above it.'

'Ah!' I said, beginning to understand the situation. 'So it's not a witch's skeleton after all then?!'

'No, Stephen,' said Sophie impatiently.' It's just a skeleton from the churchyard that happens to have fallen through.'

I could feel myself relax a little.

'So where's the coffin then?' I asked, warming to the task.

'There might not have been one,' said Sophie,' or it might have rotted away. In the late 17$^{th}$ century there was an Act of Parliament that stipulated that the dead had to be buried in woollen shrouds. This skeleton, which is obviously pretty low down in the ground above, could easily date from that period.'

'Buried in wool?' I said.' What on Earth for?'

Sophie laughed.

'It was an attempt to prop up the English cloth trade, which was in steep decline at that period. I saw a couple of suspected burials in wool at one of the archaeological sites we visited on my course. They were only mandatory for a short period – 20 years or something – but they were pretty widespread at the time.'

'Interesting,' I said. 'I'm just pleased that it wasn't another witch.'

Sophie touched my arm to reassure me.

'Shall we get on?' she said.

Just as we were about to set off down the tunnel again, Sophie stopped suddenly and put her hand on my arm. I stopped as well.

'What is it?' I asked.

She motioned for me to remain silent. I cocked my head to one side and listened carefully.

'It sounds like wailing!' I said.' Oh please God no, not another Skeleton Cat!'

'No!' said Sophie, dismissively. 'It's voices. Muffled human voices.'

We remained silent for another moment. I listened more carefully.

'You're right,' I said.' It's coming from the far end of the tunnel!'

We made our way cautiously to the end of the tunnel and, as it began to rise again beyond the skeleton area, we could see ahead of us in our collective torchlight that there was some kind of bricked-up doorway at the end of it. When we reached it, I ran the palm of my hand over the bricks and we both

250

pressed our ears to the wall.

'It's definitely voices,' says Sophie. 'It sounds like singing.'

'These bricks are loose!' I said, pulling one of them out.

'It's very poor quality mortar,' replied Sophie, examining the stuff. 'It was probably done in a hurry.'

I took another brick out.

'We can have these out in no time!' I said.

Between us, Sophie and I began the process of removing the bricks, stacking them up neatly on the floor along the sides of the tunnel behind us as we did so. The human voices got louder the more bricks we removed. A large number of them were loose; others became so as we removed the ones adjacent to them. We soon had a decent-sized gap to look and step through.

We could see that behind the bricked-up doorway there was a really tattered curtain hanging down across the opening, attached above it on the other side. I went to move the curtain aside but it disintegrated into clouds of dust as I moved it. We had to put our hands up to cover our faces, as we'd left the dust masks in the farmhouse cellar. We stood there for a few moments while the dust settled gently onto the tunnel floor.

Sophie grabbed my arm in excitement.

'Look at the thickness of this wall!' she said. 'What with this and the singing, this has to be the east wall of the church crypt beneath the chancel! I told you this tunnel would lead to the church!'

I shone my torch around the edges of the

doorway. The wall was certainly thick, and made of the same stone as the church. The dark brick infill that we had by now largely removed looked incongruous against the white stonework that had been revealed.

'I think you're right,' I said, 'but why is there a door here and why was it bricked up?'

Sophie shrugged.

'It's eighteenth-century brick,' she said. 'It must have something to do with Grace and the smugglers. Maybe it was the smugglers' escape tunnel to the sanctuary of the church, or maybe it was just another part of their underground distribution network? I reckon they sealed it up with brick because they thought that would provide better protection against Grace's magic than a wooden door. This is the church after all – they would presumably not want witchcraft going on in there!'

Behind where the curtain had hung was the back of a big wooden object, which we could not see either the top or the sides of and which was essentially blocking our view of whatever was beyond. It was standing about a foot out from the other side of the wall. I stepped over the bricks that were still in place at the foot of the doorway and into the space between the wall and the object. I could see, as I looked along it to the left, that there was a narrow passageway I could fit through between it and the wall. I shone my torch up the passageway and it lit up some more white stonework in the distance.

'There's a room here,' I said. 'It's probably the crypt, as you say. If we edge along to our left here we should be able to get out from behind this big wooden object and out into the room. It looks a bit of a squeeze, but it should be doable.'

'Okay,' said Sophie, enthusiastically. ' Let's give it a go!'

I turned sideways and squeezed between the big wooden object and the inside of what we took to be the church's crypt's eastern wall. I inched my way sideways along the narrow space like a crab. I could feel the rough stone wall catching on the back of my clothes as I did so, but I was less worried about that than getting splinters in my nose! Eventually, after a bit of twisting and turning, I reached the end of the object and almost fell out into the room beyond as I exited the narrow space. Sophie followed in the same fashion and we soon found ourselves standing together in an underground room. I located a light switch and switched it on.

'This is definitely the church,' said Sophie. ' Listen! You can hear the congregation singing a hymn!'

I craned my neck so that my left ear was facing upwards. I could indeed hear the strains of ' Be still, for the presence of the Lord' coming through the ceiling.

' Well, well!' I said. ' That's amazing!'

It was the first time I had ever been in the crypt. I didn't even know it was there. It had a calm, peaceful feeling about it, in contrast to the cupboard which had poor old Grace in it. We listened for a few moments to the joy of the vocal and the beautiful piano accompaniment, the louder and more powerful notes of which resonated through to us as we stood still together in a moment of harmony. Sophie held my hand and I kissed her on the nose.

'So what on Earth is this big wooden thing then?' she said, at length.

We let go of each other's hands and moved out into the centre of the room so that we could get a better view of it. It was a pipe organ!

'Well, most of a pipe organ,' replied Sophie, to my out-loud exclamation. 'It looks like it was dumped here ages ago and hasn't moved since.'

'Hence the piano upstairs,' I said, rolling my eyes towards the ceiling. 'I reckon they removed the bits of it that could be removed and dumped the rest of it down here.'

'Yes,' continued Sophie, 'it's actually in three parts - there's a bit over there and a bit more over there.'

I followed her gaze and nodded in agreement.

'Well,' I said, 'whoever put the organ there obviously didn't think to have a look behind the curtain! If they had have done they would have found the bricked-up doorway to the tunnel!'

'If someone else had found the Skeleton Cat first,' said Sophie, 'it would have saved us a lot of trouble!'

We began to look around the crypt while the congregation above us completed their hymn. It was dusty in there, though nowhere near as bad as the cellar of the farmhouse. There were some metal racks with old books on them and a big metal two-doored cupboard, standing about six feet high, with a rusted chain wrapped round the door handles and a padlock holding the chain in place. I pulled at the

IAN YEARSLEY

padlock but it was locked.

'I don't think this has been opened for a while!' I said.

I rocked the cupboard on its base, firstly away from me and then back towards me.

'It's really light though,' I said. 'There can't be anything in it? Why lock a cupboard if there's nothing in it to steal?'

'Who knows?' said Sophie. 'We probably ought not to be trying to find out either. Technically this is a private part of the church and we are undoubtedly trespassing.'

I laughed dismissively.

'Who's going to know?' I said. 'The congregation are engrossed in their service.'

'I don't think they are,' said Sophie. 'It sounds like Reverend Grant is wrapping it up to me.'

I stopped my examination of the contents of the crypt and listened again to what was going on upstairs. The singing had indeed finished and Reverend Grant's deep bass tones were now the only thing breaking the silence. I could hear the congregation periodically and collectively repeating the word 'Amen'.

'I ought to start going to church more myself really,' I said.

'I think we both should,' said Sophie.

There was some muffled shuffling of feet upstairs and it sounded like the service had ended and the parishioners were getting ready to depart. Just at that moment I spotted another old rotting curtain which was identical to the one that had covered the bricked-up entrance to the tunnel

255

behind the organ. It was covering an object that was propped up against the south wall of the crypt. I walked across to it and snatched up the curtain to see what was beneath it. Just like the previous one, the curtain disintegrated into clouds of dust. Sophie and I temporarily found ourselves in a thick fog.

'For goodness sake, Stephen!' said Sophie, clearly not amused. 'What did you do that for?'

'Look,' I said, waving my arms about furiously, so as to waft the dust away,' it's an old coffin!'

Sophie came over, her interest piqued, and we both stared at the coffin, which was propped up almost vertically against the wall and had been previously hidden from sight by the now-disintegrated curtain.

'That is old!' said Sophie, the archaeologist inside her coming to the fore again.' Late eighteenth- or early nineteenth-century, I should think, judging from the nails that are holding the planks of wood together.'

She tried to remove the coffin lid, but it was nailed in place.

'Sophie!' I said. 'You just told me that we shouldn't be poking around in other people's stuff!'

She laughed.

'This is different!' she said. 'It's a relic from the past!'

'So is that cupboard!'

'Don't you want to know what's inside it, Stephen?' asked Sophie.

'I'm not sure I do,' I said. 'I've seen enough skeletons recently to last me a lifetime!'

Sophie laughed again.

'It's not going to have a skeleton inside it if it's propped up against the wall like this!'

'I'm not so sure about that!' I said. 'Look at this brass nameplate on the top of it.'

I pointed to a small brass plaque on the top end of the coffin which had the words 'John Mason, Lord of the Manor of Home Farm in Cannow's End, died 1807' engraved on it.

'John Mason?!' said Sophie.' Wasn't he mentioned in that book about the village?'

I nodded, rocking the coffin slightly like I had done with the cupboard, to try to gauge its weight.

'I think there is something in it,' I said, 'but nothing loose like a skeleton. It's more like there's something really dense and heavy inside. Sand or something. Get something to prise it open with.'

Sophie looked at me with surprise.

'Oh, so we are going to break it open after all then?!' she said, with mock alarm.

I was momentarily torn, so I hesitated, first moving one way then the next, then stopping altogether.

'Well,' I said, 'how about we see if we can prise it open easily? If we can, we'll have a look at what's inside; if we can't, we'll go and tell Brian about it and ask his permission to open it up. He'll probably be as interested to know what's in there as we are!'

'Yes,' said Sophie sarcastically, 'why don't we just go upstairs and ask him now. He's going to love us appearing out of the crypt while he's locking up upstairs. It'd be like a couple of ghosts coming out of the bowels of the Earth!'

I hesitated again, but eventually decided to go and look for something to prise the coffin lid open with. However, my uncertainty over which direction I was going in had left me a little unsteady on my feet and I tripped over them as I set off in search of something. I fell headlong onto the floor and into the big metal cupboard, pushing it back against the wall. The top of it hit the wall, making it tip back towards me again. As I lay there on the floor looking up at it, it was as if it was all happening in slow motion, the cupboard teetering on the brink of toppling onto me. Would it or wouldn't it fall?

I could hear Sophie shouting: 'Stephen!'

The cupboard fell.

I scrambled to get out of the way and as I did so I swung my legs around to kick the cupboard away from me. This successfully prevented it from landing on my head but I had unwittingly kicked it in the direction of Sophie and the coffin. Sophie jumped back out of the way just in time, but the cupboard fell smack bang on top of the coffin and broke it in two. The kick, the sound of the metal making contact with the wood, and the cupboard crashing down onto first the coffin and then the stone floor of the crypt made a Hell of a racket! A thin layer of dust leapt up off the floor and hung momentarily in the air like a blanket of gently falling snow.

'Christ!' I said. 'That was close.'

'You've broken the coffin, you idiot!' said Sophie, coming over to check if I was alright, which thankfully I was.

Before we could say or do anything else we heard

the sound of movement behind us and turned to
see Reverend Grant coming down a set of previously
unseen stairs in the distance. Aunt was behind him.
  'We're in for it now,' said Sophie.

# Stephen Varley's Journal, Sunday 12th November

*8pm, continued*

Neither Brian nor Aunt were too impressed.

'What in Heaven are you two doing down here?' asked Brian, with a mixture of surprise and anger.

'And what on Earth is all that racket about, Stephen?' added Aunt for good measure, correctly deducing from the fact that I was lying on the floor that I was the cause of it.

Sophie helped me to my feet and I dusted myself down.

'It's a bit of a long story,' I said, sheepishly.

They both stood there expectantly.

'We thought we'd follow another one of the tunnels from the room under the lock-up,' explained Sophie, pointing vaguely in the appropriate direction, 'and it came out through a doorway behind the organ.' She pointed more specifically this time.

'There's a room under the lock-up?' repeated Brian, incredulously. 'And a tunnel from that came out behind the organ?'

'Yes,' said Sophie. 'The tunnel from the farmhouse that you saw us beginning to excavate led to an underground room beneath the old village lock-up and a tunnel from that room leads here.'

Brian raised his eyebrows.

'So the church is connected to the tunnel network too, evidently?'

'Yes,' said Sophie. 'We think there are connections with the Lord of the Manor as well.'

'The Lord of the Manor?' repeated Aunt, with

surprise in her voice. 'Which one?'

'John Mason,' said Sophie. 'He was mentioned in your book that Stephen read at my parents' house when we first arrived.'

'So,' said Brian, interrupting the discussion and drawing various threads together, 'you were exploring the tunnel from the lock-up to the church, you came in here and you, what, knocked a cupboard over?'

'Yes,' I said. 'That was my fault: I tripped over my own feet. Sorry.'

Brian shook his head.

'Well, let's get the cupboard up first,' he said.

Brian and I bent down and lifted the cupboard up until it was vertical again.

'It's lucky it isn't heavy,' I said, trying to lighten the mood.

'There's not a lot in it,' said Brian.

'Reverend Grant,' said Sophie, quietly, like a child about to admit to some hitherto undiscovered misdemeanour, 'I am afraid we have damaged your coffin.'

Brian at last laughed.

'My coffin?' he said. 'Hopefully I won't be needing one of those for a good while yet!'

Sophie forced a smile.

'No, I mean that one. It's actually John Mason's coffin, judging from the nameplate on it.'

Sophie pointed at the now-broken coffin and Brian followed her gaze.

'Well!' he said. 'I didn't know that was there! I thought there was just a load of old junk in this vicinity. Wasn't there a blanket or something covering up the things in this area?'

I looked sheepish again.

'It was an old curtain,' I said, pointing to a few small remnants of it that lay strewn about.' It was so old that it fell to pieces in my hands.'

'Dear, oh dear, Stephen,' said Aunt.' You shouldn't have been poking about in here in the first place!'

Brian went over to have a look at the coffin and I could see clearly that the wooden lid had virtually snapped in half and one of the sides of the coffin had been badly damaged by the cupboard falling onto it. A lot of the nails holding the lid down had come loose. He crouched down and wrenched one half of the lid off of it. Inside the coffin itself we could see some white material, folded up and jam-packed into the small space.

Sophie drew a sharp intake of breath and put her hands over her mouth.

'It's silk!' she said.' Eighteenth-century silk!'

The four of us crowded round the coffin and Brian began gently to extract the folded white material from within it. I crouched down next to him and felt it. It was definitely silk, slightly greying with age but fundamentally pure white, like it was ready to be made into dresses or other artefacts. Brian passed some of the material up to Aunt and Sophie for their inspection.

'This is beautiful,' said Sophie.

'Just like you, dear,' said Aunt, warmly.

Sophie blushed and held some of it up to her face.

'This would make lovely material for a dress,' she said.

'It must be the smugglers again,' I said. 'They must have hid the silk in the coffin, as if it was a dead body. Nobody would have suspected seeing a coffin in a churchyard! I bet some of the locals even doffed their caps to it! This must be how they moved some of the goods around. Presumably, as it's got John Mason's name on it, it must have been a duplicate coffin or something, or he was perhaps in on the whole thing?'

Brian reeled the extended lengths of silk back in from us and placed the material loosely back in the coffin. He then stood up and I found myself doing the same.

'Come over here,' he said. 'I've got something to show you.'

The three of us followed him to the big metal cupboard, where he got out a key from his pocket and undid the padlock.

'I thought that was an old padlock,' I said, 'and that nobody had opened that cupboard in years!'

Brian laughed.

'It is an old padlock,' he said, unloosening the chain and passing it through the door handles to release them, 'but the cupboard has been opened very recently. I found the padlock on the floor, with the key still in it. The chain was there as well. There was something I wanted to lock away for safekeeping. I'll show you.'

He let the padlock and chain drop to the floor and slowly opened the doors of the cupboard. There was a metal shelf near the top of the cupboard, about three-quarters of the way up, but the rest of it was empty. On top of this shelf, no doubt having been thrown about a bit when the cupboard fell down and was righted again, was an old red book. Brian reached up and got it down.

'It's one of the original parish registers,' he said, 'and it has some very interesting entries in it that I think you might like to see.'

He took it across to one of the old wooden organ parts and rested it on top of it where there was sufficient room to open the book out. The cover of the book said, 'All Saints church, Cannow's End, Burial Register 1757-1803'.

Brian opened the book and flicked through the pages until he came to what he was looking for.

'Have a look at this,' he said.

The three of us stood around him and we all leaned forward in unison to look at the pages in front of us.

Across the top of the double-page spread that was open before us were the printed words 'Register of Burials'. The pages themselves were ruled into columns, with a heading at the top of each column. The headings were also printed, reading from left to right 'Number of Entry', 'Name of Person Buried', 'Rank or Profession', 'Sex', 'Age', 'Place Where Death Occurred', 'Date of Death' and 'By Whom Burial Ceremony Performed', like this...

| Number of Entry | Name of Person Buried | Rank or Profession | Sex | Age | Place Where Death Occurred | Date of Death | By Whom Burial Ceremony Performed |
|---|---|---|---|---|---|---|---|
|  |  |  |  |  |  |  |  |
|  |  |  |  |  |  |  |  |

All the entries in the table below the column headings were hand written, in a very swirly script, quite difficult to read in places.

'Have a look at the dates,' said Brian.

'I'm not sure what I'm looking at,' said Sophie, slightly despondently. 'There are entries for 1783, 1784, 1785 and 1786 on the page, from a wide spread of months.'

'Yes,' said Brian. 'That's what we would expect.'

He flicked the book forward a few pages.

'Now look at this,' he said.

Sophie raised her eyebrows.

'All the entries on this page are from 1793,' she said.

Brian turned the page.

'And on this page,' he said. He turned another page. 'And on this one.'

'Wow!' I said. 'A lot of people died in 1793!'

Brian nodded knowingly.

'Look at the cause of death,' he said.

'"Plague",' read Aunt from the pages in front of us. 'There are a handful of entries showing other causes - "tuberculosis", "old age", someone "fell off a horse" - but the entries mostly say "plague".'

Brian grinned.

'They do indeed,' he said. 'According to this book, 327 people in Cannow's End died of plague in 1793 and were buried in the churchyard.'

'Jesus!' I said. 'That's a lot of burials. It must have been an epidemic!'

Brian nodded, wincing almost imperceptibly at my unintentional blasphemy.

'It is a lot of burials, Stephen,' he said, 'but there's a problem: it's actually more than the population of the village at the time.'

There was a moment's silence while we all pondered what Brian had said.

'Do you think plague victims were brought here from neighbouring parishes?' asked Sophie.

'No,' said Brian. 'I don't.'

'Why not, Reverend?' asked Aunt, curious.

Brian grinned again. The details were coming out as he had planned them.

'Because I studied plague for my "Themes in Biblical Theology" module at University - and 1793 was not a plague year!'

'What?!'

Sophie, Aunt and I all spoke simultaneously in surprise.

'It must have been,' I said. 'Look at the number of burials in the book!'

Brian laughed.

'Don't believe everything you read, Stephen,' he said. 'You, as a novelist, should know how easy it is to create a fictitious world. I think we have evidence of that happening here.'

There was another moment's silence.

'So if these entries are fake, Brian,' said Aunt, musing aloud, 'which is essentially what you are saying, then someone has faked them, and they've done that for a purpose.'

'Yes,' said Brian. 'That's what I'm thinking.'

'And what would that purpose be?' asked Sophie.

'I wasn't sure until now,' said Brian, wiping the back of his hand across his brow,' but having seen that coffin I think I have an idea.'

I interrupted his narrative.

'They were fake entries of fake burials to explain the large number of coffin movements that was presumably taking place in the churchyard in that year!' I said, suddenly realising where this was going. 'The coffins had silk and presumably other smuggled goods in them, but to maintain the veneer of reality the smugglers faked the Burial Register entries to cover up what they were doing!'

'That's what I think was going on,' said Brian. 'I don't know how we can prove it, but I can't think of any other explanation.'

'Does that mean that there are another 326 silk-filled coffins around here somewhere, maybe even buried in the churchyard?' asked Sophie, her eyes brightening as she spoke.

Brian scratched his head.

'I don't think so,' he said. 'There certainly aren't any upstairs and when I had a rummage around down here the other day, looking for anything I could sell to raise money for the church restoration fund, I didn't even notice the one that you found.

I can't believe that that many coffins would have been formally buried in the churchyard. One or two may have been, but 326 is a huge undertaking. There probably wouldn't be the space for them. I reckon the smugglers had a man on the inside who faked the registers in return for payment in smuggled goods, while the coffins themselves came and went - presumably through the tunnels at times - when opportunity allowed.'

'Who was the man on the inside?' asked Sophie.

Brian shrugged.

'It would have to be the rector or the curate,' he said. 'No-one else could have tampered with the books so much without it being noticed. Not everyone was literate then, either.'

'And who was the rector at the time?' asked Aunt.

'According to the rectors' board in the church,' said Brian, 'it was Randolph Herbert, but he was largely absent from the parish during his incumbency. It would have to have been one of his curates, I would think, and we don't have the names of all those.'

'Probably a friend or relative of Hard Nut Blyth's!' I said.

'Undoubtedly,' said Brian.

We spent some moments musing on all this when Brian suddenly asked:

'Are you going to show me the tunnel entrance then?'

'Of course!' I said, enthusiastically, well past my previous animosity towards him and feeling that I owed him something for the damage that I had caused. 'It's over here!'

I led the party to the narrow gap behind the section of the organ that Sophie and I had squeezed through.

'It's down there,' I said. 'You have to edge sideways along this gap to get to the tunnel entrance.'

'Well I can assure you I won't be doing that, Stephen!' said Aunt from over Brian's shoulder.

'I wouldn't mind having a go,' said Brian, 'but I'm not sure I would fit. I'm larger than either of you two!'

We all laughed.

'Come in through the farmhouse,' said Aunt, kindly. 'You can explore the whole tunnel network from there.'

'Would that be alright?' asked Brian, glancing at me, then Sophie.

'Of course it would!' I said. 'It's the least we can do, to show you how we got here!'

# Stephen Varley's Journal, Sunday 12th November

*8pm, continued*

So we all made our way back to the farmhouse and spent the rest of the day showing Brian the tunnel to the lock-up, the underground room and the tunnel to the church. We explained the finds of the witch and cat skeletons but left out the part about Vinegar Tom coming to life!

'Why have you plastered over this part of the wall?' asked Brian.

Sophie adopted an uncharacteristically feeble demeanour.

'The skeletons spooked me out a bit,' she said, employing a little white lie.' I asked my dad to seal them up out of sight.'

We then took Brian down the tunnel to the church and showed him the back of the organ, returning to the room beneath the lock-up without going into the crypt. We then collectively turned our attention to the remaining tunnel, or at least to the last door left that we hadn't yet been through.

'This has to lead into the village somewhere,' said Sophie, by way of introduction. 'We think it probably led to Hard Nut's grocery shop.'

Brian nodded as he perused our tunnel map that Sophie had brought with her and now held up for him to view.

'That would seem to be the most logical explanation,' I continued. 'It's heading in that direction and we have evidence of smuggling in both the farmhouse and the church, so why would there not be a smuggling aspect behind this door?'

Brian paused for a moment.

'So where was Hard Nut's shop?' he asked.

Sophie and I both went to answer his question simultaneously, but we remained open mouthed. As I stood there wondering what to say, I realised in that moment that locating the shop was a glaring omission from our research. Sophie looked at me and then back at Brian.

'We don't know,' she said, forlornly.

'We haven't really had a chance to find out,' I added.

Brian rubbed his chin with his hand.

'There's a book in the church,' he said, clearly trying to remember its details, 'that was given to Alf – my predecessor – by one of the old parishioners. It contains a perambulation of the High Street in 1841, derived from the details of that year's census. It goes up one side of the High Street and down the other, explaining what each building was then and who lived there. I remember looking through it when I first came here. There were more shops in the village then because villages in those days had to be much more self-sufficient: the butcher's, baker's, grocer's, etc. were all within walking distance in the village, not a car journey away to a supermarket in Thamesmouth or some out-of-town retail park. Although Hard Nut's grocer's is no longer there, we can find out from the census data in the book where it used to be. We could then have a look above ground at the building in question – assuming it's still there, of course – and then we'll know where exactly we're heading to through the tunnel.'

I looked at Sophie. It seemed like a good idea.

'Ok,' I said. 'Lead the way to the church!'

The three of us went back up into the building in question, via Home Farm, as it was easier. Brian disappeared momentarily into the vestry and reappeared shortly afterwards with a book.

'This is it!' he said, triumphantly, holding it up for us to see as he approached. It looked quite modern, maybe about 10 years old or so.

'<u>Cannow's End through the Ages</u>,' I said, reading the cover aloud.

Brian rested the book on the back of a pew and Sophie and I gathered round to see what he had to show us. He opened the book on the contents page and began to scan down the list of chapters with his index finger.

'Here we are!' he said. '"A Perambulation of Cannow's End in 1841".'

He flicked to the page in question, where there was a map of Cannow's End High Street and some accompanying text.

'The perambulation starts at the church,' he said, 'and progresses eastwards from there down the High Street on the north side and then returns on the south side back to the church. We're probably going to have to work our way through the whole thing. Remember, we're looking for a grocer's shop, or perhaps anyone with the surname "Blyth".'

The three of us scanned the text in silence as Brian turned the pages. The chapter was organised into sections by property, so that for the church it had a short heading of "All Saints Church", the name of the then occupant, in this case the rector, William Atkins, and a short description of the building. After the church came "The Lock-Up", which had the words "Erected in 1773, not a residence" written beneath the heading. There were very few numbered properties, most of them had individual names like 'Rose Cottage', 'Black House', etc.

'There don't seem to be that many places listed,' said Sophie, with mild dismay. 'I would have thought that there would have been more houses than this.'

Brian nodded.

'You've got to remember, though,' he said, 'that the population of Cannow's End was a lot smaller in 1841 than it is now. Most of the development here, according to a later chapter in this book at least, has taken place since the Second World War. Hence we get entries like "Here is the Three Acre Meadow" in between individual properties.' He pointed to the place in question. 'There's a photograph somewhere in here which was taken from the top of the church tower in about 1905. A lot of the High Street was still undeveloped even then.'

We worked our way methodically through the entries along the north side of the High Street, but everything appeared to be either residential or agricultural. Only when we got to the eastern end – the furthest from the church but nearest to the main road which skirts around that part of Cannow's End – did tradesmen's premises begin to appear.

'Oh look!' said Sophie, suddenly, pointing to an entry on the page.'"The Old Blacksmith's".' She then read aloud from the entry. '"The Old Blacksmith's, which is now a residence, unsurprisingly takes its name from a former trade that was practised on the premises. This building was a blacksmith's as early as 1789 and continued in that trade until 1927. It is shown as such in the 1841 census. The property was converted into a house c.1930 and has been residential ever since."'

'Yes,' said Brian,'that's exactly the kind of thing we are looking for.'

'Here's another one!' I said, spotting an entry lower down the page.'" Number 6 in the High Street was formerly a wheelwright's shop. It appears as such on all the censuses from 1841 to 1901. It was used briefly as a cart lodge around the time of the First World War, but was converted into a house in 1921. You can still see evidence of its former uses in the internal structure." Pity it doesn't say what the evidence is.'

'Indeed,' said Brian.' There's not much else in the way of " shops" on the north side by the looks of it, because the perambulation now crosses over to The King's Head on the south side and then comes back westwards towards the church.'

'" The King's Head",' said Sophie, reading aloud from the book once more, '" has been a pub since the early 17$^{th}$ century, when it was known as The Sailor. The name was changed sometime in the 1640s, probably as a result of the strong local support for the Royalist cause hereabouts during the Civil War. The original building has been extended a number of times over the years, but the demarcations between it and the extensions can be easily detected inside the building. Timber-framing and wattle-and-daub walling is still very much in evidence inside."'

274

We worked our way, in virtual terms at least, westwards along the High Street back to the church. On the way we uncovered a former butcher's, a former baker's and, almost unbelievably, a former candlestick maker's, but as yet there was no grocer's.

'At least there are more former business premises on this side of the street,' I observed.

'Yes,' said Brian. 'It looks like the north side was predominantly houses and fields, whereas the south side was houses and businesses. I suppose most businesses operated from what were originally people's homes. The blacksmith, for example, would have set up his business in front of his house and gradually adapted his premises as his business expanded; it probably went from being a house with a business on the front to being a business with a house on the back. I reckon that was true of many of the "shops" in the village in those days.'

Sophie shuffled uneasily.

'We're not finding any grocer's though,' she said, impatiently. 'Do you think the author of the book missed it out?'

Brian raised his eyebrows.

'I wouldn't have thought so,' he said. 'I let a couple of the old village residents have a look at the book a few weeks ago and they were reminiscing about all kinds of memories that the book triggered off. They seemed to be of the opinion that it was accurate. This section is also based on the census, don't forget, and that was based on the facts of the day.'

He turned the page and we could see from the

blank space at the bottom of the right-hand page that what now lay in front of us were the final few entries in the chapter.

'Well if there's no former grocery shop here,' said Sophie, despondently, 'it'll be back to the drawing board, I'm afraid.'

We all looked intently at the final few entries. One-by-one we dismissed them until there was just one building left: Church Cottage – Aunt's house. I felt sick. We must have missed it.

'Hold on a minute!' said Brian, beginning to read aloud from the book. 'Look at this! "Church Cottage dates back to at least the 16$^{th}$ century. It was residential in 1841 and has, in fact, always been residential, apart from a short period in the late 18$^{th}$ century when a small grocer's shop was opened on the premises by William Blyth, a churchwarden at nearby All Saints church."'

'Oh my God!' I said, taking a few moments for the words to sink in. 'Blyth's grocery shop was in Aunt's cottage!'

The three of us looked at one another in amazement.

'That means,' said Sophie, taking up the narrative, 'that if there is a tunnel behind that final door in the room beneath the lock-up, then it must lead straight across the road into Aunt's cellar!'

It was incredible! If our suppositions were correct, then we now knew where both entrances to the final tunnel were and, more than that, we had access to both of them!

'I'll go and get Amelia,' said Brian, at length. 'She went back to her cottage after the service. Little

276

does she know what might be lying beneath it! You two go and open the door in the room under the lock-up and Amelia and I will go down into her cellar to try to find an opening from there!'

# Stephen Varley's Journal, Sunday 12<sup>th</sup> November

*8pm, continued*

Sophie and I returned excitedly to the farmhouse and went down into the room under the lock-up as planned. We were almost running as we went and my heart was racing as we did so.

'Get the key!' I said. 'And the torches!'

We made our way down to the room and successfully turned the final key in the lock of the one remaining door. The door immediately swung open away from us and the familiar damp tunnel smell came out to us from the space beyond. I shone my torch into the void, revealing the usual clay floor and arched brick walls and roof. There was an old wooden tea chest standing square in the middle of the floor of the tunnel, about 12 feet down it; it looked like it had been placed there deliberately. Beyond the chest my torch beam picked out a second door at the other end of the tunnel, about the same distance from the tea chest in that direction. Sophie and I entered the space.

'Another door!' said Sophie, shining her own torch beam on it in unison with mine. 'It must lead into Aunt's cellar!'

We made our way to the tea chest, which we found to be rectangular.

'Another smugglers' relic!' observed Sophie. 'Eighteenth-century again!'

I nodded.

'We must be dead centre under the road here,' I said. 'The number of times I've walked along the

278

street above! You would never know that this was
here!'

We stood with one of us either side of the tea
chest, which was placed lengthways along the tunnel,
so that we each stood on one of the longer sides,
bending our heads forward slightly to accommodate
the arched roof. We shone our torches onto its lid
and Sophie tried to lift the lid off.

'It's nailed in place,' she said. 'Just like the
coffin lid!'

'Wait here!' I said.

I ran back to Dave's tool bag and rummaged around
for a few moments until I found the crowbar that
I had used to take the 'KEEP OUT!' board off the
front door of Home Farm with and I then ran back
to meet Sophie in the tunnel.

'This should do the trick!' I said, brandishing
my find.

I put my torch down while Sophie kept hers
focussed on the tea chest. In the light of her
torch I lifted up the crowbar, inserted one end of
it under the tea chest lid and pushed the other end
of it downwards to prise the lid open. It jumped up
suddenly from its nail anchorage, and once part of it
was loose I was able to use the crowbar to work
around the remaining edges of the lid and gradually
prise the whole thing off. Just as it became
completely loose we heard some noise coming from
the other side of the door at the Aunt's cottage
end of the tunnel.

'Stephen? Sophie? Can you hear me?' came the
sound of Brian's muffled voice from behind it.

We left the tea chest, with its lid loose but

balanced on top of it, and ran over to the door.

'Yes!' cried Sophie excitedly as we did so. 'We can hear you, Brian!'

'Ok!' came the voice from beyond the door. 'Stand back! I'm going to open the door from this side.'

We did as we were instructed and heard a key turning in the lock. The door swung open towards us and there behind it in the bright electric light of Aunt's yellow-painted cellar stood Reverend Brian, with Aunt behind him.

'Goodness gracious me!' said Aunt, with evident surprise. 'I never knew this was here!'

Sophie and I stepped forward and peered into Aunt's cellar.

'There was another big old wardrobe blocking the door here,' explained Brian. 'We had to move it out of the way. It was a bit of a struggle.'

'It's always been down here,' said Aunt, by way of explanation. 'I've never stored anything in it because the cellar is a bit damp, and I've never had the need or ability to move it, so it has just stood there all these years. The key to this door was on top of it.'

'Just like at my great uncle's!' I said, grinning at Sophie.

She laughed.

'That wardrobe was guarding the entrance to the tunnel, Aunt!' she said.

Brian smiled.

'So what's that you've found?' he asked, indicating the tea chest behind us. It was better illuminated from that direction, as the light from the table lamp in the tunnel beyond the room was picking out its shape quite clearly in the darkness.

'It's a tea chest,' I said. 'We were just about to open it. Come and have a look!'

I led the way back to the tea chest, followed by Sophie, then Brian, then Aunt. Sophie and I stood on opposite sides of it again, with Brian and Aunt coming to a standstill at the narrow end of it that was closest to Aunt's cottage.

'What's in it, dear?' asked Aunt, excitedly.

'We're about to find out, Aunt!' I said. 'Here, take these.'

I took Sophie's torch from her and gave it to Aunt. I then gave mine to Brian.

I motioned to Sophie to take hold of her side of the lid and we lifted it off with ease.

'Mind the nails,' I said, seeing some protruding from the lid as we did so.

Aunt and Brian directed their torch beams into the space that was revealed and we all four of us leant forward and craned our necks to see what was in the tea chest.

There were two things. The main one was another, smaller chest, iron-bound and made of a dark wood. On top of it was a large old copy of the Bible, bound in worn brown leather, the book's title, and the words 'Cannow's End' below it, embossed in gold lettering. Sophie reached in and lifted the book out. Its spine was a little loose and we could immediately see that this was because some of its pages were missing. She opened it out in the torchlight in front of us.

Aunt put her hand to her mouth and drew in her breath.

'It's Hard Nut's Bible!' she said. 'The one the

stories say that he used to tear pages out of to wrap his groceries in!'

Sophie flicked through the pages, allowing them to fall open naturally. There were gaps throughout the book.

'This could well be 18$^{th}$-century,' she said, 'judging from the font.'

Sophie handed the book to Brian, who leafed through it in a similar manner. Aunt kept her torch beam on the book as it was passed from one to the other.

'Hard Nut's Bible,' he repeated. 'This is a valuable piece of Cannow's End's history.'

He placed it carefully on a dry patch of the floor by the tunnel wall.

'What else is in there, Stephen?' he asked. 'Some kind of chest?'

Aunt and Brian shone their torch beams back into the tea chest, focussing them on the smaller chest that was inside. That chest was quite small, but sturdily made. It had three iron straps around it, each of which was padlocked at the side of the lid which opened.

'Wow!' said Sophie, surveying the iron strapwork and the padlocks. 'There must be something important in there.'

'Lift it out,' said Brian, encouragingly, 'so that we can see it better.'

Sophie and I leaned in to lift the chest out, but we couldn't shift it!

'It's really heavy!' said Sophie.

Aunt scratched her nose.

'What do you think is inside it, dear?'

I screwed up my face.

'No idea,' I said, 'but one thing's for certain: we'll never find out unless we find the keys to those padlocks!'

A light-bulb seemed to go on in Aunt's head and her eyes brightened immeasurably.

'Hold on a minute, dear,' she said. 'I'll be back in just a tick!'

With that she disappeared down the tunnel back into the cellar of her cottage and returned after a short interval brandishing a large metal hoop about four inches in diameter with three small keys hanging from it.

'Do you think these might fit the padlocks?' she asked.

I snatched the bunch of keys from Aunt's extended hand more forcefully than I had intended to, but I was so amazed and excited to see them.

'Where did you get these from?' I asked, incredulous, turning the keys over in my hand as I did so.

'They've been hanging on a nail in my cellar for decades,' Aunt replied. 'I've always wondered what they were for. I've tried them in hundreds of locks over the years without success. I didn't want to throw them out though, just in case they came in handy one day!'

I looked at Sophie with amazement.

'Give it a go, Stephen!' she said.

Aunt and Brian refocussed their torches on the left-most of the three padlocks from where I was standing and I tried the first key that came to hand in the lock. It didn't fit. I then tried the same key in the middle lock. It didn't fit into that either. We all exchanged anxious glances.

'Third time lucky!' I said.

I put the key into the right-hand lock, making doubly sure it went in properly. I turned the key and, with a click, the padlock sprang open as smoothly as if it had last been used yesterday.

'Yes!' said Sophie, half aloud and half under her breath.

'That lock is really well made, to open as easily as that after all this time,' observed Brian.

'One down, two to go!' said Aunt, triumphantly.

I put a second key into the left-hand lock and that too sprung open. I then put the remaining key into the middle lock and successfully unlocked that as well.

'Bingo!' said Sophie, excitedly. 'Let me open the lid!'

I stepped back to give her room. She reached in and began to raise it.

'It's heavy!' she said, as she started the manoeuvre.

'It's probably all that ironwork,' observed Aunt.

Sophie gradually raised the lid from horizontal to vertical. When it reached its vertical tipping point it dropped away from her over its hinges a couple of inches and fell backwards onto the top of the side of the outer chest in front of her. The torchlight glistened on something that was revealed inside the inner chest. We all leaned forward and peered into it simultaneously to see what had been exposed there.

It was packed with gold coins!

We were temporarily speechless and there was an

eerie glow as the gold reflected light out of the dark recesses of the space.

'Jesus!' said Sophie at length. 'That's a lot of gold!'

Brian appeared to raise an eyebrow at the use of the word 'Jesus', but said nothing. Aunt's eyes had grown wide and bright again.

'Is it real gold?' I asked, looking at Sophie.

'Oh yes!' she said. 'There's no mistaking that!'

Brian reached in with his free hand and picked out one of the coins, turning it over in his fingers in his torch beam as he did so.

'"Ferdinand VI D.G. Hispan. Etind. Rex 1754",' he read aloud from the coin's surface. 'This is a Spanish gold coin, minted for King Ferdinand VI of Spain in the mid-18th century.'

'Eighteenth-century coins,' mused Sophie, scooping up a handful and holding them out in the palm of her hand so that we could all see them in Aunt's torch beam. 'These will be worth a fortune!'

'Oh my goodness gracious me!' said Aunt, physically beginning to wilt.

Brian dropped his coin back into the chest and just about managed to catch her in his arms before she fainted. Both he and Aunt dropped their torches and the torch beams cast weird shadows up the curving brick walls as they landed and rolled to a stop.

'This treasure must have been left here by the smugglers,' said Sophie. 'Maybe Grace knew about it and wanted it for herself, or maybe it was hers and they stole it?'

I shrugged.

'Either scenario is possible,' I said.

Brian steadied Aunt on her feet and I motioned for her to prop herself onto the edge of the tea chest for a few moments. He collected both torches from where they had fallen and handed one to me. I shone it into the chest again.

'There's enough money here to do up the farmhouse, Aunt!' I said.

'And help restore the church too, I should think!' said Sophie.

# Stephen Varley's Journal, Sunday 1st July

2pm

The find of the gold coins last November solved all of Aunt's problems. Although we had technically found the chest underneath a public highway, the only buildings it was accessible from were Aunt's cottage, Aunt's farmhouse and the church, so we agreed between us that we would say that we found it in the cellar of Home Farm. We decided to sell the coins to a collector colleague of the man from Norfolk who'd bought the barrel of brandy and keep the profits.

Aunt donated a third of the proceeds to the church restoration fund – she has been a regular worshipper at All Saints for decades – and kept the remainder for herself to do up Home Farm and carry out a few minor repairs on ' my little cottage', as she insisted on calling it. Sophie and I were very happy with that outcome. Apart from the episode with the Skeleton Cat, we had enjoyed our adventure and our time back in Essex and had been delighted to see things turn out so well for both Aunt and Brian.

When Sophie, Aunt and I were all standing together in the farmhouse kitchen one day, Aunt suddenly came out with an old question.

'I asked you once before,' she said, 'and I'm going to ask you again. Why don't you two live in Home Farm?'

Sophie and I looked at one another.

'We hadn't forgotten your kind offer, Aunt,' I said. 'We _have_ thought about it. Northumberland is a long way off and south-east Essex is Sophie's home patch. We have friends and family in the locality, too.'

I was becoming more used to, and consequently less uncomfortable with, all the weird local witchcraft stuff. Our recent adventures, not least the encounter with Old Liz in the Thamesmouth shop, had quite piqued my interest in it, to be honest. I was interested to find out how she had known about the Skeleton Cat and the reason we had gone to her shop in the first place! I felt more confident about things now that Grace and Tom had been laid to rest and I wanted to pay a return visit to Old Liz to ask her if there was some kind of offering she could recommend for us to make that would help them to sleep soundly in their hidden graves off the underground room. All in all, living at Home Farm did sound like a potential plan.

I looked at Sophie again. Her eyes were imploring me to say 'Yes'.

I looked back at Aunt with gratitude.

' Why not?' I said, rhetorically. ' If you're sure? It will give us a new project to work on and we can be close by to look after you!'

' Oh Stephen!' she said, hugging first me and then Sophie.' You've made an old woman very happy.'

So in due course Aunt gave us some of the money and Sophie and I moved into Home Farm, terminating the lease on our Northumberland property. Over the six months or so between then and now we have used the funds to repair and restore the farmhouse - with Dave's help, of course - and to tidy up the garden. We have converted the bedroom above the kitchen into a new modern bathroom and have smartened up and improved the layout of the old bathroom/utility room downstairs. We have even hung the old garden gate back on its hinges, though we decided to cut the 'KEEP OUT!' board in half and take it to the tip. It seemed a symbolic moment, as we watched it disappear into the crusher: there was no need for us to keep out of the farmhouse now. The 'Welcome to Hell' and 'Do not open' signs went the same way, but we have held on to the 'No cursing' sign as a souvenir.

Dave blocked up all three tunnel entrances from the cellar and the one from the church, but Aunt wanted to keep the one from her cottage open.

'Just in case I ever need to go down it again,' she said, with a twinkle in her eye.

I know that she does periodically do exactly that, to visit the room beneath the lock-up to pay her respects to the memories of Grace Cartwright and Vinegar Tom. Sophie and I have been down there with her once, for that very purpose.

I hugged Sophie tightly on the night that Home Farm's restoration was completed and we were finally left to ourselves once Dave and his fellow builders had gone. Despite some unexpected events and scares on the way we both really enjoyed our temporary return to Cannow's End and we have been glad to have been able to move back here on a permanent basis. Sophie can even put our tunnel project on her archaeology CV!

'I'm so pleased to be back in Essex,' I said to her. 'It was never the same in Northumberland.'

Sophie kissed me on the lips in return.

'Yes,' she said, 'I know what you mean. I'm

delighted to be back here in Cannow's End myself. It's a wonderful village, with an atmosphere all of its own. We've had some great times here already; who knows what other adventures await us in the future?'

## THE END

IAN YEARSLEY

Lightning Source UK Ltd.
Milton Keynes UK
UKHW021250300522
403724UK00008B/1384

9 781782 225348